Here's what critics are saying about the *Hollywood Headlines Mysteries*:

"Gemma Halliday's witty, entertaining writing style shines through in her new book! I look forward to seeing lots more of Tina as this series continues. A fun read!"
—*Fresh Fiction*

"(*HOLLYWOOD SCANDALS*) is a great start to a new series that I will definitely be following as Halliday writes the kind of books that just make you smile and put you in a great mood. They're just so enjoyable and I would without a doubt recommend this book to romance and mystery readers alike."
—*Enchanted By Books*

"(*HOLLYWOOD SCANDALS*) is very well written with smart and funny dialogue. It is a well-paced story that is thoroughly enjoyable with a mystery, a little romance, and a lot of laughs. Readers are sure to enjoy this delightful tale which is highly recommended."
—*Romance Reviews Today*

"The latest in the Hollywood Headlines series is 320 pages of pure fun. Halliday has created yet another laugh-out-loud whodunit. She breathes life into her mystery with a rich cast of vivid, pulp-fiction type characters and a heroine worth rooting for. 4 1/2 stars!"
—*RT Book Reviews*

D1559532

BOOKS BY GEMMA HALLIDAY

Marty Hudson Mysteries
Sherlock Homes and the Case
of the Brash Blonde

High Heels Mysteries
Spying in High Heels
Killer in High Heels
Undercover in High Heels
Christmas in High Heels
(short story)
Alibi in High Heels
Mayhem in High Heels
Honeymoon in High Heels
(short story)
Sweetheart in High Heels
(short story)
Fearless in High Heels
Danger in High Heels
Homicide in High Heels
Deadly in High Heels
Suspect in High Heels

Tahoe Tessie Mysteries
Luck Be A Lady
Hey Big Spender
Baby It's Cold Outside
(holiday short story)

Hollywood Headlines Mysteries
Hollywood Scandals
Hollywood Secrets
Hollywood Confessions
Hollywood Deception

Jamie Bond Mysteries
Unbreakable Bond
Secret Bond
Bond Bombshell
(short story)
Lethal Bond
Bond Ambition
(short story)

Young Adult Books
Deadly Cool
Social Suicide

Other Works
Play Nice
Viva Las Vegas
A High Heels Haunting
Watching You (short story)
Confessions of a Bombshell
Bandit (short story)

BOOKS BY ANNA SNOW

Barb Jackson Mysteries:
Bubblegum Blonde
Illegally Blonde
The Blonde Before Christmas
(holiday short story)

Hollywood Headlines Mysteries
Hollywood Deception

HOLLYWOOD DECEPTION

a Hollywood Headlines mystery

GEMMA HALLIDAY

AND

ANNA SNOW

HOLLYWOOD DECEPTION

CHAPTER ONE

The set was jam packed, and it was only 9:00 a.m.

Several production assistants wearing headsets hustled to and from other members of the crew with coffee drinks in hand. Lighting and camera people moved large pieces of equipment around the set, readying for the perfect shot. Makeup and wardrobe artists buzzed about in a flurry of activity, rushing powder puffs and starched shirts across the sound stage to the talent, hidden away in their trailers.

I took a sip of the iced coffee one of the countless PAs had handed me the moment I'd sat down. I must admit I was a bit envious of the talent in those trailers. I had a slight obsession with fashion and could only imagine what it would be like to have a personal stylist and makeup artist of my own. But on my tabloid reporter budget, all I could afford was to watch *Project Runway* and use my imagination when I hit the consignment shops in Studio City.

I reached down and adjusted the hem of my short black miniskirt then crossed my legs and checked the neckline of my pink top. I'd been trying to land this interview for a couple of weeks now, and thanks to my persistent nature—and my ample cleavage, which was always a bit hard to contain but had seemed to impress my quarry's manager—I'd landed an exclusive with none other than Bobby Baxter, host of the hit television series *Bobby Tells All*.

Bobby Tells All was an hour-long show where Bobby proved the truth about everyday common misconceptions and myths while providing the audience with a healthy dose of humor and sarcasm. He got to the bottom of just about every question a person could think of, from *What's Really in That*

Sausage You're Eating? to *Can a Bundle of Balloons Really Carry a Person Away?* and everything in between. The show was fun, quirky, and had been an instant ratings hit when it had debuted last year, making Bobby a household name—at least among cable TV watchers.

He'd also become something of a B-list celebrity. A status Bobby seemed to enjoy even more than busting myths, quickly becoming a fixture in the tabloid headlines for his "bad boy" antics.

Case in point: a couple of weeks earlier, Bobby had assaulted a fan at Beverly's, an upscale restaurant in Hollywood. Paparazzi had been on the scene, star watching, and had caught photos of the aftermath—the fan with a bloody nose. It had quickly gone viral, but neither party had made any comment on what had started the altercation.

Until now. Somehow I had been able to land an exclusive with Bobby (see cleavage-versus-manager comment above) and was about to get his side of the story. I had a feeling it was going to be good. Okay, so it wasn't exactly hard-hitting investigative reporting that would have CNN beating down my door with offers of field correspondent positions. But as far as the kind of stories the tabloid paper I worked for, the *L.A. Informer*, published, this was front page gold.

Bobby's personal assistant had assured me that Bobby would "fit me in" today between takes as he filmed his latest episode. Though, when that might be, I had no idea. A quick look at the enormous clock on the far wall told me that filming should've started nearly an hour ago. Not that running a bit behind wasn't par for the course in Hollywood, but I certainly hoped Bobby hadn't changed his mind and wasn't actively avoiding me—something I'd become used to in my line of work.

The tinkle of my phone sounded from the bottom of my purse. I forced my eyes away from all of the frenetic activity and dug around until I came up with the little pink device. I checked the display. It was a text from my boss, Felix Dunn.

Get the story yet? Make it good, Allie. Our front page is bare. :)

I grinned down at the little smile emoticon then fired off a response.

On it, boss.

At least I hoped. I glanced up at the clock again, praying Bobby wasn't blowing me off. Working as a reporter for the *L.A. Informer* wasn't exactly a prestigious position. The *Informer* was often described as a combination of *People* magazine meets the *Enquirer*, but without the aliens and three-headed anything. We posted up-to-date information, most of it true, on celebrities, their television shows, movies, love lives, and of course all of the deliciously naughty trouble they tended to get themselves into. Most celebs had a love-hate relationship with us. They hated the way we followed them around like little puppies with cameras, poked fun at their outfits, and could blow a little thing like a bad hair day up into a sensational headline. But they hated it even worse when we stopped talking about them altogether.

Another text came in.

Are we still on for tonight?

I nibbled my bottom lip. Even though it probably wasn't the best idea I'd ever had, for the past few months, I'd been dating my boss. I hadn't exactly meant to. It had sort of happened by accident. But as much as I knew it wasn't the best career move, there was something about Felix that was hard to resist.

For starters, he was hot. Like volcanic. Blond hair, blues eyes, and a British accent that could make a girl melt. He was charming in a rough-around-the-edges way but gentle in the moments when it counted. In truth, he made me kinda giddy, like a high school girl around her crush.

I was just about to text him back, thumbs poised over the screen of my phone, when Bobby finally burst onto the set. I say "burst" because as soon as he appeared, the crew scattered like bugs.

"What is taking so long? Where is my latte? Where the hell is makeup?" he demanded of several people all at once. The assistant director made some rapid arm movements toward the crew, no less than three PAs ran off to presumably find a latte, and a thin woman carrying an overstuffed bag quickly appeared at his side and began powdering his forehead.

This was the first time I'd seen Bobby in person, and while I'd recognize the chiseled jaw and dark good looks anywhere, it appeared that his easy smile was something he reserved for the cameras. His mouth was set in a grim line, and his eyebrows were drawn together in a scowl.

I sent a quick response to Felix.

Yes. Be ready at eight. Bobby's on set now. Gotta go.

I set my phone to silent, slid it back into my purse without awaiting a response, and turned my attention back to Bobby. He was saying something to wardrobe now—an older woman in a flowy dress. His voice was low enough that I couldn't hear what, but from the way the scowl had deepened and he was gesturing to his clothes, he didn't look happy. He looked immaculate to me in a white dress shirt and pair of black slacks that hugged his legs perfectly. Not one shiny brown hair on his severely gelled head was out of place.

He finally finished his tirade at the wardrobe woman, who slunk away like a dog with her tail between her legs, and made his way onto the sound stage. Today it was set up like a science lab, and I'll admit I was kind of eager to see what myth he'd be busting in it.

Two lighting guys with instruments to check the white balance descended on Bobby, who tried to swat them off like flies. "Didn't you check this with my stand-in?" he yelled.

The guys didn't answer, instead slinking off in much the same fashion as the wardrobe lady.

I raised an eyebrow, making a mental note. It seemed Bobby Baxter was a diva with a capital *D*. The show fan in me was disappointed, but the reporter in me was giggling on the inside as I mentally began writing my article on the "Divalicious Mr. Baxter."

I relaxed back into the surprisingly comfortable canvas director's chair and watched as the crew took their places to begin filming. The minute action was called and the cameras started rolling, Bobby's scowl was replaced with the friendly grin I had come to associate with him through my hours of DVRed *Bobby Tells All.*

He smiled at the camera. "So as you can see, the dental industry has a long standing history of using poisonous products to clean your teeth. But what happens if we delve deeper into the ingredients found in your mouthwash?"

I watched as Bobby went through a two-minute spiel where he moved mouthwash around in various beakers, all the while totally grossing me out with what was really in it. Involuntarily I felt my tongue trying to wipe my teeth as he talked. I was going to have to pick up some of that natural toothpaste next time I was in Whole Foods.

"And that, my friends," Bobby said, wrapping up the segment, "is the whole *tooth* about your mouthwash."

"Cut!" the director yelled. "That was great. Let's go one more time."

"What for?" Bobby argued, the scowl immediately back.

"Let's just do one more for safety." The director smiled at Bobby, though I could see a hint of fear behind it. Geez, this guy had the entire crew on edge. "Okay, Bobby?"

"Was there something *wrong* with the way I did that take?"

"N-no. I just think we should—"

"Then we're moving on." Bobby stared the director down as if challenging him. I felt my eyes, along with the entire crew's, ping-ponging back and forth between the two men.

The director paused, took a deep breath, and then blew it out on a resigned sigh. "Okay, moving on." I thought I saw Bobby smirk as the makeup woman descended on him again, adding more powder to his nose as the crew moved props for the next scene.

The next couple of hours went on much the same. The cameras went on, Bobby smiled and joked with the viewing audience, the director yelled "cut," and Bobby morphed into Diva Man, instantly jumping on whichever crew member was closest for not doing their job up to his standards. The light was weak. The mic was in his way. The prop should have been on his left, not his right. With his winning personality, I was honestly starting to wonder how Bobby *hadn't* gotten in more altercations lately.

I checked the clock. I'd been on set for well over three hours. Bobby hadn't so much as glanced my way. I wondered when he planned to "fit me in" as I shifted in my chair to get a little feeling back to my right cheek.

The director called another scene number, and the crew once again reset for the next shot. An old-fashioned mailbag was brought out, and I recognized the upcoming segment immediately.

At the end of every show, Bobby read a letter sent in from a fan, usually a child or their teacher or parent, and proved or disproved their question. I loved this portion of the show. Kids came up with the coolest questions, and it was fascinating to see the conclusion of the experiments Bobby performed.

Bobby reached into the bag, the director yelled "action," and our charm-oozing host began reading a selected letter. It was from a local elementary school teacher concerning what would happen if a person ate Pop Rocks and drank soda at the same time.

"Well, let's test this theory out," Bobby told the camera. "As you can see, we have a bag of popping candy here and a bottle of soda. Now the carbon dioxide trapped in the candy will have a reaction with free carbonation in the soda, but will it cause an explosion? Only one way to find out—that's it!" Bobby's happy face melted, and he slammed the little black package of candy onto the table. Tiny red rock candy burst all over the stage like confetti. "I cannot work like this! Are you kidding me?!"

I looked around in confusion. What in the heck had just happened? Everything had seemed to be going great, at least to me. What had I missed?

The director hurried up onto the set and stopped in front of Bobby. They talked heatedly for a few seconds, though in low enough tones this time that I couldn't make out the words. Finally Bobby threw his hands into the air, turned on his heel, and stormed off the set toward his trailer.

"Take five, everybody," the director called out wearily then made his way past the camera equipment and out of sight. I figured he was most likely looking for a bottle of vodka. Not that I could blame him. I had a feeling that my interview—if I ever got one—was going to be about as pleasant as a case of poison oak on my bikini area.

I shifted in my chair, wondering just how long this "five" was going to be. How long did it take to sooth the savage diva ego?

After half an hour had passed and Bobby still hadn't appeared back on set to finish filming, I decided to go in search of someone who could tell me what was going on before my entire day was wasted waiting around for an interview that wouldn't happen. With a quick sweep of the area, I found Bobby's personal assistant, who had originally greeted me on set. He was standing to the left of the set, talking animatedly on the phone. I stood, adjusted my skirt, rolled my lips to even out my lip gloss, and wove my way through the crowded set. My pink high heels clicked on the cement floor beneath my feet as I approached him.

The assistant saw me walking toward him and held up one finger. I stopped a few feet away from him so that he could continue his call in private as I tried to remember the guy's name. Harry? Hunter? Something with an *H*.

He was short for a man, only a few inches taller than my 5'3", and slim. His medium brown hair was thinning, his skin was pale, and his eyes were rimmed in dark circles that spoke of too many hours doing Bobby's bidding and not enough sleeping. He wore the same earbud and microphone combo I noticed most of the crew sporting, though his dangled from his ear as if he'd pulled it out to make the phone call. He finished quickly then shoved the phone back into the front pocket of his jeans.

"Ms. Quick?" he greeted me.

"That's right. From the *L.A. Informer*," I said with a smile. I pointed at him and raised an eyebrow. "And you were…"

"Henry. Henry Klein," he supplied.

I nodded in recognition and committed that name to memory. "I'm supposed to have an exclusive interview today with Bobby? About the incident with the fan."

"Right. So sorry to keep you waiting. Bobby's…" He trailed off with a wave of his hand in the direction Bobby had stomped off to, as though he was trying to come up with a polite word for jerk.

"That's alright. I understand." I smiled and patted his forearm as I went into reporter mode. Henry wasn't Bobby Baxter, but as his personal assistant, I'd bet he knew a lot about Bobby. There was always a chance that he could tell me something I'd never get out of Bobby himself. I put on a little extra charm and stepped closer to him.

"While we wait for Bobby to come back out, could you tell me a little bit about what happened the night that he had that run-in with the fan at Beverly's?" I smiled up at him as sweetly as I could and pushed my chest out just a bit as I patted his arm.

While I was keen on feminine equality as any woman, I knew you could catch a lot more flies with honey—or in my case a pair of ample Ds—than with vinegar. A little flirting went a long way to getting the answers I wanted, especially in Hollywood.

"Me?" Henry squeaked out, his voice about an octave higher. "Oh, I don't know…"

"It's just that anything you might be able to tell me would really help me out. And help Bobby. I mean, you'd be saving him time by filling me in now."

Henry shifted uneasily. "I just don't know if that's a good idea. I'm sure Bobby will tell you everything about that night as soon as he's finished taping the show."

"Oh, I'm sure he will, too." I batted my lashes at him. "I was just hoping that maybe you could tell me what you know or what you might have heard about it all. You know, just in case Bobby forgets something small. I like to get all of the details so that my story is completely accurate. I'm sure you understand." I continued smiling.

"Well, I guess it can't hurt." He finally returned my smile. "But I only know what I saw."

"You were at the restaurant with Bobby on the night of the altercation?" How lucky could I get? Henry was an eyewitness.

Henry nodded. "Yeah. Sort of. I mean, I was there, but Bobby likes me to hang back a bit. He says I scare off the ladies."

I resisted the urge to roll my eyes. Bobby was a regular pal. "Any lady in particular with Bobby that night?"

Henry glanced around like Bobby was going to jump out from behind a wall with a pink slip if he saw him talking to me. "No. He was alone at the bar, sitting on a stool and talking to whoever passed by." He frowned. "He'd, uh, maybe had a bit too much to drink."

I raised an eyebrow. "Oh? What makes you say that?"

Henry licked his lips. "Well, he was being loud—well, louder than usual. Kind of...um, maybe bothering some of the other patrons."

Translation: diva turned obnoxious drunk.

"Go on," I prompted. "Was the fan he hit one of those patrons he was bothering?"

Henry shook his head. "No. I mean that guy seemed friendly enough from where I was sitting. He just walked up to Bobby and started talking to him."

"The guy wasn't being confrontational?" I asked.

"Not at all." Henry shook his head. "They talked for a minute, and then the next thing I know, Bobby hauls off and punches the guy right in the face. I've seen Bobby in a mood, but I've never seen him hit someone."

"What happened then?" I asked.

"The guy fell to the floor. Then all hell broke loose. Security guards came running out of nowhere and grabbed Bobby by the arms. Of course, Bobby was yelling for them to let him go and fighting to get out of their holds. Then the cops showed up and arrested him. He was still yelling and acting like a fool when they shoved him into the cop car and drove away."

"Did you happen to hear what the fan and Bobby were talking about before Bobby hit him?"

"No. Sorry." Henry shook his head. "I was too far away."

"That's all right," I said. "I'm sure I'll get the rest from Bobby." I checked my watch again. "If he ever comes back out here."

"Let me go back to his trailer and see if I can get him to come out. He did promise you an interview, and it wouldn't be right to make you wait around all day. Give me just a second."

I watched Henry jog outside the warehouse to where Bobby's trailer sat beside two others labeled *hair and makeup* and *wardrobe*.

I hoped Henry could coax Bobby out. Unfortunately, the assistant hadn't told me much more than I'd already known from the social media accounts of the evening. What I really wanted to know was what the fan had said that ticked Bobby off so much. I'd seen firsthand today how easily Bobby could fly off the handle. But hitting a complete stranger seemed a bit much, even for him.

I meandered over to the Craft services table while I waited, picking up a pair of blueberry mini muffins and a fresh coffee. I was just polishing off the second tiny treat when Henry finally appeared again. The expression on his face told me all I needed to know.

I wouldn't be getting my exclusive today, if ever.

He hurried up to me. "I'm so sorry, Ms. Quick." He held up his hands pleadingly. "But Bobby's refusing to talk to anyone. I know you were promised an interview, but when he gets like this, there's no changing his mind. He did say he would talk with you tomorrow morning if you're willing to come back then."

"Of course." I nodded. "I can come back in the morning." What was I going to do? Refuse and lose the story? Not likely. I didn't really have much of a choice. On this, like it or not, Bobby was calling all of the shots.

"Again, I'm so sorry about today."

"It's not your fault," I assured him and patted his arm again. "Does he get like this often?" I motioned toward the trailer.

Henry shook his head, and a lock of his thin brown hair fell over his forehead. "To be perfectly honest with you, he's always a bit of…a handful. But things have been worse since his arrest. Snapping at people, always late, paranoid."

"Paranoid?" I jumped on the word. "How so?"

Henry pursed his lips as if thinking twice about confiding in a tabloid reporter. Smart man. "Well, it's not one thing in particular, but it just feels like he's always looking over his shoulder, you know? I don't think anyone else has even noticed. Maybe I'm just imagining it." He shrugged then pressed on his little earpiece as if getting a call. "I'll be right there," he said into the mic. "I'm sorry, Ms. Quick, but I have to go. Duty calls."

"Oh, no worries. I understand," I told him.

"Be here around ten in the morning, and we'll get you that interview with Bobby before he starts filming."

"I'll see you then," I called after him.

I watched him jog away to take care of whatever crisis needed dealt with. Then I tossed the strap of my purse over my shoulder and made my way back to the golf cart that I'd ridden to the set. I hopped inside and steered in the direction of the studio visitors' parking area.

Henry hadn't exactly been a fountain of information, but the bit about Bobby seeming excessively agitated and paranoid since the incident made me even more curious as to what was said between him and the fan he'd smacked around. Was Bobby hiding something? Did he know the fan personally? Did the fan know something about Bobby that he didn't want getting out? Did Bobby have something on the fan? My reporter brain spun in circles with a zillion questions.

I parked the golf cart in its assigned slot by the main entrance, waved at the guard manning the gate, and hurried to my car. I'd sat on the set most of the day only to be told to come back tomorrow.

An entire day wasted.

I didn't lead a glamorous, exciting life, but I did have a life, and I enjoyed what there was of it too much to waste my days. And I didn't like the idea of depending on someone as volatile as Bobby Baxter for my article. What if he decided to give the interview to another reporter?

I slid into the driver seat of my Volkswagen Beetle. The white vinyl seats seared the back of my thighs. I'd been so excited at the thought of interviewing Bobby that I'd forgotten to put the sunshade over the windshield. I shook my head at my mistake and cranked up the air conditioner. The cool air blasted against my face, and I almost sighed aloud. L.A. was hot no matter what time of year it was, and today I could practically feel my makeup melting off of my face. While the interior of the car cooled, I flipped to my favorite radio station and pulled my phone out of my purse, turned my ringer back on, and texted an update to Felix.

No interview today. Diva drama. I'll explain over dinner.

The phone chimed with a response almost immediately. *See you at 8.*

I tossed the phone back into my purse and tossed the bag onto the passenger seat before putting the car in gear and pulling through the studio gate. I made a quick stop at the nearest drive-thru and grabbed a chocolate shake. It would take hours on the elliptical to burn off that little cup of deliciousness, but with the day I'd had, it was worth it. I mean, when wasn't chocolate worth it?

After what felt like an eternity of being stuck in traffic on the 2, I finally turned into my neighborhood and onto my street. My standard gray apartment building was a small fourplex on the outskirts of Glendale, hugging the foothills of the San Gabriel Mountains. Nothing terribly fancy, but it didn't break the bank either.

I pulled into my assigned parking spot in front of the building and took a minute to appreciate the semi-quiet (for L.A.) neighborhood. Tall trees lined each side of the street, and on a good night when the smog was at a thin layer, I had a clear view of the mountains, which in my mind was almost as good as living in the Hollywood Hills. Almost.

I killed the ignition, grabbed my purse, hopped out of my Bug, and made my way up the stairs to my apartment door.

The new sprinkler in the side yard area was blasting away, coating the grass in cool water and making a racket on the side of the building with every rotation. I pulled my keys from my purse and let myself inside. I had one hour to get fab for Felix…and I intended to put it to good use.

CHAPTER TWO

———

My cat, Mr. Fluffykins, greeted me by winding himself around my legs. I reached down and gave his head a generous scratch as I tossed my purse on top of my hand-painted pink coffee table.

I love the color pink. It might sound silly to some, but the color pink, in all shades, made me happy. And who couldn't use more happy in their lives, right? Especially in my line of work, I felt that pink kept me from becoming jaded…like certain of my coworkers. I'd hand painted and sewn most of the items in my tiny apartment, including the pink coffee table, the kitchen table, which I'd painted gerbera daisies—my favorite—on, and the hot pink throw pillows with gold tassels on the corners that adorned the sofa I'd found on Craigslist.

I was a do-it-yourself kind of girl. Mostly because my paycheck from the *Informer* wasn't big enough to be a hire-a-decorator type yet.

I kicked off my heels and padded to the kitchen, where Mr. Fluffykins meowed and gave me his *feed me now, peasant* look. I complied, pouring him new bowls of food and water.

"You wouldn't believe the day I had, Mr. Fluffykins," I said as I pulled a bottle of water from the refrigerator. I'd poured my heart out to my sweet kitty on more than one occasion over the years. He probably knew more about me than anyone else in the world. I was glad that cats couldn't talk, because if he could and ever got mad at me, he'd have plenty of blackmail fodder.

He looked up at me and meowed then dug into his meal.

"I was supposed to interview Bobby Baxter, but he stood me up. Rude, right?" I continued.

Mr. Fluffykins grunted—though whether it was in response or simply a byproduct of inhaling his food, I couldn't say. I went on anyway. "I hate to say the guy's a jerk before I even meet him…but I'm pretty sure the guy's a jerk." I shook my head and took a sip of the water.

"And now I have a date with Felix in…" I checked the clock on the microwave. "Less than an hour. I better get ready. Can't keep the boss waiting!" I grinned as I gave Mr. Fluffykins another quick scratch and hurried down the short hallway to the bathroom.

I took a quick, hot shower, dried myself off, and wrapped my hair in a hot pink towel.

Felix and I had been out together several times over the past few months, but our relationship status was still somewhat ambiguous. While I wouldn't quite call him my boyfriend yet—at least not to anyone but Mr. Fluffykins—if I saw him with another woman, I think I'd be justified in clawing her eyes out. Or his. Not that I thought there were any other women in Felix's life, but the "exclusive" talk was one bridge we'd yet to cross. While I knew Felix had lived in L.A. for years, he still held on to his typically British aversion for discussing emotion in any form. For the most part that worked for me.

I let the towel fall from my hair and grabbed my blow dryer from the small pink hook on the wall and blasted my hair. Once my blonde locks were dry, I piled them in loose ringlets on top of my head and secured them with crystal-tipped bobby pins. I kept my makeup fairly light but added an extra coat of lengthening mascara on my lashes. Then I finished the look off with a swipe of Tickled Pink lip gloss on my lips.

I stepped into my tiny bedroom closet and pulled out my latest consignment shop find. A silver spaghetti strap dress with a low cut front that accentuated my "girls," and a short hemline that barely reached midthigh. The dress was backless with the exception of half a dozen thin crystal-adorned silver chains that dangled low toward my hips. Consignment shops in L.A. could be amazing if you knew which ones to hit. Most of my closet consisted of gently used finds. I had a bit of a shopping habit, but as long as it was in secondhand stores, it was a habit I could afford to indulge in.

I applied a thin layer of my favorite Virgin Mint Mojito body butter then slid the dress on over my head, secured some areas with lingerie tape just to be safe, and topped the ensemble off with a pair of matching silver stiletto heels and an electric pink sequined clutch for a pop of color.

With one final look in the full-length mirror, I grinned. I was going for sex kitten, and I think I succeeded. This dress was sure to make Felix sweat. I grinned at the thought.

While our relationship was flirting with the exclusive territory, the one thing that had me second-guessing our status was a distinct lack of overnight visits. We'd been seeing each other for a few months now, and the grand total of times he'd spent the night was three. That's it. Just three. I'm not some sex-crazed maniac or anything, but I read *Cosmo*—I knew that was not normal. Not that I had any complaints about the glorious three times. And I guessed there was something to be said for taking it slow. But some days I felt like I was in a relationship with a nun.

I slid on a silver cuff bracelet, a long silver necklace with a teardrop shaped pink faux sapphire that dangled between my breasts, and matching dangling earrings. I dared Felix to resist me tonight.

Mr. Fluffykins hopped up onto the bed and stretched out to watch me.

I glanced over at him. "What do you think?" I asked and spun in a circle.

He meowed and rolled over onto his back.

"What a lot of help you are." I laughed.

The doorbell rang. A quick look at the bedside clock told me Felix was early. As usual.

"Be good." I pointed at Mr. Fluffykins and hurried into the living room. With a deep breath, I opened the door.

Felix stood on my porch. I watched as his eyes did a quick head to toe. He must have liked what he saw, because the corner of his mouth quirked upward, along with one perfectly arched eyebrow.

"Something wrong?" I asked.

"On the contrary," he said, the other corner lifting up in a true smile. "You look amazing, love." He stepped forward, wrapped his arm around my waist, and pressed his lips to mine in a quick kiss. "That dress." He grinned and shook his head.

"Do you like it?" His palm heated the skin of my lower back where it rested.

"*Like* isn't a strong enough word." He winked. "Are you ready to go?"

"All set. I just need to lock up."

I closed and locked the door behind us and dropped my keys into my clutch. I said a silent prayer about our transportation for the night as I followed him down the steps.

Felix normally drove an old beat-up junker that had seen better days. And those better days were back when people were still doing the Macarena. The last time I'd ridden in it, the seat belt had snapped, and I'd almost fallen out the rusted passenger door when he'd taken a quick left. I had no idea why he hadn't ditched the bucket of bolts for a newer model a long time ago. The truth was he could more than afford it.

Felix was what one would call a cheap rich man. Not only did he make a decent salary as the editor in chief of the *Informer*, but his family was old money. I'd even heard a rumor or two around the newsroom that he was titled gentry back in England and distantly related to the queen. Despite that, he lived a frugal lifestyle—drove an old car, wore off-the-rack (and I sometimes suspected that was the clearance rack), and rarely carried more than $20 in his wallet.

I must have made enough of a fuss over his duct-taped seats damaging my Valentino gown when we'd covered a recent red carpet event that he'd taken note, because the last time we'd gone to a nice dinner, Felix had miraculously sprung for a car service, allowing us to arrive in appropriate style. I mentally crossed my fingers and chanted a "please, please, please," hoping for a repeat of that experience (and not the junker one) as we descended the stairs.

I peeked around the corner of the building and spotted the black town car waiting at the curb. Yes! Not that I was superficial, but I did want to make it to dinner alive.

When we reached the car, he opened the door for me before sliding in beside me.

The driver pulled away from my building, and we were on our way.

"Where are we going tonight?" I asked, secretly hoping it would be somewhere private, romantic, and delicious. All I'd had since breakfast were the mini muffins and a chocolate shake.

"I made a dinner reservation at Beverly's. I hope that's all right."

I shot him a look. "Purely coincidence that's where Baxter had his fight?"

He turned his face to the window so I couldn't see his expression. "You know I don't believe in coincidence."

I narrowed my eyes at the back of his head. "So, this is a working dinner then? Not a date?"

He turned toward me, a charming smile in place. "There's no reason it can't be business *and* pleasure."

It didn't escape my notice that he was talking to my cleavage. Which, in this case, I didn't completely mind.

"Fine. But I'm totally ordering the lobster now."

I thought I saw him cringe at the thought of the expense, but he quickly covered it with a peck on my cheek. "Anything for you, love."

"I'll keep that in mind for later," I mumbled.

"What was that?"

"Nothing." I shot him a big toothy smile.

While the thought of lobster at Beverly's was making my stomach rumble, it wasn't my first choice for a romantic evening out. Beverley's was the type of place people went to see and be seen. So while I had a good chance at catching a glimpse of my fantasy crushes, the chance of a quiet romantic dinner was slight. Especially since I knew Felix had the Baxter story on the mind—which likely meant paying off waitstaff for any dirt he could get them to spill.

"So what happened to the interview?" Felix asked, as if he could read my mind.

I sighed. "Did you know Bobby Baxter was a class A diva?"

Felix shook his head. "No. I know he's had a few scuffles with the paparazzi, but nothing out of the ordinary. Why? What happened?"

I told Felix about how I'd shown up on set to watch the taping of *Bobby Tells All*, how Bobby was a total jerk to everyone who crossed his path, and how he'd had a tantrum and stormed off the set.

"His assistant promised me an interview in the morning."

"Well, let's hope Bobby keeps his word this time. I'd hate for you to waste another day on his nonsense. If you can't get the interview in the morning, then come back to the office. You can write a piece on how he stood you up, how he behaved on set, or something along those lines."

"Not exactly the same as an exclusive," I said.

He shrugged and smiled. "We could always make something up."

We both chuckled at his joke. (At least, I was *pretty* sure he was joking.)

Thin laugh lines fanned out at the corners of his eyes, and I had the urge to lean over and kiss them. But I controlled myself. Instead, I placed my hand on his and enjoyed his easy company until we arrived at the restaurant.

* * *

I'd lived in Southern California all of my life, but I never failed to be a bit starstruck when out for a night on the town. There was a clash of realities when walking through a crowded restaurant and bumping into the likes of Julia Roberts and Jennifer Lawrence—people who normally greeted me from my TV screen. As our car pulled up outside Beverly's main entrance, I couldn't help but crane my head to see if anyone interesting was hanging around outside. Unfortunately, all I saw were a few members of the paparazzi, smoking and leaning against the building, cameras in hand in case anyone noteworthy pulled up. They jumped to attention when we exited our car, cameras poised…until they realized we were no one of importance. Still, I felt more than one set of eyes on my back as we walked through the doors.

"Felix Dunn. We have an eight thirty reservation." Felix gave his name to the maître d' at a slick black podium.

The gentleman flicked his fingers across a tablet and smiled. "Of course, Mr. Dunn," he said in the most fake French accent I'd ever heard. If this guy was an actor, he needed a few more lessons. "The hostess will seat you." He held open a second set of double glass doors and allowed us to enter.

The inside of Beverly's was absolutely beautiful with all the latest modern touches—chrome and glass décor, big dishes with tiny portions of food that looked like they were plated by Jackson Pollock, and servers-slash-wannabe-actors whose pretentiousness was only rivaled by the patrons.

After the hostess checked her list and led us to our table, I spotted someone Felix and I both knew seated at the bar. *Informer* photographer and paparazzo extraordinaire, Cameron Dakota, and her current boy toy, movie star Trace Brody.

Trace was one of the most drool-worthy action stars on the big screen at the moment, and he and Cam were just a couple more hot dates away from getting their own celebrity nickname—like Tram or Cace. If I didn't know he was Cam's, I'd be sorely tempted to go chat him up myself. Purely for story fodder, of course. But Cam wasn't a slouch in the looks department herself, standing close to six feet tall, with blonde hair and blue eyes of her own, a rocking body, and legs that went on for days. She'd started her career as a model, only stepping behind the camera when she'd had enough of being the "body."

There were times my petite self envied Cam's supermodel height. I also envied the fact that everyone at the paper liked her and no one ever tried to scoop her stories…the same I could not always say for myself.

"Is that Cam?" Felix asked, spotting the couple as well.

I nodded. "And Trace."

"Trace Brody?" Felix perked up. "Let's go say hello."

I shot him a look. "Say hello—yes. Nose out something on Trace to print tomorrow—no."

Felix put a hand over his heart and gave me a look of mock horror. "Who, me? Never."

I grinned. "Right." But I followed him to the bar anyway.

"Here comes trouble," Cam said cheerfully and raised her glass toward us in greeting. "What are you two up to tonight?"

"Just having a little dinner," I answered quickly before Felix could mention Baxter. Hey, if he had to work a story while we were out, it was going to be *my* story. "How about the two of you?" I asked.

"The same," Cam said lightly.

"It's good to see you, Allie. Felix." Trace stood and kissed me on the cheek, shook Felix's hand, then retook his seat next to Cam.

"You just get here?" Cam asked.

I nodded.

"Try the baked ziti. It's to die for tonight." Cam laughed and laid her hand on my arm momentarily. I glanced at her champagne glass. Empty. I wondered if they were celebrating something tonight.

"Thanks, but I've got my sights set on the lobster." I winked at Felix. He pretended not to notice.

"You come here often, Trace?" Felix asked casually.

Too casually.

I narrowed my eyes at him. What was he up to?

"Oh, yeah. All the time," Trace replied. "Of course, I still have to deal with the paparazzi buzzing around." He tilted his head toward Cam.

"Funny, smart guy." Cam whacked him playfully on his arm. "No camera tonight, see?" She held her empty hands up.

"You didn't happen to be here the other night when Bobby Baxter was arrested, did you?" Felix asked.

There it was. I barely contained the urge to roll my eyes.

Luckily for him, Trace shook his head. "No, but from what I understand, it was quite the scene."

"I imagine it was," I said, shooting Felix a look. Ix-nay on interrogating our iends-fray.

He must have seen it, as he put on his charming smile again. "Well, we'll let you enjoy your evening. It was good to see you again, Trace."

"Take it easy you guys," Trace said as we turned to walk away.

I gave a small wave to Cam and Trace and let Felix lead me back to our table. The comforting heat from his palm seeped into my skin at the small of my back, making me instantly forgive his nosey nature. Let's face it, who was I to judge?

He pulled out my chair, and I sat. He then took his seat, leaned back in his chair, and raised one eyebrow at me.

"What?"

"Like you wouldn't have asked Trace about Baxter?"

I laughed. "Okay, fine. Yes, I totally would have."

He grinned. "I know. Which is why I love you so much."

I felt myself blush and covered it by picking up my menu. His tone was teasing, which left me with a funny feeling of giddiness and self-doubt at the words. I tried to brush it off as I scanned the wine list.

A few minutes later the waitress came by and took our orders. I decided to take pity on Felix and go for the baked ziti, on Cam's recommendation. Felix went with the chicken parmesan. Both were delicious. I knew because Felix fed me bites of his meal across the candlelit table. Despite being in the middle of one of Hollywood's busiest restaurants, I had to admit it was kind of romantic after all. The romance was only interrupted at brief intervals when Felix pumped the passing waitstaff for info about what they may have seen the night Baxter was arrested. I couldn't blame him, because he was right—I'd have done the same thing if he hadn't done it first. Unfortunately, no one had any new information to add to the bare bones we already knew. Fortunately, the wine was warming, the meal indulgent, and the company witty and hot enough that by the end of the meal, I was really hoping the *business* part of our evening was over and we could get to the *pleasure*.

"That was a lovely meal," I told Felix, snuggling against his arm outside as we waited for our driver.

"I agree. And the company wasn't bad either." He grinned down at me, and my knees melted a little.

"And the wine was divine."

He grinned again. "I noticed you enjoyed it."

I swatted him playfully on the arm. "What's that supposed to mean?"

"Nothing. I just might have liked a taste."

I swatted him harder this time, and he laughed in response, clearly enjoying the rise he was getting out of me. Okay, so maybe I had drunk a bit more than my fair share of the bottle. I was young, in a hot dress, and with a gorgeous man on my arm. Why not have a little fun?

"Well, I tell you what," I said, going back in for the snuggle as our car came into view. "I have another bottle at home that's almost as good. I'm happy to share it with you."

Felix gave me a brief smile but didn't answer as our car pulled up and he helped me in.

Hmmm…not exactly encouraging. Okay, maybe he hadn't gotten my hint. I tried again as we pulled away from the curb.

"Or, if you'd rather, we can go to your place?"

Again with the brief smile. Maybe even briefer this time. "I don't want to keep you out too late."

Translation: I don't want you to stay over?

I gave myself a mental shake, telling myself I was reading too much into it. I pulled out what I hoped was my most seductive smile, leaning toward him until the thin strap of my dress fell down my shoulder ever so slightly. "We could just stay in at my place tonight then."

This time his smile was not only brief, but it held a touch of something I couldn't quite put my finger on. I prayed it wasn't pity.

"I'd love to, Allie, but I have a long day tomorrow, and you have that interview with Baxter in the morning. How about a rain check?"

I blinked at him. Was he serious? I was in the hottest dress known to man, he'd just said he'd loved me at dinner (okay, I was pretty sure that had been teasing levity, but still!), and I was practically throwing myself at him after admittedly drinking a bit too much wine. If he was looking for an opening to take me to bed, there wasn't going to be a better one.

"Sure. Rain check." I tried to sound understanding as I adjusted my shoulder strap, but in all honestly, I didn't understand at all. A horrible thought occurred to me. Was Felix losing interest?

The rest of the car ride back to my place was quiet. Felix held my hand but barely said half a dozen words the entire time. The car pulled up outside my apartment building, we got out, and Felix walked me to my door.

"I'll see you tomorrow after your interview. Sleep well, Allie."

Felix leaned down and pressed a quick kiss to my lips. Then he turned on his heel and walked back to the car before I could respond.

I closed my apartment door and locked it behind me, watching out of the side window as the car pulled away and disappeared out of sight.

Mr. Fluffykins meowed and wound himself around my legs. I bent down and scooped him up into my arms.

"I have no idea what his deal is," I confided to my furry pal as I carried him down the hall and sat him on the bed. On a normal day, I might have kicked him out to the living room to sleep on his pink pillow bed. But tonight I needed the extra snuggles, even if they were feline.

With a sigh, I kicked my shoes off and slid the dress off, letting it pool on the floor. My top dresser drawer was partially open, and my sky blue pajamas with little sheep on them were poking out. I grabbed them, pulled them on, and climbed into bed.

Could he really be losing interest already? That was fast. But tonight he'd acted like I had cooties and he hadn't had his yearly cooties shot.

I briefly wondered if I was just a fling to him. Felix was, admittedly, at least a decade older than I was. I didn't know whether it was my age or not, but there were times when I got the feeling he didn't take me quite seriously.

I snuggled down into my fluffy linens and closed my eyes. "Maybe he just needs a little more time, Fluffykins," I said as my kitty curled up against me and I cuddled him close. Maybe he was shy. Maybe it was a British thing. Maybe—

I was just drifting off to sleep, counting my maybes, when my phone rang.

I grabbed it off of the nightstand. Felix's name appeared on the display. A thrill of excitement shot through me. *Maybe* he'd changed his mind about that early morning. I grinned as I answered the call.

"I was hoping you'd change your mind…"

"Allie, something's happened." Felix's voice came fast and serious, and I was instantly on high alert.

"What's going on?" I sat up in bed.

"It's Bobby Baxter…"

I groaned. "Great. Tell me he didn't cancel our interview again."

"No." I heard Felix take a deep breath. "He's dead."

CHAPTER THREE

——

Almost an hour later I was standing on a street corner in downtown L.A. in jeans and a hastily thrown on T-shirt, staring at a dead Bobby Baxter.

Crime scene tape sectioned off the sidewalk, and the paparazzi crowded the street, snapping pictures while reporters shouted questions at the police on the scene. I spotted Tina Bender, a fellow reporter at the *Informer,* jotting down notes on her tiny notepad. Her black clothing and purple streaked hair stood out in the crowd. She looked up and spotted me, narrowed her eyes, and then went back to her notes.

I wanted to kick myself for allowing her to beat me to the scene. Tina and I had been in a kind of competition for the best stories since the day I'd arrived. I'd had something to prove—that Felix hadn't hired me just because I was a D cup— and she'd had something of her own to prove to me—that she was top dog, and I better not think of stealing her bone. Of course, I'd done just that. Hey, what better way to show you could run with the big dogs than to take the big doggie's fave toy? What I hadn't counted on was that Tina wasn't the *forgive and forget* kind. She was more the *we can coexist, but stay off my turf* kind.

Only, Bobby was my story and my turf. And now I had to play catch up. Damn. I hated playing catch up. There was no telling what kind of information Tina had gotten before I'd arrived.

I weaved my way through the crowd until I was standing up against the crime scene tape. Thankfully, I'd made it in time to see the body before the police covered it with a tarp. Just seeing the body alone answered many of my questions. Bobby was lying face up, eyes open, with a bullet hole in the center of his forehead. Cause of death—pretty straightforward. Blood pooled beneath his head and upper body and dripped off the curb into the street.

As much as I was trying to be the cool, unemotional reporter, I felt bile begin to rise in the back of my throat and had to look away. The fact that I'd seen this man so full of life— albeit angry life—just hours ago hit me harder than I thought it would. Tears pricked the back of my eyes, and I took deep breaths to try to keep the scenery from spinning.

Reporters were shouting questions all around me, all of which the police ignored. I scanned the crowd, purposely *not* looking at Bobby again, and spotted another familiar face. Cam. She was still in the cocktail dress I'd seen her in earlier, though she'd covered it with a trench that felt more appropriate for the gritty scene than sparkly sequins.

I worked my way through the crowd, stepping on toes and dodging elbows until I was by her side.

"Can you believe this?" she asked when I stepped up beside her. Gone was the celebratory smile she'd had earlier. Instead her face looked grim and decidedly sober. "Total madness."

She wasn't lying. The street was full of reporters, and fans were starting to crowd as well, blocking traffic.

"Hey, didn't you interview this guy?" she asked as she raised her camera and fired off a few shots in rapid succession.

"I was supposed to today, but he put it off until tomorrow morning. Have you heard anything?" I almost had to shout for her to hear me as she held her camera up and fired off more shots.

"Just that he was shot, which is pretty obvious." She nodded toward the body with a hole in its head. "I overheard the coroner say he'd been dead about an hour or so when I got here."

I checked the time on my phone. That put the time of death at somewhere near midnight. "Did anyone witness the shooting?" I asked.

"Not that I've heard. This corner of the street isn't usually busy this time of night, so I'm not surprised."

Neither was I. It's not like a killer was going to just walk up and kill someone, especially someone as famous as Bobby

Baxter, on a busy street corner. Not if he wanted to get away with it, that was.

"But I'll tell you one thing," Cam said, snapping off more pictures. "If you want to get the lowdown on this story, you better get a move on. Tina's here, and she's determined."

I looked over at my competition again. Tina might not like me, but I'll admit I admired her. She was one hell of a reporter, and she'd proven in the past that she wasn't afraid to take some wild chances to get her story. Even if they were usually at my expense.

"Thanks, Cam. I'll see you at the office in the morning."

"Take it easy," she said and continued to work.

I made my way through the worst of the crowd, listening for anything that I could print. The chatter was all the same. Someone had killed Bobby Baxter. No one had seen anything. The police weren't talking to the press.

I hung around for a few minutes, but the officers on the scene stonewalled all my questions with curt "no comment"s. As the coroner's van showed up to move Bobby, and the crowd began to disperse, I realized I wasn't getting anything else here tonight. I trudged back to my car and headed in the direction of my apartment.

* * *

I stepped off the elevators the next morning at nine fifteen, just *slightly* late for work. Already the hum of activity was high. Keyboards clacked as reporters like myself typed out stories and columns. A symphony of voices taking calls from informants and following up on "anonymous" sources collided, creating a dull roar of noise. And various assistants and interns raced between their cubicles and Felix's glass-walled office in the center of the room, with hot tips and tepid coffees. Felix looked up from the copy he was approving as I walked past, giving me a nod. I gave the chief a little salute before settling at my desk in my own cube near the windows.

The first thing I did—after getting my own tepid coffee, that is—was assemble my meager notes from my trip the day before to the set of *Bobby Tells All* and jot off a quick story on

Bobby, his death, and his altercation weeks before. It wasn't much, but I hoped my insider look at the show at least added some extra interest over whatever Tina was cooking up. I quickly emailed it to Felix. It wasn't my best work, but it would have to do until I could get to the heart of the real story—who had killed Bobby Baxter.

The interview that I would now never get was scheduled for ten o'clock, and while I clearly couldn't talk to Bobby, there was a chance I could talk to his personal assistant again. While I wasn't counting on getting lucky enough that Henry would know who killed Bobby, I had a strong hope that he could at least tell me where Bobby had been the night before and who he'd planned to be with. I only hoped that Henry had been too distraught to remember to have my name removed from the studio visitor's list.

Twenty minutes later I pulled up to the gates outside the studio where *Bobby Tells All* was filmed and stopped at the guard shack.

The same plump, balding man who'd allowed me entrance the day before leaned out of the shack window and smiled.

"Back again today, Ms. Quick?"

"I sure am." I smiled up at him.

He flipped some pages on his clipboard and nodded. "There you are," he said as he scanned the sheets of paper.

I let out a mental sigh of relief.

"Have a nice day." He sent me a small salute and raised the wooden arm barring my car's way. I drove through, made a right, and parked in the visitor parking area. I grabbed a visitor golf cart and steered in the direction of the *Bobby Tells All* set.

From what I'd seen of Bobby's behavior the day before, I couldn't help but wonder if he'd finally pushed someone he worked with too far and if they'd lost it and knocked him off. The thought wasn't too farfetched. Bobby appeared to be a major pain. I'd read stories of people being killed for a lot less.

I parked outside the giant warehouse that was home to *Bobby Tells All* and walked inside. The set was quiet, but many of the crew members were still milling about looking unsure what to do. Clearly the memo hadn't gotten to everyone last night that the star of their show was dead. I spotted the director talking quietly to a couple of men in suits—likely from the network—near the side of the stage that was still set up like the lab from yesterday's segment. I spotted the makeup girl and the wardrobe woman sitting near the Craft services table, chatting in low tones. To my surprise, the wardrobe woman was dabbing her eyes with a tissue. Either she had a very kind heart, or maybe Bobby hadn't always been a jerk to her. A couple of feet away I spotted Henry, his headset dangling around his neck and a cup of coffee in hand. If possible, he looked more tired and spent than the day before.

My ballet flats—which perfectly paired with my curve-hugging white linen jumpsuit—tapped quietly today as I made my way over to where he was standing.

"Henry?" I asked. "Allie Quick from the *L.A. Informer*. Remember me?"

"Of course, Ms. Quick." He appeared surprised. "I didn't expect to see you here after..." He trailed off, clearly not sure how to tactfully refer to his boss being found shot in the head.

I nodded and tried to look appropriately sympathetic and understanding.

"I heard about what happened to Bobby. I'm so sorry for your loss."

Henry cleared his throat. "Thanks. But it's not like we were close."

I raised an eyebrow at him. "Oh?"

"Bobby wasn't exactly the type to get personal." Then he frowned as if suddenly realizing what he was saying. "Don't get me wrong. I'm sorry he's gone. No one deserves that." He paused, as if mentally envisioning *that*.

"I noticed yesterday that Bobby wasn't exactly the warm fuzzy type," I said, hoping to draw a bit more out of him.

Henry shrugged. "Hollywood. What can you do?"

"How long did you work for him?"

"Three years."

"That's a long time. You must have gotten to know each other pretty well."

He shook his head. "Like I said, Bobby wasn't interested in getting personal. He didn't know anything about me except that I did all of his grunt work for him."

While Henry was clearly shaken at the turn of events, he didn't sound all that torn up about Bobby being gone. Then again, who could blame him? From what I'd seen of Bobby, I couldn't say I'd miss him much either if I'd had to do his grunt work.

"Do you know anyone who would've wanted to hurt him?" I said, asking the obvious question.

Henry shrugged. "Bobby was...let's say, abrupt...with almost everyone. You couldn't throw a rock around here without hitting someone who'd had a run-in with him at some point. But I don't know of anyone who would've actually killed him, if that's what you mean."

"Did he have any arguments with anyone on set lately? Maybe more heated than normal?" I added, fearing the answer could encompass just about everyone.

Henry shook his head. "He might not have been the easiest guy to work for, but he was the reason we all got paychecks, you know?"

He had a point. I glanced around at the shell-shocked crew. Without Bobby, *Bobby Tells All* was done for, and they were all out of a job. I didn't know anyone who'd throw away their livelihood simply because the guy they worked for was a jerk.

I decided to try another avenue.

"Bobby uncovered a lot of the secrets on his show, didn't he?"

Henry shrugged again. "I guess so. I mean, that was the whole point—uncover the stuff big business doesn't want you to know."

"Did anyone he ever profile on the show retaliate? Maybe file a lawsuit or threaten Bobby himself?"

"Sure. All the time."

Oh boy. Bobby's winning personality was making the suspect pool hard to narrow down. "Any stand out to you?"

Henry shook his head. "Not really. Legal handles all of that. Besides, none of them would have a reason to kill Bobby. The shows have already aired."

"What about shows that haven't aired yet?" I asked. "Do you know what Bobby was currently working on?"

Henry leaned back against the wall and crossed his arms over his chest. "We had a few shows in production that hadn't aired yet. But they're really no big secret. They're posted on the website."

I made a mental note to check out Bobby's site.

"What can you tell me about them?" I smiled, hoping to appeal to his good nature to indulge me.

He sighed. "Well, there were three that he was developing at the moment."

I pulled out my phone, hitting the record function to take notes as Henry began giving me the details.

"The first one just wrapped shooting yesterday—you saw the tail end of it."

I nodded encouragingly.

"It was called 'The Tooth and Nothing but the Tooth.' It was a tell-all about oral hygiene. Like, what your dentist doesn't want you to know. The truth about flossing and mouthwash and all that." He shrugged, seeming unimpressed with the show idea himself. "The one we finished before that was called 'Hair Today Gone Tomorrow.' It was another exposé type of show that was supposed to tell the good, the bad, and the really ugly about laser hair removal."

"And the last show?" I asked.

"The last show that I know about was still in the research phase. It was called 'Takin' Out the Trash.' It was supposed to uncover the truth about what really happens to your garbage and recycling after it reaches the plant. Where it ends up, how recycling really works, if it's actually environmentally friendly with all the chemicals and water used. Stuff like that. It's supposed to air later this spring."

None of these shows sounded like they could lead to a man's murder. Homicidal dentist? Angry estheticians? I mean, how bad could recycling be? I tried not to let my disappointment show. So far, my one *in* with this story was turning out to be a dud.

"One last thing," I said, feeling I was quickly losing Henry's attention. "Do you know what Bobby's schedule was last night? Where he was going, who he planned to be with?"

Henry shook his head. "Sorry. I had the night off."

Fab. But I pasted on a smile anyway and told him, "Thanks, Henry. You've been a big help."

"Hey, you're welcome. Now, if you'll excuse me, I need to start looking for another job." He gave me a wan smile as he walked away.

I hurried back to the golf cart I'd driven to the set and steered in the direction of the visitor parking lot and my car. Then I hopped into my Bug and pulled past the guard shack and onto the 10 freeway in the direction of the *Informer*. As I went over what Henry had told me, I couldn't help but worry how Tina was faring. It was clear from her presence at the crime scene last night that she intended to try to scoop me. I wondered if Felix knew Tina was trying to steal my story out from under me. Not that he'd care, really. As much as Felix was a hot date and a protective guy when it came to us as a couple, when we were in the office, it was all business. And Felix was in the business of printing the most salacious, scandalous stories he could get—no matter where they came from. If Tina came in with something juicier than I did, I knew he wouldn't think twice about killing my story and going with hers.

That thought had me pushing the accelerator just a *tad* harder than I should as I hit the 101 and raced under one of the massive overpasses.

It wasn't until I spotted the telltale black-and-white of a CHP officer's car at the side of the road that I slowed. Luckily for me, he already had a small sports car, with an angry-looking driver behind the wheel, pulled over at the side of the road. The CHP must have been hiding under the overpass and caught the sports car speeding. I thanked my lucky stars it was him who'd been caught in the speed trap and not me. The thought of having to pay a speeding ticket threw a bucket of cold water on my desire to get to the office any quicker than legally possible.

Fifteen minutes later I pulled up in front of the *Informer*.

The *L.A. Informer* offices were housed in a three-story, square, dingy beige stucco building with peeling paint and a rickety fire escape that would probably kill you faster than the fire you were running from. It was located on Hollywood Boulevard, just on the border of where tourist shops selling maps to stars' homes gave way to crack houses selling stuff that could make you see stars.

I locked my car in the lot behind the building and hurried inside. I rode the sketchy elevator up to the second floor. The doors dinged open, which startled me because they hadn't dinged in weeks. Someone must have sprung for a repair finally. I stepped off into the controlled chaos that was my place of employment.

I passed by Cam in her cubicle sorting through her shots of Bobby Baxter's extremely dead body, and Tina in her cubicle talking animatedly on the phone while simultaneously clicking her computer mouse. She looked up, saw me, frowned, and then turned her chair in the opposite direction. Great. She probably had a hot lead, while I had stories about dentists and trash.

Felix glanced up and spotted me as I passed by. I gave him a small smile. He nodded once at me then bent his head back to the work on the desk in front of him. I ignored his cool *we're at work* demeanor and continued toward my desk.

"Hey, Allie." Max Beacon popped his gray head up from his cubicle as I approached.

"Hey, yourself."

"You heard about Bobby Baxter?"

I nodded.

"Gonna be a hell of an obit," he said. Max was somewhere between 65 and 105, had a balding head of pure white hair, droopy bloodshot eyes, a prickly growth of gray stubble covering the lower half of his face, and a faint aroma of whisky, probably from the flask he kept not-so-hidden in his bottom desk drawer. He wrote the obituary column, and he'd been at the *Informer* longer than anyone. And he vowed he'd be here until we were ready to print his own obit, which he had prewritten, detailing how he'd died of cirrhosis of the liver.

"I heard you were supposed to interview the guy," Max said, leaning on the outer edge of his cube.

"Today in fact," I told him. "Just my luck."

"Could be worse," Max answered. "You could be Baxter."

"Very good point." I paused. "You have his obit done yet?" While I was *pretty* sure it wouldn't contain much I didn't already know, no stone unturned, right?

Max grinned as he sat back down behind his computer. An ancient one with an even more ancient monitor. Sometime around 1995 Max had refused to upgrade his equipment any further, which suited Felix's frugal nature just fine. "Funny, Tina just asked me the same thing."

I thought a dirty word. "You give it to her?"

Max shook his head. "I wasn't done yet."

"And are you done now?" I asked, batting my eyelashes at him.

His grin widened. "It just so happens that I am."

Finally the blonde catches a break! "So, can I see it?" I shot him another eyelash-fluttering smile.

He cackled deep in his throat. "It's good for my old heart to have pretty young girls fighting over me." He pulled a sheet of paper from his printer and handed it to me. "But know that if Tina asks, I'm not keeping anything from her either."

I waved him off. That was fine with me. As long as I got it first.

I took the paper and read it over. "Bobby was married?"

"It appears so." Max nodded. "Marilyn Baxter is her name. They're separated now, but they hadn't divorced yet, from what I understand."

That would explain why no one had mentioned a wife to me so far. It also put a whole new spin on who could've killed Bobby. Wasn't the wife always the best suspect?

"Thanks, Max," I said, turning toward my desk. "I owe you one."

He grinned at me. "If you need anything else, you know where to find me."

I hurried to my desk and ran a quick search for Bobby Baxter on a website for public records. As Max had said, no divorce on record. There were, however, two properties in Bobby's name. A large home in the Hollywood Hills purchased two years ago and a condo in Culver City, near the studio that had just been purchased a few months ago. When the happy couple split, perhaps? Putting my money on the Hollywood Hills place as the wife's residence, I jotted down the address, shut down my computer, grabbed my purse, and practically ran to the elevator. As the doors slid shut, I spotted Tina eyeing me. She knew I was up to something.

The fact that Marilyn Baxter was separated from her husband was interesting. Clearly there was trouble in paradise, and clearly if a divorce was imminent, she stood to have her assets cut at least in half—possibly more if Bobby'd had her sign a prenup. But since her husband died before the divorce became final, she stood to inherit everything.

I needed to talk to the wife.

I hopped off of the janky elevator, jogged across the lot, and once inside my Bug, sped off in the direction of the Hollywood Hills.

CHAPTER FOUR

———

Half an hour later I'd wound my way up into the swanky Hollywood Hills that separated the Valley from Hollywood proper. The hills were a little piece of paradise, nestled between the graffiti-filled basins, that were ripe with mature trees, spectacular nighttime views, and celebrity neighbors on all sides. It took me another fifteen minutes of searching the lush, private neighborhoods to locate the Baxter residence.

Once I did, my hopes of talking to Bobby's wife plummeted. Half a dozen cops and paparazzi had already beaten me here.

I parked against the curb across the street and two houses down from the Baxter place and took a minute to survey the surrounding area.

The home was nice but not overly decadent. Long, paved driveway, two-story house with a Spanish tiled roof, and landscaping that looked impeccably well cared for. It spoke of money—but TV money, not movie star stuff.

The gates leading up the drive were standing wide open, and three police cars were parked in front of the house.

Apparently the authorities had the same idea about the wife that I did.

I started the car, drove about a block away, and parked against the curb in a turnaround. Then I got out of the car and started walking toward the Baxter residence. I figured that there was no way to talk to the wife alone with the police there, but I could still look around. I was at the edge of the wrought iron fence surrounding the property when I spotted an older Hispanic woman in an apron coming around the side of the house, pulling a large green trash bin behind her.

Mrs. Baxter had a housekeeper. I quickened my steps just a bit, glad I'd decided to wear ballet flats instead of my usual heels.

"Good morning," I said with a smile.

The woman looked up at me, surprise on her face. "Good morning."

"I'm Allie. I just moved in down the road a ways and was out checking out the neighborhood."

The housekeeper nodded, her tightly curled salt-and-pepper hair bobbing as she did. "I'm Marta, and welcome. This is a very nice neighborhood."

"Have you worked here long?" I motioned in the direction of the house.

"A couple of years."

I scrunched up my face like I was thinking hard and asked, "Isn't this where that host of that tell-all show lives? What was his name..." I snapped my fingers and looked away as though trying to remember.

"Bobby Baxter," Marta said. "But he doesn't live here. Only Mrs. Baxter is in residence. And I stay in the guest house."

"Oh? They split up?"

Marta nodded.

"Did you work for them when the couple was together?"

Again she nodded, bobbing her curls. "Si. I've been with them since they moved here."

"That's so sad. Did they argue a lot?"

Marta wiped her hands on her apron. "All of the time."

"About what?"

Marta paused, eyeing me suspiciously. Oops. Too far?

I cleared my throat. "I mean, well, between you and me, my husband and I just separated. It's...not pretty." I looked down, pretending to wipe a tear.

"Oh, I'm so sorry." Marta sounded so sincere I almost felt bad for lying to her.

Almost. "Thanks. It's been rough. I, well, I just imagine it must have been rough for Mrs. Baxter too."

Marta nodded. "Yes. Divorce is never easy. But I'll tell you one thing—cheaters always get what they deserve in the end."

My ears pricked up at that. Now we were getting somewhere. "Cheating? That's why they broke up?"

Marta paused. "I shouldn't say anything. Not with Mr. Baxter gone." She made the sign of the cross over her chest then leaned in and whispered, "He was killed last night."

"I did hear something about that on the radio this morning," I lied. "I can't imagine how Mrs. Baxter must have felt when the police showed up at her door last night."

"I don't think she knew until this morning," Marta said. "She wasn't in when the police came last night."

"Wait—Mrs. Baxter wasn't at home last night?"

Marta blinked at me, suddenly realizing maybe she'd said too much. "I, uh, I don't know. She wasn't in when I went to sleep."

"What time was that?"

"A-around one thirty," she said, glancing back over her shoulder at the house.

Bingo. The wife didn't have an alibi. I was liking this more and more.

"Do the police think that she did it? Is that why they're here?" I pressed.

"I don't think so," Marta said, suddenly in a hurry to secure the lid on the trash bin. "Mrs. Baxter might argue and yell, but she wouldn't kill someone." She paused. "She wouldn't do anything that might get her hands dirty."

The way Marta's expression shifted on that last note told me Marilyn Baxter might not be a model employer. Maybe not even a nice person.

"I have to go," she said, turning back to the house.

"It was good talking to you!" I called after her. "It's a nice neighborhood." But I wasn't entirely sure she still believed my story at this point.

I turned and jogged back up the block. A teenager on a skateboard was trying to execute some sort of complicated flip thing near my car. He looked up as I approached, and moved to shove off.

"Hey, wait a minute," I hailed him.

He put his foot down and kicked his board up into his hands. The kid was about sixteen or seventeen, had copper colored hair, fair skin dotted with a smattering of light freckles, and green eyes. He wore a black beanie, a T-shirt sporting the name of some gaming site, and jeans.

"'Sup?" He nodded at me once then let his eyes run me up and down. He must have liked what he saw, as his mouth turned up in a crooked smile.

"Do you live around here?" I asked.

He nodded. "Just there." He pointed to a house sitting across from the hub of activity.

"I was wondering if you could do me a favor." I smiled at him sweetly.

"That depends. What's in it for me?" he asked, eyes rooted to the low cut neckline of my jumpsuit.

I reached into my purse, pulled out my wallet, fished around inside, and came out with a few twenties.

I held them up.

"I'll give you a hundred bucks if you'll watch that house and call me if the woman who lives there leaves."

His eyes bounced between my cleavage and the money.

"Sure. Is that it?"

I grabbed a business card out of my purse and scribbled my cell number on the back. "Call or text this number the minute that woman leaves the house."

He took the card and the money. "You got it, babe."

"And keep this just between the two of us," I said with a wink.

"No problem." He dropped the board on the sidewalk and rolled away.

I jumped back into my car, hoping I hadn't wasted my money. Or, technically, Felix's, since I was totally expensing this to the *Informer*'s account.

Once I was out of the hills, I swung by the drive-thru at my favorite coffee shop and grabbed a frappe and a scone, which I nibbled on the way back to the office.

I rode the elevator up to the second floor and stepped off.

Felix glanced up at me as I passed by, and I waved my frappe cup at him.

He did a palms-up and mouthed the words *Where's mine?*

Cute. I shrugged and gave him an apologetic look.

I noticed Tina wasn't at her desk. That was concerning. I fleetingly wondered if Cam knew where she was and what I'd have to do to bribe her into telling me.

Max stuck his head up and waved as I passed then went back to work on whatever he was typing away on.

I dropped my purse on the floor beside my desk, sat my frappe down next to my monitor, and took a seat.

At a temporary dead end where Marilyn Baxter was concerned, I figured I'd shift focus to whom Bobby had been "telling all" about. I started by searching for the show's website that Henry had told me about. I pulled up a search engine and keyed in Bobby Baxter, quickly finding it was the top hit.

I clicked the link, and a photo of Bobby flashed on the screen. With his big toothy smile and slicked back hair, he looked more like a greasy used car salesman than the host of a popular television show. Or maybe that was just because I now knew the personality that went with that mug. I clicked around on the site menu until I found a *coming soon* link.

Following the link, a list of upcoming shows and their blurbs appeared.

The only three shows were the same ones the personal assistant had told me about when I'd questioned him earlier in the morning.

I clicked the first show link.

"The Tooth and Nothing but the Tooth." From what I could tell, the theme for the show was basically telling people that they didn't need to go to the dentist as often as they thought. I skimmed the rest of the show's page, and the most scandalous thing I came across was the line about not having to floss often, as long as you rinsed well with mouthwash.

While I suddenly didn't feel half as guilty about my flossing habits, there was no way someone had killed Bobby over this info. Not unless a convention of crazy, homicidal dentists had come to town. I closed that show's page and clicked on the second link.

"Hair Today Gone Tomorrow."

The plot was along the same lines as the dentist show but was about the truth behind laser hair removal and how it might only work if you have fine, unnoticeable hair to begin with. Again, I didn't see anything that would send someone into a homicidal rage. It was highly doubtful someone had killed Bobby over hair removal.

I clicked on the last link, and a page for "Takin' Out the Trash" popped up.

There was little information posted about it, which fit what Henry said about it still being in the research phase. Unfortunately, it also gave me nothing to go on. I grabbed my cell and pulled up Henry's office number.

He answered on the third ring.

"Henry Klein."

"Henry? This is Allie Quick with the *L.A. Informer*."

"Yeah, I remember. Is there something I can do for you, Ms. Quick?"

"Actually, there is," I said and tapped my pen on the desk gently. "I was wondering if you could tell me a little bit more about one of the shows Bobby was working on. 'Takin' Out the Trash'?"

"Why do you want to know about that?" he asked.

"I'm still working on a story about Bobby, and I took a look at his website like you suggested. There's the bare minimum about it listed on the site. Do you happen to know what kind of info Bobby was planning to tell all about?"

"I don't really know," Henry said easily. "To be honest, I'm not sure the show was going to be that big of a hit really. Who wants to watch a show about trash?"

"Is that all the show was about?" I asked.

"As far as I know. It was basically just explaining how recycling isn't really that environmentally friendly. You know, with the amount of water and chemicals they use to process the trash."

"Did the show feature any one person or company in particular?"

"Um, I think he mostly focused on one company. Hang on. Let me pull up my contacts."

I tapped my pen on my desk in a frantic staccato while I listened to Henry fiddling with his phone.

Finally he came back on. "Sunshine Sanitation."

I wrote the name down. "Any particular reason he profiled them?"

"Not that I know of," Henry answered. "They have the biggest recycling contracts in the L.A. basin, though, so it's not totally surprising."

I feared I was chasing down another dead end. Mostly likely, Henry was right. The only thing odd about this show was that Bobby had chosen to do a show on trash altogether.

"Thanks, Henry. I appreciate your help."

"Anytime."

I ended the call and dropped my phone into my purse. Since I had nothing better to do, I googled Sunshine Sanitation. The company's website popped up. A giant yellow sun with a smiley face and sunglasses filled the screen. An animated *Keepin' It Clean!* popped up on the screen in hot pink lettering.

I raised my eyebrows at the extremely bright and flashy advertisement. I loved bright and flashy as much, if not more, than the next girl, but for a sanitation company? Whatever worked, I guess. I clicked around a bit, but nothing popped out at me as odd. Other than how happy they seemed to be collecting people's trash. Just to cover all bases, I picked up my phone and dialed the number listed on their contact page.

A bubbly woman answered after the first ring.

"Keepin' it clean with Sunshine Sanitation. This is Ellen. How can I help you?"

"This is Allie Quick from the *L.A. Informer*," I introduced myself. "I understand that your company was the focus of an episode of *Bobby Tells All*, 'Takin' Out the Trash,' and I was hoping to ask you some questions about your experience with Mr. Baxter."

The woman's bubbly personality quickly turned cold. "We have no comment," she said. Before I could say another word, she hung up on me.

So much for that. Though, I didn't blame her. If Bobby's show had been all about how recycling wasn't really all that great for the environment, it probably didn't paint the cheery company in a good light. Though, honestly, I couldn't see them killing over it. It wasn't like people were going to watch Bobby's show and immediately stop recycling. And since the city gave contracts to utilities like garbage and water, it wasn't as if Sunshine Sanitation was in danger of losing customers either.

All of which left me right back where I'd started—nowhere.

My stomach rumbled. I glanced at the clock and realized that it was after five. Max had already left, and Tina was still nowhere in sight. I looked at Felix in his office. He was talking animatedly on the phone. It looked like something definitely had him fired up. Felix wasn't very good company when something had him riled up, so I squashed the idea to invite him to dinner, until he was in a better mood.

I powered down my computer, grabbed my purse, and headed for the elevator.

Traffic was so thick that the drive back to my place took nearly an hour. When I finally stepped foot into my apartment and closed the door behind me, I leaned my back against the door and sighed with relief. Mr. Fluffykins raised his head from his comfy spot on the sofa, meowed at me, and then lay back down. Apparently my arrival wasn't anything to celebrate.

"It's nice to see you too." I tossed my purse on the coffee table and went into the kitchen. Mr. Fluffykins ignored me as I made my way past his perch.

I opened the freezer. Three Lean Cuisines: mac 'n cheese, chicken penne, and green enchiladas. I decided to make it a fiesta and grabbed the enchilada box. I popped a couple of holes in the plastic and stuck it in the microwave. Mr. Fluffykins came into the kitchen, meowing in what I knew was his way of demanding fresh food and water, so I refilled his dishes, patted his head, and then washed my hands.

The timer on the microwave dinged, and I was just about to pull my dinner out, when my phone rang.

I jogged the five steps into the living room to my purse, fished around inside, and pulled out my phone. A number I didn't recognize flashed on the display. I pressed the phone to my ear.

"Allie Quick."

"Hey, this is Shane."

"Hi," I said, hesitantly, trying to remember if I knew a Shane.

"You gave me your card today and asked me to call you if the lady across the street left her house, remember?"

Right. The teen on the skateboard. "Of course. Has she left?" I asked, my heart rate kicking up a notch.

"It looks like she's about to," he said with a hint of excitement in his voice. "I saw her toss a black bag into the backseat of her car, and then she went back inside."

"That's great, Shane. I'm on my way. Keep an eye on her. Text me if she leaves before I get there. There's an extra fifty in it for you if I catch her."

"You got it!" he agreed eagerly before ending the call.

I tossed my phone back into my purse and hurried out the door.

CHAPTER FIVE

———

I gunned my little Bug, ignoring the speed limit. I had to catch Mrs. Baxter leaving her home before she got too far ahead of me and I lost her. I'd just rounded the last curve leading to the Baxter estate when a black BMW zoomed past me. I recognized the car as the one that had been sitting in the Baxters' driveway earlier in the day when I'd been talking to Marta. A second later a text pinged in from Shane.

She just left

I turned around in front of the Baxters' house, quickly heading back down the hill after the BMW. As soon as I caught sight of her, I hung back. The last thing I wanted to do was spook her into thinking she was being followed. I let her weave through the turns a few car lengths ahead of me, staying just close enough to keep her in sight.

Once we made it out of the hills, she stayed on Highland, following it all the way to Wilshire. I stayed behind her one lane over and to the right to avoid being spotted. We bobbed and weaved through the evening traffic until she pulled up to the Grand Hotel and Spa.

Checking into a hotel for the night? That might explain the bag Shane had seen her toss onto the backseat of her car.

I pulled around the building and parked in a slot marked *Visitor* instead of valeting my car. After paying off Shane to spy for me, I was a smidge low on funds. I jogged back around to the front of the building just in time to see a woman I assumed was Marilyn Baxter get out of her car. She was a tall, extremely thin, platinum blonde with high cheekbones and obviously enhanced lips. And boobs. And butt. I wondered if there was anything on her that wasn't man-made. From my vantage point, she appeared to be your typical trophy wife. I silently wondered how long she and Bobby had been together.

I watched her hand a bellboy a black overnight bag and a tip and stroll inside. I followed a step behind, pushing through the revolving door. She was at the check-in desk. I busied myself looking at some magazine racks in the gift shop until she thanked the clerk and made her way down the hall toward the spa.

I waited a two-Mississippi count then followed. She chatted with a short brunette at the spa's front desk for a moment. Then she was led into another room, where I could see pedicure chairs set up in neat little rows. Mrs. Baxter sat and put her feet into one of the tubs before the brunette walked away.

My piggies immediately whimpered with jealousy inside my ballet flats. It had been more than a month since my last pedicure. I wiggled my toes. A pedicure would be a great excuse to strike up a conversation with Marilyn. I mentally calculated just how much room I had left before hitting my credit card limit. I could pay a couple of bills a little late, couldn't I? I mean, who really needed electricity?

Mind made up, I walked into to the spa and up to the reception desk.

The woman manning it smiled at me in greeting. "Welcome to the Grand Hotel Spa. I'm Elizabeth. How may I help you?"

"I'm Allie. I was wondering if you happen to have an opening for a pedicure?"

Without even looking at her book, she beamed at me. "Of course. We have several chairs open at the moment. Are you a guest of the hotel?"

"No, I'm just stopping in," I said and returned her smile.

"No problem. I only ask because hotel guests are automatically given a discount."

She then waved over a woman of average height with brown hair and a pale complexion.

"This is Callie. She'll take good care of you."

"Thanks," I said and followed the young woman to the line of chairs along the back wall. Callie sat me one chair away from Marilyn. I toed off my shoes and placed my feet in the warm bubbly footbath Callie provided.

"Peppermint, lavender, or vanilla?" she asked me and motioned toward a line of scented oils.

"Vanilla please," I answered.

She placed a few drops in the bath. "I'll be back in a few minutes. You just sit here and relax." She smiled and then walked away.

The scent of smooth, creamy vanilla wafted up to meet me, and I had to fight the urge to close my eyes and relax against the soft cushiony seat.

I shook myself out of the little heaven I was enjoying and set my mind firmly back on the reason I was splurging on the little luxury my feet rested in.

I glanced over to Marilyn. She was wearing a short skirt, which was the designer version of a knockoff I had in my own closet, and a red sleeveless blouse. Her hair was piled high atop her head, and white gold and ruby chandelier earrings dangled from her earlobes. She was reading the latest copy of *Vogue* magazine and completely ignoring the world around her. I made a mental note to see if my copy had come in the mail when I got home. I spotted her shoes, a pair of black Christian Louboutin's, sitting in the chair between us.

"I love your shoes," I said and smiled.

She glanced at me then said in a bored tone, "Thanks. They were a gift from my husband."

"Wow. Lucky girl."

"If you say so," she said with a slight shrug and continued perusing her magazine.

I could see that she wasn't going to be an easy nut to crack. Just my luck. So I decided to just play it straight.

"You're Marilyn Baxter, aren't you?"

This time, she looked at me fully. "Yes. Who are you?"

"I'm Allie Quick. I'm a reporter for the *L.A. Informer*. I had an interview with your husband set up for yesterday, but he rescheduled, and then he was killed last night."

"And you think I can tell you something about that?" She pursed her blood red lips and narrowed her eyes at me.

"Your husband wanted to tell me his side of the story. About this altercation with that fan at Beverly's. I was hoping maybe you could help fill in the blanks."

She snorted. "You were, huh?"

"For example, where were you last night when he was killed?"

At that moment, her nail technician came over and shut off Marilyn's footbath, drying her feet in a large, fluffy towel.

"Listen, Abby," Marilyn said.

"Allie," I corrected her.

"Whatever." She waved a dismissive hand in the air. "I don't know how you got in here, but I'm not talking to the press. Least of all the *tabloids*." She said the last word as if it had a foul odor.

I let it roll off of me. This wasn't the first time I'd been subjected to rude comments concerning my career, and if I was doing my job right, it wouldn't be the last.

"I hear he was cheating on you," I said, almost offhandedly.

She froze. "Who told you that?"

I shrugged. "A source."

She shook her head, her eyes spitting fire at me. "You people are relentless. This is why I checked in here for the week in the first place. To get away from the likes of you!"

With that, she stood, grabbed her shoes out of the chair, and followed her tech to another area of the spa before I could say a single word in response.

So much for questioning her about her whereabouts. But at least I knew where she would be for the next week. I guess some women figured a spa week could fix anything, even their husband's murder.

Since I was already there, and probably already obligated to pay, I let Callie finish my pedi. An hour later I was back at home with a fresh coat of perfectly pink polish on my toes. I reheated my enchiladas, which were the consistency of cardboard at that point, then tossed those and microwaved the mac 'n cheese instead. It wasn't bad, especially when paired with a glass of chardonnay that I felt I had so earned after the day I'd had.

Once I'd drained my glass, I grabbed a quick shower and slid into a pair of pajamas with little purple pigs on them then pulled my laptop out.

Felix was online. Most likely working late. He was a bit of a workaholic, although he'd never admit it. I PMed him.

How was your day?

Busy, he responded.

Want to come over and relax a little? I can make some popcorn, and we can watch a movie? I asked. I knew chances were slim, but a girl had to try when she could.

Rain check? Got work to do still tonight.

Gee, he was really racking up those rain checks. At this point, he was close to a monsoon.

I was about to type back when he shot off, *I'll talk to you tomorrow*, and then a second later he signed off without awaiting a response.

I stared at the computer screen for another minute longer then closed it and set it on the nightstand. I tried to shut down the niggling worry that Felix was blowing me off. Could it be he didn't want to see me anymore? I realized that we hadn't actually said a word to each other all day at work. Granted, we'd both been busy. But it still felt odd.

Was this what it was like breaking up with someone you worked with? Would he be awkward and silent around me at work? Then blow me off in private? Oh God, would I need to find a new job? I'd barely gotten the one at the *Informer*. Would Felix even give me a reference? How did that work with ex-girlfriends?

I closed my eyes. I took a deep breath. I counted to ten.

Get a grip, girl. Felix was not breaking it off with me. I was being melodramatic. Probably.

I switched off the bedside lamp, snuggled my cat, and closed my eyes, trying not to think about it.

* * *

The next morning I was moving at a surprisingly decent pace through traffic on the 5, when I decided to take a quick detour to check out Bobby's apartment in Culver City before hitting the office. While I was sure the police had been all over it already, I figured it was at least worth a stop. They'd been looking for evidence of a crime, not necessarily the makings of a great story. Granted, solving the crime would make for the best story, but I was in *take what you can get* mode.

Culver City sat just west of the city of Los Angeles, nestled conveniently between the two main arteries of the region, the 405 and the 10 freeways. While the landscape wasn't much to write home about—mostly filled with tall concrete and glass buildings—it was prime real estate for studios, mega-agencies, and network headquarters. Bobby's condo was just off Jefferson, near the park—one of the rare units in town with a view of something green.

I found an empty spot at the curb a couple of blocks up from his building, parked, and adjusted my pencil skirt as I got out. The building looked roughly the same as all of the other ones on the block. Stucco exterior, balconies on the upper floors, underground parking for the residents, and a small lobby in front with mailboxes and an elevator. I took it up to the third floor, where Bobby's address was, but as soon as I approached his unit, I knew something was off.

Yellow crime scene tape fluttered along the sides of the door, which was partly ajar. I bit my lip, looking over both shoulders.

Reporter Me said, *Awesome! We can get inside. Just push the door open and let's look around!*

Coward Me said, *Are you freakin' nuts!? What if whoever broke in is still in there?*

I did an "eeny, meeny, miny, moe," and in the end, Reporter Me won out. I'd just do a quick little look around. And I'd leave the door open so I could make a fast escape if needed. And I pulled out a pair of latex gloves and slipped them on—no sense in leaving any fingerprints behind in case the police weren't done here. Then I grabbed my phone and let my finger hover over the icon for the *Informer*'s number in case anything went wrong.

I took a deep breath and pushed my way in, my eyes sweeping the place from my spot in the doorway. It looked like your average bachelor pad. A leather couch sat in front of a big screen TV, a small kitchen—looking largely unused—sat to the left, and a hallway led to the right, presumably to bedrooms. A balcony sat off the living room, offering a view of the park and a gas station the next block over. Nothing looked terrifically out of place, but then again, I had no idea what this place had looked like when Bobby had inhabited it.

I took a hesitant step forward, listening for any signs of life. "Hello?" I called out.

The only answer I got was silence.

I let out a little sigh of relief and took a few more steps in, leaving the front door partially open behind me. "Anyone here?" I asked as I moved through the living room toward the hallway. Four doors opened up off the hall. I peeked my head in the first one and found a guest bedroom. Queen bed, chest of drawers, and a chair by the window. Nothing that looked personal. I moved on.

The second doorway led to a guest bath, and the third to what looked like a home office with a desk and a couple of bookcases flanking the high window.

If Bobby had any personal notes or correspondence on the shows he'd been working on, I had a hunch this was where he'd keep it. I quickly moved around the desk. No computer, I noticed. Bummer. But if there had been one here, presumably the police would have taken it with them. They had left a cordless phone, but no lights blinked indicating messages. Not surprising. If Bobby was like most people, anything interesting or personal would be on his cell anyway—which was again likely in the custody of the police.

I randomly pulled out drawers, finding the usual mix of items like pens, rubber bands, stamps, and sticky notepads. Nothing terribly interesting. The first bookcase held mostly nonfiction and a lot of tell-alls. The second was devoted to file folders, notebooks, and what looked like shooting scripts. I pulled one out. *Love: Myth or Just Hormones.* I grinned, feeling a bit of sad nostalgia that there would never be any more clever revelations from Bobby Baxter. As much as he'd seemed a diva and a jerk in person, I really had been a fan of the show. I set the script back on the shelf.

And that was when I heard it.

A dull thud from the end of the hallway.

I froze, my hand midway from the bookcase, ears straining to hear more. I was not alone in the condo. Damn, why hadn't I listened to Cowardly Me?

I tiptoed to the doorway and gingerly peeked out. The last door off the hallway led to the master bedroom. And someone was in there. I took a deep breath, counted to three, and then took one tentative step into the hallway. If I made a quick sprint of it, I could maybe get to the front door and out of here before whoever had broken in saw me. Maybe. If they didn't have good reflexes. Or a gun.

That last thought shot a new round of adrenaline through me. I took one more step…

"Freeze!"

I screamed as a figure appeared in the master bedroom doorway, brandishing some sort of weapon high above his head.

Or, *her* head, I noticed as I paused in my banshee screech just long enough to register what I was looking at.

"Tina!" I shouted, taking in the purple hair, the poison green boots, and the retro Strawberry Shortcake T-shirt over trendy black jeans.

She blinked at me, her breath coming fast. "Allie! God, what are you doing here?" she asked. She lowered the weapon to her side. Which I now noticed was *not* a gun but a hair dryer.

I grinned. "I think the better question is, what are *you* doing here? Need a little styling before work?" I gestured to the hairdryer.

She frowned and tossed it onto the bed behind her. "It was the closest thing I could grab when I heard you. Cripes, you scared me. I thought you were an intruder."

"Ditto," I admitted. "You the one who broke the crime scene seal?" I asked as I took a step forward, joining her in the master bedroom.

She shrugged. "The crime scene tape had already been cut, and the door was open when I got here."

"Open?"

She shrugged. "Unlocked."

Close enough.

"Well, you scared me half to death," I told her, looking around. Bobby's bedroom was sadly as void of personal effects as the guest room had been. A king-sized bed took up the majority of the room, flanked by two nightstands, and an entryway on the left opened to a master bath. "So, find anything interesting?" I asked.

Tina smirked. "Right. Like I'd share it with you."

That was what I figured. "Tell you what—how about you show me yours, and I'll show you mine?" I offered. Which seemed like a safe enough trade considering I really didn't have much.

She narrowed her eyes at me, seemingly considering this. "I dunno. How do I know that you've got anything useful?"

Dang she was clever. "How do I know *you* do?" I countered.

She sucked in her cheeks and pursed her lips in thought. "Okay," she said finally. "You first. What's in the office?" she asked, gesturing to the room I'd just exited.

"Scripts, books, a landline."

She nodded. "And?"

"And that's it," I told her truthfully.

She rolled her eyes. "Well, that's not anything!"

"Hey, I didn't say I had anything. I just said I'd share."

Her eyes narrowed again. "Fine. Bobby's got a toilet, a sink, and a shower. Now I've shared."

My turn to roll my eyes. "Okay, this is pointless. The condo is a bust. But surely you've uncovered something about Bobby worth sharing?"

She crossed her arms over her chest and shook her head in the negative. "You. First."

I blew out a breath. "Okay, fine. Look, I know Bobby was working on three stories when he died. It's possible one of them might have been connected to his death." Which was true. Anything was *possible* at this point.

"What were they about?" Tina asked, her stance softening.

"The first was about dental hygiene, the second about laser hair removal, and the last one focused on a recycling plant called Sunshine Sanitation."

Tina nodded, obviously making mental notes. "Any idea which one might have involved something worth killing over?"

I shook my head. "Not yet."

She shrugged. "Well, it's a start."

I cleared my throat and shot her an expectant look.

Tina smiled. "Okay, fair is fair. Bobby and his wife had a prenup."

"Oh, really?" This was good news. Well, for me. Maybe not for the wife. "What did it say?"

"Standard," Tina responded. "If she is convicted of a crime, she gets nothing. If she cheats, she gets nothing. If they divorce before their tenth anniversary, she gets nothing."

I thought back to the records I'd seen. They'd only been married a few years at best. "Wow. Nice motive for murder."

"Yeah, you think?" Tina's grin was a mile wide.

"How did you find this out?" I asked.

"His lawyer."

"His lawyer *told* you?"

Tina turned her head away, averting her eyes. "Not exactly."

I didn't want to know. It was probably illegal. Better to stay nonculpable.

"Anyway, there's really not much here. I did find this." She turned behind her and grabbed a slim tablet from the nightstand on the right of the bed. "But there's not much on it. Some ebooks, Candy Crush, Angry Birds—the usual junk."

I grabbed it and immediately swiped it on. A screen with a bunch of apps and documents came up. Tina was right—the home screen had several books, scripts, and a few games and various apps.

"The police took his computer. I'm surprised they didn't take this," I mused out loud.

"Well, it was kinda hidden."

I raised an eyebrow her way.

"He had it tucked between a couple of magazines in the bathroom. Looks like Bobby liked to read while…you know."

Ew! I looked down at the tablet in my hands, trying to calculate how much hand sanitizer was going to be needed to shake the cooties feel from my fingers.

I was about to drop the offending object like a hot potato, when one of the programs on the main screen caught my eye. A calendar. I quickly clicked it open while Tina grabbed the hair dryer and returned it to the bathroom.

The first page it opened to was this week. I scanned the entries. Several appointments were noted—mostly with his network, agent, and writers for the show. A couple of entries later in the evenings looked like they might be personal, though he'd only noted times and locations that looked like restaurants. I swiped through to the day he'd died, mentally crossing my fingers.

Three entries for that afternoon—all the usual meetings. That evening, however, he'd noted: *SB DeVitto's 9pm.*

"Anything good?" Tina emerged from the bathroom, wiping her hands on a towel.

I quickly closed the program. "Not really." My sharing streak only lasted so long.

She shrugged. "I'm gonna check out the kitchen. You wanna tag along?"

I shook my head, setting the germ-infested tablet back on the nightstand. "I'm good. I'll see you back at the office," I called over my shoulder as I hightailed it out of the condo.

CHAPTER SIX

———

As soon as I got to the *Informer,* I googled "DeVitto's." Turns out it was a restaurant and bar in downtown L.A., about three blocks from where Bobby had been killed. If he'd been meeting "SB" there at 9:00 p.m., it was possible that his dinner companion had still been with him at midnight when he'd been killed. Or…even possible that his dinner companion had killed him?

I dialed Bobby's assistant, Henry, who answered on the second ring.

"Hi, it's Allie Quick again," I told him.

"Hi, Allie. What can I do for you?" he asked, his voice tired and like he really didn't want to do anything. I could only imagine how many calls he'd been fielding since his boss's death.

Out of sympathy, I got right to the point. "I was wondering if you could tell me if anyone connected to Bobby's show has the initials *SB*?"

There was a pause on the other end. "Honestly? I really couldn't tell you. We've got tons of people working on the crew."

Dang. "Any way I could get a roster of them all?"

"I suppose I could send over the latest credits list…" he hedged, sounding like he'd rather not.

"Thanks!" I said quickly before he could change his mind.

He sighed into the phone. "Okay. I'll email it over to you now," he promised before hanging up.

I tapped my pen on my desk as I waited, and five minutes later an email popped into my inbox from Henry. I quickly downloaded the pdf attachment and scanned the list. He was right. There were tons of people connect to the show, from crew to assistants to the research team. I printed the document out then pulled out a pink highlighter and started going through names. Twenty minutes later I had pink lines through Sandra Butler, a PA; Sanjay Bastil, on Bobby's research staff; and Sarah Baker, the harried makeup woman I'd seen on set. I had no idea why Bobby would want to meet for dinner with any of them on the night he'd died, but at least it was somewhere to start.

I was just googling the makeup artist when Felix stuck his head out of his office.

"Allie. I need to see you. Now." Not exactly the words of endearment every girl longs to hear from her paramour. But, I did enjoy being employed, so I went into Felix's office.

"What's up, *Boss*?"

If he caught my sarcasm, he didn't let on.

"Have a seat."

I took a seat in one of the old vinyl-covered chairs in front of his desk and crossed my legs.

His eyes lingered on my bare thighs below my skirt a moment longer than was considered appropriate before he met my gaze. Good. At least he still noticed me.

He cleared his throat. "Where are you on the Bobby Baxter story?"

"I talked to the wife yesterday, but she didn't give me anything useful. I plan to look into another couple of avenues today." What those avenues were, I wasn't sure, but I wasn't about to tell him that.

He nodded. "Tina's working a lead as well." He paused. "But you already know that."

"Of course I do. She guns for all of my stories," I said.

Felix shot me a look. "Don't start. I'm not playing referee to you two again."

"Who, me?" I blinked innocently at him.

His look didn't soften much, but the corner of his mouth hitched up ever so slightly.

"What's her angle?" I asked, wondering if the prenup info meant she was going with a "the wife did it" line.

Felix shook his head. "She didn't say. She's playing it pretty close to the vest until she has something substantial."

Of course she was. Oh well, it was worth a try.

"Speaking of angles…what's yours?" he asked.

"I, uh…don't think I should share until I have something substantial either," I lied. The truth was I had no idea what my angle was. So far I had floss-happy dentists, bright-and-flashy trash men, and a wife who loved pedicures and hated tabloids. Not a smoking gun among the bunch.

"Well, you better come up with something fast. And better than Tina's, if you want me to run with it."

"I'll get the story," I assured him.

"Good." He stood, signaling the interrogation was over.

I stood to leave as well, but I turned around at the door to face him. "Will I see you later?" I hated how desperate that sounded the second it left my lips.

Felix paused then nodded. "Maybe. If I can get finished up here early enough, maybe we can get a drink?"

"That'd be nice." I smiled genuinely at him and practically skipped back to my desk. Whatever misgivings I'd had last night, I shoved to the back of my mind. Felix wasn't breaking it off with me. He was just busy. And he wanted to get a drink after work. Drinks were good. Maybe not staying-over good, but it was a step in the right direction. Who knew—if I got enough drinks into him…

My phone buzzed, shaking me out of that thought. I grabbed it and checked the display. It was Shane, the skateboard kid.

"Allie Quick."

"Hey, Allie, it's me, Shane. I was, um, just wondering if you, um, still need me to keep an eye on that lady?"

"Has she come back?" I asked.

"No, I was just curious."

I thought about it for a moment. "It wouldn't hurt to keep an eye on her. If you don't mind."

"It's no trouble. Will you be, uh, be coming back around sometime?"

I could practically hear his blush through the phone. Cute. The kid had a crush on me.

"Maybe. I need to talk to her, but she isn't too keen on speaking to me right now."

"So you want to surprise her," he said with understanding.

"I guess so," I said. I hadn't really thought about my next move with Mrs. Baxter yet. But it didn't hurt to have a pair of eyes watching the house. You never knew what might turn up.

"I'm on it!" Shane assured me with enthusiasm usually saved for finding a rare Pokemon.

"Thanks," I said and ended the call.

With Shane's eyes on the Baxter house and the wife taking a hiatus at the hotel and spa, my investigation into Bobby's death was left dangling in the breeze. I tapped my pen against my lip. I looked over at Tina's cubicle. She was on the phone, animatedly talking to someone. Great. Her sources seemed chatty. I felt my story slowly slipping away.

I pulled up a new blank document on my computer and titled it *SUSPECTS*.

Right below that I typed *Marilyn Baxter*. Under that I added the elusive *SB*. Then I drew a blank

There had to be more people who wanted Bobby dead. The guy was a jerk. But who?

Wait—what about the guy Bobby had assaulted?

I pulled up the notes I'd originally written to take with me to the interview with Bobby and found the fan's name: Ritchie Mullins.

Bobby had decked him in a very public place. What if Ritchie held a grudge? Or what if he'd wanted revenge? I wish I knew what the two had been arguing about.

On the list, I wrote down *Ritchie Mullins*. There. That was looking more like a respectable suspect list now.

While smart money was still on the wife, the fan was an interesting idea. I did a little searching and found a social media profile for Ritchie. He had an impressive 3,041 friends, had graduated from Encino High, and worked three days a week as a personal trainer at the Oceanside Gym in Santa Monica.

I grabbed my purse and phone and left the office.

About half an hour later I found a spot on the street a block away from the gym where Ritchie worked. Today I'd chosen to wear my favorite off-the-shoulder baby pink dolman top with a black pencil skirt and matching pink sling-back high heels. The sun beat down on my bare shoulder and face as I made my way down the sidewalk to the gym.

One of the entrance doors was propped open. The smell of sweaty men and the sound of grunts and weights clanking together met me as I strolled inside.

I spotted a reception desk and hurried over. The young man behind the desk gave me a quick once-over and smiled.

"I'm Alex. Welcome to Oceanside Gym. Can I help you?"

His black hair glistened in the overhead light, and his chubby cheeks made him look barely old enough to even have a job.

"I was wondering if Ritchie Mullins is working today?"

"Sure. Just a minute."

Alex left the desk, and I watched as he made his way toward the back of the gym. He stopped and said something to a very large man in a red long-sleeved shirt that said *Oceanside* across the chest. The man looked up at me. Then he nodded at Alex and followed him back to the front desk.

"I'm Ritchie," the guy said as he wiped his hands on a clean towel before extending it my way. "You looking for a personal trainer?"

I shook the offered hand, momentarily speechless. This guy was huge. I mean, like Incredible Hulk without the green paint huge. How on earth had Bobby decked this guy and gotten away with it? If this guy put his finger on my head and pressed down, I was sure I'd go through the floor like a thumbtack.

"Not exactly," I said, trying to gather my wits. "I'm Allie Quick from the *L.A. Informer*. I was wondering if I could ask you a few questions about the night of your altercation with Bobby Baxter."

Ritchie narrowed his eyes at me. "That's old news, sweetheart. Bobby's dead."

I silently wondered if this guy'd had anything to do with that. "Indulge me," I said.

His eyes went from my face down to my neckline and all the way south to my bare legs. His stare was so intense I could almost feel it. Ick. I tried not to shift uncomfortably under his gaze.

"I suppose," he finally decided. "What do you want to know that I haven't already told the press?" He directed me to a table and chairs to our left, next to a smoothie bar, and we sat down.

"I was wondering if you could tell me your side of the story. What happened the night of the assault?"

Ritchie tried to hide his look of irritation but failed. "I was a fan of Bobby's show. I saw him at Beverly's. I was there with a couple of coworkers for a birthday dinner. I approached him, told him I was a fan. He told me to piss off."

"Harsh," I said.

"I thought so, too, so I asked him what his problem was. He got irate and punched me."

"And you didn't fight back?" I asked, still unable to believe that Bobby'd had the guts to smack around a guy who looked like he could bench press a Buick.

"Nah. There were people taking pictures all over the place. He was ruined before the security ever grabbed him. What would be the sense in me kicking his ass?"

"So you're a 'live and let live' kind of guy?" I asked.

"You could say that."

"You at work the night before last?" I asked.

Ritchie frowned. "Why do you ask?"

"Just curious."

He narrowed his eyes at me. "Curious if I killed Bobby that night, you mean?"

I shrugged. "Your words, not mine."

"Look, honey, Bobby was an a-hole, but I didn't even know the guy. If I killed everyone who tried to take a swing at me, I'd be on death row many times over."

That was hardly convincing me of his character.

"And, yes, for the record, I was working that night. Now, if you don't mind…" He scooted his chair back. "I have a client to get back to." He stood and without another word walked away.

I sat there a little longer and watched Ritchie rejoin his client at the free weights.

Something about his story just didn't add up. Sure, I could see Bobby being rude to a fan. But Bobby wasn't dumb by anyone's account. And while he'd been good-looking in a TV sort of way, he'd hardly looked like he spent time in a gym. I just didn't see David taking a swing at Goliath for no reason.

Which begged the question—why was Ritchie lying?

As I was walking out of the gym and down the sidewalk to my car, I spotted a coffee shop and couldn't resist. I crossed the street and went inside. The cool air from the stainless steel ceiling fans blew down on me, and I almost sighed aloud.

The barista, a woman probably in her late twenties, brushed a strand of auburn hair behind her ear and smiled a greeting at me. A tiny little diamond stud on her nose glinted in the overhead light.

I gave her my order of an iced vanilla latte and orange crème scone and took a seat at a table while I waited.

From my vantage point, I could see into the glass storefront of the Oceanside Gym. I wondered why Ritchie would lie about what had caused Bobby to hit him. Maybe they'd known each other—had some sort of past grudge? Maybe Ritchie owed him money, and with Bobby gone, he now thought he could skip out on the debt? Maybe Ritchie had just been a bigger creep than he'd admitted to, and Bobby had snapped?

The coffee shop wasn't busy, and instead of calling out my name, the barista brought my order to me. "If you need anything else, just let me know." She smiled, set down my coffee and scone, and then walked away.

I took a sip of my latte. If only I'd been there to see the assault happen.

Then it hit me.

Hadn't Ritchie said lots of people were filming the incident? Maybe someone had caught footage of the moments just before the assault had taken place. Of course, tracking down every single person who might have had a cell out at Beverly's that night could be daunting. Unless, of course, someone already had.

I pulled my phone out of my purse and dialed Cam.

"Cameron Dakota."

"Cam, it's Allie."

"Hey, Allie. What's up?"

I stirred the ice in my coffee with a straw. "I need your help."

"With what?" she asked.

"I was wondering...did you guys put out a call for footage on the night Bobby assaulted that guy at Beverly's?"

"Of course. As soon as word hit, we sent out a Twitter alert."

Bingo. While Cam was always quick to a scene with her camera when good gossip was going down, in the digital age, I knew our website often relied on cell phone footage from people in the right place at the right time to fill in blanks. Which our devoted followers loved for two reasons: one, we often had video footage of embarrassing moments as they happened, and two, we paid a nice bounty for any cell footage that we did end up using. In fact, there were several freelancers who often pulled in monthly paychecks from us just for being "in the right place" when celebrities did embarrassing things like wearing UGGs with Daisy Dukes to pump their gas.

"I don't suppose you got anything good?" I asked.

"Nothing usable," Cam replied. Which I already knew, or else it would have been on our website.

"Do you still have it?"

"Sure. It's all in raw form though. Meet me at the office in fifteen, and I can show you."

"I'm on my way," I said as I tossed my napkin in the trash can, grabbed my coffee and purse, and hurried out of the shop and back to my car.

The trip back took closer to thirty minutes, but once there I rode the elevator up to the second floor. Cam was watching for me and waved me over the moment I stepped off of our death trap of an elevator. I looked around for Tina, but she was nowhere to be found. I hurried over to Cam, pulled an extra chair into her cubicle, and took a seat.

"I've got it all cued up. We only got a handful of submissions. Most don't really show much action, unfortunately."

"That's okay. I'll take what I can get," I said.

"Here's the first one." Cam clicked her mouse, and a slightly slanted picture of the bar area at Beverly's appeared on the screen. Cam pointed to an elbow in a blue shirt. "That's Bobby there."

I rolled my eyes. "Wow. An elbow. How incriminating."

Cam grinned at me. "Sorry. Like I said, most of it is unusable."

I watched as the elbow lifted a glass off the bar a few times. Then it abruptly moved out of frame. The would-be photographer swiveled his phone just in time for us to see Bobby being pulled off of Ritchie Mullins by security.

"Nothing we didn't know there," I mused out loud.

Cam clicked on the next file, and a similar scene played out, but this one had a large potted palm obscuring most of the action. Three more similar videos from other equally terrible vantage points later, and I was starting to think this was another dead end.

"Last one," Cam told me, clicking on another file.

This one looked like it had been shot by another patron at the bar, as it showed Bobby in profile.

"That's him," I said and motioned to the monitor. So far Henry had been telling the truth. Bobby looked like he was drunk and being loud, waving his arms in the air, laughing animatedly.

"And here comes the fan," Cam said.

We both leaned forward to get a better look at what was happening. The film was grainy, so reading the men's lips was out of the question, but it was easy to identify Bobby and Ritchie.

Ritchie walked up to Bobby and tapped him on the shoulder. Bobby turned around, and the jovial smile he'd been sporting disappeared from his face the second he saw Ritchie.

"He doesn't look happy," Cam said.

"Definitely," I agreed. "But he does look like he recognizes him."

I saw Ritchie's mouth move as he said something. Bobby's face contorted with rage, and then he cocked his arm back.

Unfortunately, that's when our amateur Scorsese dropped his phone, and all we could see were pairs of feet.

"Damn," I muttered.

"I know." Cam shook her head. "This could have been primo video."

By the time the phone was picked up again, we saw Bobby on top of Ritchie, trying to get another hit in as security pulled him off. Finally they succeeded, hauling a kicking and flailing Bobby out of the restaurant.

Ritchie stood, rubbed his jaw, then smiled in the direction the men had carried Bobby.

"Wow. I wonder what he said to piss off Baxter?"

That was the question of the day. But I knew one thing was for sure. Baxter and Ritchie had definitely known each other.

"Thanks, Cam. I owe you one," I told her, heading back to my own desk.

I started searching all the databases at our disposal for all I could find on Ritchie Mullins. Bobby had definitely recognized Ritchie and hadn't been happy to see him. Had Ritchie confronted Bobby a second time…maybe this time with a gun in hand? There had to be a connection between the two men, and I was determined to find it.

An hour of shifting through boring personal stats later, my eyes were starting to water. If there was any connection between Bobby and Ritchie, it was well hidden and off-line. My stomach rumbled, and I looked at the clock. Well past lunchtime. I grabbed my purse and made for the elevator.

Normally, my lunch consisted of a quick sandwich or salad at one of the takeout delis nearby. But instead of cruising down Hollywood Boulevard, I pointed my car toward downtown L.A., and half an hour later pulled up in front of DeVitto's Italian restaurant. It didn't look overly crowded at this time of day, though the outdoor patio along the side of the building held a decent number of patrons. I was greeted by a friendly hostess who promptly seated me at a table for one on the patio near the door.

I perused the menu as I waited for my server, noting that the prices were way outside of the usual deli fare. I would be expensing this meal to the *Informer* account for sure.

"Hi, my name is Brian, and I'll be your server today," a friendly, young guy said, approaching my table. He had a big, toothy smile and close-cropped brown hair, and he looked vaguely familiar. "Can I start you off with something to drink?"

While the wine list he handed me was impressive, I answered with, "Just an iced tea, please."

If he was disappointed at the instant reduction in the bill size, he didn't show it. "Perfect. I'll get that right out to you."

"Uh, Brian," I stopped him.

He paused, giving me his megawatt smile. "Yes?"

"I was wondering…any chance you know if any servers working today were also on two nights ago?"

He frowned, indicating he was not yet of the Botox age. "What day was that?"

"The 10th."

He nodded, the smile coming back. "Sure. I actually picked up a shift that evening." He paused. "Why? Was there something wrong with the service that night?"

"No, nothing like that," I reassured him. "I was actually just wondering if you noticed this man here?" I pulled up a photo of Bobby on my phone and showed it to him.

Brian squinted down, shielding the screen from the sunlight as he studied the face. Finally recognition dawned, resulting in another big smile. "Yeah, Bobby Baxter. Shame about what happened to him."

I nodded my agreement. "Did you wait on him?"

Brian shook his head. "I wish. Man, I'd love to get a spot on his show. This is just my day job. I'm an actor," he explained.

It dawned on me why he looked so familiar. "You did that soap commercial!"

I didn't think it was possible for Brian's smile to grow bigger, but somehow he managed to sprout an extra few teeth. "You've seen it?"

I nodded. "Of course! You get all muddy playing rugby, and the green soap lathers and refreshes away your day," I said, repeating the company slogan. "You were awesome in it."

"Wow, thanks." Brian blushed.

"So, um, about Bobby," I said, having appropriately buttered up my witness. "Did you get a look at the person he was dining with that night?"

Brian tapped his pen to his lips. "Let me see…I'll admit I was more focused on Bobby. We don't get a lot of celebs in here, so it's always kind of fun when we do."

"Do you remember if it was a man or woman?"

He nodded. "Man. Kind of an older guy maybe? I remember he had salt-and-pepper hair."

I frowned. That ruled out Sandra Butler and Sarah Baker. I wondered how old Sanjay Bastil was. Though I wasn't sure what motive a member of Bobby's own research crew could have for murdering him. Admit it girl, this whole thing was a long shot.

Though, as I thanked Brian and ordered the salmon salad, at least I knew one thing: Bobby hadn't been alone on the night he'd died.

* * *

After a delightful lunch that cost way too much and a mostly traffic-free ride back to the office, I was at my desk looking for anyone in Bobby's life who fit the description of his last supper companion. Parents? Both deceased. Uncles? All living in his native Midwestern small town. Agent? Not even close. I supposed it could have been a network executive, but if that was the case, I couldn't think of any reason for them to off their star.

Felix stepped up beside my desk. "Hard at work?"

"Always," I answered. I swiveled in my chair to face him. "What's up?"

"I just got a look at the ballistics report on Baxter."

I raised an eyebrow at him. "How did you get that?"

"I know some people." He smiled mischievously.

I wished I knew more people. "So, what did it say?" I asked, lowering my voice to a whisper as I glanced around for any sign of Tina.

"She's not here," Felix told me with a knowing grin.

I felt a sheepish blush creep into my cheeks. "So what did the report say?"

"Death from a single GSW to the head."

"No surprise there," I added.

"Nine-millimeter caliber weapon…wait for it…registered to him."

"He was killed with his own gun?"

"It's a cruel world, kid," Felix said, shaking his head.

I'll say. It also killed my theory that Ritchie had come back better armed to confront Bobby.

"Ballistics came back a match to his weapon after they compared it to an old police report involving gunshots at his residence last year," Felix continued. "Bobby claimed the gun went off when he was cleaning it. But the police suspected possible domestic dispute, so they took the bullet then. Striations were an exact match to the one that killed him."

"Any idea where the gun is now?" I asked.

Felix shook his head. "Either the police don't know, or they aren't saying."

I chewed on that info. "Thanks for the tip."

"Anything for you, love," he said, shooting me a wink before he disappeared back into his office.

I watched his retreating back, but my mind was on the information he'd just given me. If Bobby was killed with his own gun, that meant either he had brought it to meet his killer, or the killer had had access to it. And I could think of one person who might have easy access...and a possible "domestic dispute" with the deceased.

I dialed Shane's number as I grabbed my purse and headed for the elevator.

"Allie?" he answered on the first ring.

"Yeah, it's me. Has Mrs. Baxter come back to her house since the last time we talked?"

"Nope. I've been watching. I can see in the house perfectly from my bedroom window. No one's been there except for the housekeeper."

"Great. Thank you, Shane." I jumped into my car and pulled out onto the street.

The hotel I'd followed Marilyn Baxter to the day before was about a forty-five-minute drive from the office at this time of day. I pulled into a visitor parking slot again and hurried inside. I wasn't sure how I was going to find Marilyn. The concierge wouldn't just hand out room numbers to whoever asked. I was going to have to think of something else.

I walked through the lobby slowly. Marilyn had looked like the typical trophy wife, and my one brief interaction with her hadn't disproved that theory. Maybe I'd get lucky and she'd be in a public area, showing off her trophiness? She'd already hit the spa. I peeked into the bar off the lobby. All but three of the tables were empty, and two men sat at the bar. None of the people at the tables were Marilyn. I walked through the hotel to the only other place I could think of: the pool.

I stepped just outside the glass door and looked around. Sure enough, I spotted a red-bikini-clad Marilyn in a white lounge chair, soaking up some sun by the pool. Maybe my luck wasn't all bad today. I wasn't exactly dressed for sunbathing, but she already knew who I was, so beating around the bush wasn't an option anyway.

I walked over and took a seat on the lounge chair beside her.

She glanced my way and let out a large sigh. "You again. Didn't I say I wasn't talking to the press right now?"

"So don't talk," I said, stretching out on the chair. "We can just enjoy the sunshine together."

"What do I have to do to get away from all of you vultures?"

I shrugged. "Hey, I'm just enjoying an afternoon at the pool."

She huffed again, shifting in her chair. "I could call security," she threatened.

I glanced over at her. "And tell them what? That I had the nerve to sit next to you?"

I could just barely see the death glare she gave me from behind her huge, dark sunglasses. "Look, you, I don't know who you think you are or what you want from me, but I am very distraught right now. My husband just died." And then she did something totally unexpected. She sobbed. She quickly covered it with a hand to her mouth, but I could see tears leak from beneath the rim of her glasses.

Wow. Who knew the ice queen had a heart. I suddenly felt bad for her. Maybe she wasn't as cold as she was pretending to be.

"I never got to tell you how sorry I am for your loss," I told her.

"Thanks," she said, sniffing.

"I was never formally introduced to Bobby, but he seemed like a...great actor," I finished, fishing for something truthful.

She let out a short laugh. "That's one way to describe him."

"Look, Ms. Baxter, a lot of people are going to be printing stories about Bobby, saying all kinds of things. All I want to do is print the truth."

She sucked in her cheeks as if thinking about it. "I didn't kill my husband, if that's what you're thinking."

That was totally what I was thinking, but I just nodded sympathetically.

She removed her sunglasses and tapped them on her tan thigh. Her eyes were red-rimmed, and her expression was so sad that I was almost tempted to believe she really did miss her husband.

However, that didn't mean she hadn't been the one to get rid of him.

She sighed. "I don't know what you think I can tell you."

"Well, for starters, what was your relationship with Bobby like?" I asked gently. At this point, Marilyn was like a baby deer, and I wanted to ease into this line of questioning as gently as I could to avoid spooking her.

She blew out another sigh, this one resigned. "It was all right, I suppose. We were separated, but I'm guessing you know that already."

I nodded. "What happened?" I asked, the housekeeper's line about cheaters ringing in my ears.

She shrugged. "What ever happens in relationships? We got along really well at first. He was fun, interesting, took me out all the time."

"When was this?" I asked, thinking back to the prenup Tina had uncovered. "Before or after *Bobby Tells All* started airing?"

"After."

"So Bobby was already a celeb."

She shot me a look. "He's got a show on cable. It's not like he's a Kardashian or anything."

While her words belittled his status, my guess was if he'd been a plumber, she wouldn't have given him a second look. Mrs. Baxter looked like the type who enjoyed staying a week at the Grand Hotel and Spa without her bank account blinking an eye.

"So what happened?" I pressed.

"After a while, all we did was go out, you know? He'd take me to clubs or restaurants to be seen with a hot wife. But when we were alone, he started getting distant. Then he was always busy with work and avoided being alone with me at all."

Ouch. I couldn't help but be able to relate to that a teeny bit. "Sounds familiar," I muttered before I could stop myself.

"What?" she asked.

I waved it off. "Nothing. Just this guy I'm seeing. Anyway, so you and Bobby separated?"

She nodded. "I loved him, but I couldn't live like that anymore. As the cliché 'ignored trophy wife.'" She snorted again, though it sort of turned into a sob at the end.

"Do you know who had access to Bobby's gun?" I asked, trying to steer the conversation before she started crying in earnest.

She shook her head. "I don't know. I didn't even know Bobby still had that gun until the police told me about it this morning."

"He didn't keep it in the house?"

"No. He moved into a condo in Culver City after we separated. You could check there."

I nodded, keeping mum about the fact that I already kinda had.

"Bobby met with a man the night he was killed. Older, salt-and-pepper hair, possibly with the initials SB? Any idea who that might have been?" I asked.

She shook her head. "Sorry. Doesn't ring a bell."

It had been worth a shot.

"Do you know where Bobby kept his personal files?" I asked instead. "Like maybe show ideas, notes, that kind of thing?"

"He had a laptop. I think he kept it at work. Henry would know." She paused. "That's his personal assistant. At least I think he still is."

I paused at her wording. "*Still*? Was Henry planning to quit?" He hadn't mentioned anything like that to me.

She laughed. "As if. No, Henry was way too much of a brownnoser for that."

"So...Bobby was going to fire him?" Hello, motive.

Marilyn shrugged. "Henry had some idea for a show of his own. It was like the exposé thing Bobby did, but I guess it focused on historical events. Uncovering what really happened versus what the history books say. Like, where is Black Beard's treasure and who really shot Lincoln. That kind of thing."

I had to admit, it sounded interesting. "Was Henry pitching to Bobby's network?"

She nodded. "Actually, Bobby was supposed to be helping him get the green light on production."

"Any idea if he did?"

She shrugged again. "Like I said, Bobby and I haven't been all that close lately."

Henry hadn't mentioned anything about a new show. Though, in all fairness, I hadn't exactly asked either.

"Aren't you going to ask me again?" she asked.

"Huh?" I'd admit, I was a little lost in my own thoughts.

She sent a wry smile in my direction. "Where was I when my husband was killed."

I suddenly felt a little sheepish. But honestly? Yeah, I totally wanted to know.

"Okay, where were you?"

"I was out. Driving."

I raised an eyebrow.

"I know. It's a lousy alibi. But when I can't sleep, I like to go for a drive. It clears my head. That night, I was out driving around for an hour or so."

She was right. That was a totally lousy alibi. And my face must have shown my apprehension, as she added, "Look, if I had killed my husband, don't you think I would have come up with something better than that to account for my time?"

She had me there. With her money, she could have easily paid someone off to vouch for her.

"Oh, and by the way," she said, putting her sunglasses back on, "stay the hell away from my housekeeper, okay?"

And just like that, frosty Mrs. Baxter was back.

I pulled a card out of my purse and handed it to her. "If you can think of anything else, please call me."

She took the card and nodded. Though I was pretty sure she'd be tossing it as soon as she got back up to her room.

CHAPTER SEVEN

The drive back to the *Informer* was at a snail's pace. There was an accident blocking all eastbound lanes on the 2, and I probably could have walked back to the office faster. I cranked up the radio, pointed every AC vent in my car at my face, and contemplated what Mrs. Baxter had told me. Her alibi was pretty nonexistent. Granted, the police were probably checking into it—looking at her odometer readings or at traffic cams or something that might prove she was telling the truth. But against my better judgment I was almost inclined to believe Marilyn. Those tears had seemed real enough. Either that, or she was a top-notch actress. On the other hand, the fact that Marilyn had married Bobby, and signed a prenup, *after* he'd already hit celebrity status, likely meant Bobby'd be keeping the bulk of his estate in a divorce. All of which added up to Marilyn still having the best motive, in my book, to want Bobby out of the picture. Especially if her being the "ignored trophy wife" had resulted in her husband's attentions going elsewhere.

Though the news that Henry was looking to jump ship from *Bobby Tells All* was interesting. I wondered why Bobby was helping him. Henry had made it clear that they weren't close. And Bobby didn't seem like the type of guy who did a lot of charity from the goodness of his heart. Had he and Henry been business partners in the venture? Had something gone wrong and Henry offed him?

I realized as I finally pulled up to the *Informer*'s offices that I had a crap ton of theories but nothing based on any evidence that I could go to print with. I could only hope Tina was having the same kind of luck.

When I got back to my desk, I called Henry but got his voicemail. I left a message for him to call me and hung up. I tried looking online for any connections between Henry and Bobby as business partners—like partnership notices, copyright filings, or any scripts for the new show that might have been registered with the Writer's Guild. No luck. If the new show had gotten a green light, it was being kept under supersecret wraps.

I glanced up at the time and realized it was almost five. And I was out of leads to follow. I shut down my computer and gathered my things, wondering if I had time to go home and shower before drinks with Felix. I glanced up at his office. He was talking to his computer, probably deep in the middle of a Skype conference with someone.

I was just pulling out my phone to text him, when I noticed a delivery person step off the elevator, a bouquet of red roses in his arms.

I grinned. Lucky Cam. Trace was always doing stuff like that.

But as I watched, he walked right past Cam and approached me.

"I'm looking for Allie Quick?" he asked.

I blinked. "Are you serious?"

"Um, yes," he said, rechecking the card.

"Yeah, that's me," I answered, suddenly wary of who'd be sending me flowers. The obvious answer should have been Felix, but I knew he was way too cheap to spring for delivery.

"These are for you. Please sign here." He handed me a small clipboard. I signed my name, grabbed a few dollars from my purse and handed them to him for a tip, and then took the flowers.

"Have a nice day." He turned and walked away.

I blinked as I watched his retreating back, still thinking he must have made a mistake. I looked up to find Felix watching me through the glass wall of his office. He raised one finely arched eyebrow at me in question.

I shrugged and smiled.

The eyebrow pulled back down in a frown.

I quickly pulled the card from the bouquet and read what it said.

To Allie, the hottest babe I've ever seen.
Love, Shane

The skateboarder kid? I couldn't help the laugh that escaped me. Apparently young Shane had developed a slight crush on me. It was a sweet gesture really. Too bad it hadn't come from the grown man I was seeing.

I slid the note back into the bouquet and chanced another glance in Felix's direction. He was still staring my way, his expression stony and unreadable. I took a small step toward his office, but he quickly spun his chair around so his back faced me.

Huh. Maybe now was not a good time. Instead, I slung my purse onto my shoulder and took my roses home with me. Hey, not a terrible end to the day. I had an admirer. Granted, he was likely still in high school and had a medicine cabinet full of Proactive, but at least someone appreciated me.

I parked my car in my assigned parking spot and headed up the stairs. There was some leftover pizza in the refrigerator with my name on it and a fluffy cat ripe for some snuggling.

I stepped into my apartment and locked the door behind me before looking around.

"Mr. Fluffykins?" I called out. I tossed my purse on the sofa, laid the flowers on the table, and then went in search of my little buddy. It wasn't often that he missed greeting me two days in a row.

On my way to the bedroom, I heard something that sounded like scratching, then a little banging, then a little growling, and scratching again. I slowed down and crept the remaining three steps to my room, peeked around the doorway, and suddenly wanted to scream.

Sweet little Mr. Fluffykins was rolling around the middle of the bedroom floor with what was left of my favorite pair of black satin sling-back heels. His claws were dug into the shoe he was kneading and biting. I scanned the room for the other shoe and spotted it sticking halfway under the foot of the bed. It too had been shredded by his sharp little kitty claws.

"Have you lost your mind?" I shrieked and struggled to remember why I loved him so much.

The Evil Fluffykins, who was on his back clutching the shoe to his squishy belly, twisted his head up and gave me his best *where the heck have you been* look then had the nerve to start purring and return to shredding my shoe.

"Bad kitty. Very bad kitty!" I pinched the bridge of my nose, took a deep breath, and counted to ten. It had taken me three months to save enough money to buy those shoes, and now they were completely ruined.

"Look, I know I haven't been around much lately," I said as calmly as I could, "but did you have to take it out on my shoes? My favorite shoes!"

Mr. Fluffykins dropped the shoe, sat up, and started cleaning his paws, completely ignoring me and my obvious distress. He looked way too pleased with himself. I blew out a frustrated breath.

You love him, Allie. He's your best buddy, I reminded myself.

I let out a weary sigh and gathered the shoes then tossed them in my polka-dotted trash can on my way back to the kitchen.

I grabbed the pizza box from the fridge and shoved a cold bite into my mouth. I washed it down with a swig of chardonnay, right from the bottle. And another. And maybe one more. Then I paused, wondering if I should be swigging quite so much if I was going out for a drink with Felix later. That was, if I *was* still going out with Felix.

I plopped down on the sofa, pulled my phone out of my purse, and dialed his number. After the fourth ring, Felix picked up.

"Allie," he answered.

"Hey. We still on for drinks tonight?" I asked, trying to do light and casual and not desperate and needy.

"Tonight's not a good night for me after all. Things got busy." His tone was flat. As unreadable as his look had been earlier.

I blew out a sigh. "You're not upset about the roses, are you? Because they were—"

"None of my business," he finished for me.

"Don't tell me you're jealous?" I teased, trying to lighten the tone.

"I've got to go." He did not sound amused.

"Come on, Felix. You're not seriously going to—"

"I'll see you at the office in the morning." Then he hung up.

I stared at the phone. Seriously? What was he, twelve? He didn't even give me a chance to explain. Boy, was he gonna feel stupid when he found out they were from a kid. Though, at the moment, that thought gave me little comfort, as I was the one feeling stupid…stupid for falling for a guy who was clearly not that into me. I wondered if Felix really was jealous or if the roses had just been another great excuse to blow me off again.

I grabbed my chardonnay and took another swig. No reason to slow down now. Apparently Mr. Fluffykins was my only date for the evening. I had a sudden vision of myself as an old spinster with eighty cats and a big gray perm. I rubbed my eyes in an attempt to wipe away the depressing image.

I went into the kitchen for the rest of the pizza and settled back in on the sofa for a night of mindless television. I was finished with the pizza and halfway through a DVRed episode of *The Bachelor* when there was a knock at my door.

I checked the clock and frowned. It was after nine. Who would be at my door this late? Surely it wasn't Felix. Not after the way he'd sounded on the phone. I tossed my pizza crust on a paper plate on the table, wiped off my hands, and peeked out the peephole.

"What in the—"

I opened the door and frowned. "Shane? What in the world are you doing here?"

My not-so-secret admirer grinned and shoved his hands into the pockets of his slouchy jeans. "I just wanted to see if you got the flowers I sent you."

"Yes, I did. That was very thoughtful. How'd you find out where I live?" I asked. I couldn't help but to look around for any other surprise visitors who might be lurking in the shadows.

"I have my ways, babe." He shrugged and grinned.

I wasn't sure what was more unnerving—the fact that even a teen could find out where I lived and just show up at my doorstep, or that he'd called me babe.

"Well, do you want to tell me your 'ways,' or should I just assume that you're some creepy stalker?" I asked.

His grin quickly fled, and he shook his head and held up his hands. "No, no, that's not it at all. I'd never hurt you. Geez. Paranoid much?"

"I am now!" I sighed. "Fine. Come on in." I stepped aside and waved him in.

"Nice place." He looked around.

"Thanks. You want some pizza?" I offered.

"Nah, I'm good. Listen, I didn't mean to scare you. I just wanted to see if you liked the flowers."

I leaned my butt against the arm of the sofa and crossed my arms over my chest.

"So, seriously, how did you find my place?" I paused, something else dawning on me. "For that matter, how did you know I work for the *Informer*?"

His grin returned. "Dude, it's not like it was hard. Ever heard of Google?"

Okay, he had a point. If you googled my name, I'm sure plenty of bylines from the *Informer*'s site came up. But that didn't explain my home address. "But how did you get here?"

"I borrowed my mom's car. I *am* seventeen, you know." His chest puffed out with pride.

Good grief.

"I meant, how. Did. You. Get. My. Home. Address." I enunciated very clearly.

He shrugged. "Not to brag, but I'm pretty good with a computer. I haven't met a database yet I couldn't get into."

I blinked. "You hacked into a database to get my address?"

"Southern Gas and Electric. You can get anyone's address from those dudes."

For the second time that night, I counted to ten and breathed deeply, trying to maintain my cool.

"Listen, Shane, I really appreciated your help watching Mrs. Baxter's house."

"You're welcome."

"And the flowers were very thoughtful."

"They were awesome, right? Cost me my whole allowance."

I cringed. "But you do realize that I'm a bit older than you, don't you?"

He shrugged. "My dad is ten years older than my mom. No biggie. I mean, what are you, like twenty-one?"

"Something like that." I was flattered enough that I didn't correct him. "But this just isn't going to work out."

I was trying to let him down easy, but he just grinned and shrugged again, his red hair glinting in the overhead light. "I get it. You don't want to be a cradle robber or anything cause that would be gross."

"Exactly," I agreed.

"No sweat. I turn eighteen in just a few months. Totally legal then."

I opened my mouth to argue again, but he put his finger to my lips, silencing me.

"You don't have to give me an answer now. I'm a patient dude. Besides, I gotta get going. I'm supposed to pick my mom up from work. If you need my help with anything else, just give me a call." He waved and left the apartment.

I locked the door behind him. Fab. I had a seventeen-year-old stalker-slash-admirer now. And it was still concerning that even a kid could find my home. If he could, anyone could. With the number of celebrities I upset on a daily basis, that thought was more than a bit unnerving. Perhaps it was time to look into some kind of security system. Mr. Fluffykins didn't exactly strike fear in the hearts of people.

My cat looked at me and tilted his head as though asking me, "What the heck was that all about?"

"He's harmless." I paused. "I think. Besides, his crush on me is kind of cute in a high-schooler sort of way."

He rolled over on his back and meowed. I had a feeling it was his way of laughing at me.

CHAPTER EIGHT

———

The next morning, my first order of business was to track down Henry and ask about the show he'd been developing. I called his office, and it went to voicemail again. I left another message, but I was starting to worry that he was screening me.

When initially setting up the interview, I'd had to go through Bobby's manager first before he'd handed me off to Henry to work out the details. Simon Beckly worked out of a small office in Burbank and was known for handling mid-level talent—daytime talk show hosts, recurring commercial characters, and cable TV personalities like Bobby.

I jumped into my car, stopping only long enough to hit a drive-thru Starbucks, and headed toward Burbank. Fifteen minutes later, I was standing in front of Simon's receptionist, a redhead in a tight miniskirt, who was obviously filling in on the phones between acting gigs.

"Allie Quick," I said, when she asked for my name. "From the *L.A. Informer*. I spoke to Simon last week about an interview with Bobby Baxter."

The redhead's face fell. "Oh. Sorry. Bobby's not doing any interviews right now." She paused, leaned in close, and whispered, "Because he's dead."

I stifled a laugh at her melodrama. "Yeah, I know. That's what I wanted to talk to Simon about. Is he in?"

She nodded. "Hang on a sec." She got up from her desk, walked to a door marked *Private*, and did a shave-and-a-haircut knock before opening it a crack.

"Hey. There's someone here to see you."

I could just barely make out Simon's muffled response. "Who?"

"Some reporter. She wants to talk about Bobby."

"No comment!" I heard Simon shout in response.

"It's Allie Quick," I yelled around the redhead, hoping he'd remember my name.

"Who?"

So much for that hope. "I was here last week. About an interview with Bobby."

There was a pause. Then, "Send her in."

I breathed a sigh of relief and walked past the redhead as she opened the door for me.

"Allie, so nice to see you again!" Simon said, all jovial smiles now as he addressed my chest. Ah. It wasn't so much my name he remembered as my cleavage. Oh well. Whatever got a girl in the door.

"Nice to see you again, too, Mr. Beckly."

"Simon, please." He gestured to a pair of chairs in front of his desk, and I sat.

Simon Beckly was short, round, and had a bald head covered in liver spots. But his shiny Armani suit and gold rings on seven of his ten fingers spoke to the fact he was good at his job.

"How can I help a lovely lady such as yourself today?" he asked, all charm.

"I was wondering if I could ask you a few questions about Bobby."

Simon's smile fell, and he shook his head. "Sad business."

"I'm so sorry for your loss," I told him.

He nodded. "Yeah, it's going to be hard to replace Bobby. He was a real star."

"And a nice guy, I hear," I added, seeing an opening.

"Huh?" Simon looked at me like I was talking about the wrong Bobby. "Er, I suppose so."

"I heard he was trying to help his personal assistant get his own show with Bobby's network. Something about history myths."

"Oh that!" Simon waved me off. "Oh, Bobby squashed that show like a bug."

"Wait—Bobby squashed it?" I asked, genuinely confused. "I thought he was trying to help Henry get it on the air."

Simon shook his head. "Honey, you got it all wrong."

I was starting to get that impression. "So what really happened?"

"Well, Henry had this ridiculous idea for a show. He kept bugging Bobby about it, so finally Bobby says, 'Enough already. I'll freakin' pitch the show for you if you shut up about it.'"

I stifled a grin at Simon's stellar storytelling abilities but didn't interrupt.

"So, next time Bobby has a meeting with the network, he pitches it in a sort of offhand way. I think Bobby thought it was more of a joke than anything else. Only the joke was on him, because the execs liked it. They liked it so much they optioned it and shot a pilot."

"So the show was already in production?" I asked, my wheels turning. "Did Henry get paid?"

Simon shrugged. "Chump change. Unless the network picks a show up, we're talking token amounts of money. A few hundred bucks."

"So what happened? Did the pilot bomb?"

"Hardly!" he cackled. "It did great with test audiences. Too great. Fifty points higher than *Bobby Tells All*." He wiggled his eyebrows and nodded. "Yeah, Bobby couldn't have that. He's got no competition in the ratings right now, but Henry's show would have made Bobby's look like yesterday's news. So Bobby killed it."

"How? If the network loved it, what did he do to convince them not to air it?"

"He had me do some slick negotiating." He winked at me. "Bobby's contract was up, and he told them he'd only re-sign if they promised not to air Henry's show."

"And they agreed to that? Even knowing it was scoring higher with the test audiences?" I asked.

He nodded. "Hey, execs like a sure thing. Bobby's a proven moneymaker. They weren't going to throw that away to take a chance on an unknown, no matter how hot the pilot was."

"Wow." I thought about poor, stressed, sleep deprived looking Henry. "That's cold."

Simon shrugged. "That's Hollywood, honey. You can't take it, move back to Kansas." He cackled again at his own joke.

"Just curious…if Henry's show had been picked up, what kind of money would we be talking then?"

"Six figures," Simon said, nodding sagely. "That's per episode."

I thanked him for the info and left him with my card. As soon as I got back to my car, I dialed Henry again. Straight to voicemail.

While one couldn't help but feel for Henry, I also couldn't help but notice that it gave Henry quite a motive to want revenge on his boss. If Henry knew Bobby was the reason his show was killed, that was ample motive to want him dead. Six figures per episode? People had killed for a lot less.

I scrolled through my contacts until I found the main number for the *Bobby Tells All* production offices.

"BTA productions. This is Amelia. How can I help you?" answered a cheerful female voice.

"Hi, Amelia," I responded. "This is Allie Quick. I'm trying to get hold of Henry Klein. Is he in the office?"

"No, I'm sorry. He's not in. He's called in a personal day."

Drat. "Do you know if he'll be back tomorrow?"

"Sorry. I'm not sure."

I tried not to read anything into the fact that Henry was AWOL. "Thanks, Amelia. When he does come back, would you let me know? I have a few questions I'd like to ask him."

"I'm happy to," she said and took down my name and number.

I disconnected the call and headed toward the *Informer*. As soon as I stepped off the elevators, I noticed two things: (1) Felix was noticeably absent from his office. His desk was in the usual disarray of papers and files, but he was nowhere to be seen. I was 90 percent sure it wasn't because he was avoiding me. And (2) there was a copper haired teenage stalker at my desk.

"Shane," I greeted him as I approached.

"Hey, babe!" He stood from my desk chair, giving me a big toothy smile.

"What are you doing here?" I noticed that my computer was on and several screens were open. I swear if this kid had hacked into my email...

"I just wanted to come by and see my girl. I took the bus. I thought maybe we could do lunch."

I gritted my teeth together. "I'm not *your* girl. And how did you even get in here?" I was going to have to have a talk with Felix about security in the building.

"I told that chick with the purple streaks in her hair that I was your boyfriend, and she sent me right over."

I glanced up at Tina's cubicle. She was peeking over the top, her face red from laughter.

I thought a really dirty word.

"You have to go," I told Shane, scooting him out of the way and sitting in my chair. "I have work to do."

"You're working on a story about Bobby Baxter, aren't you? About his death?"

I spun around and shot him a look. "You know it's not nice to go through someone's computer files."

"Hey, relax. I didn't open anything personal. I just thought maybe I could help out."

I sighed. While he was getting on my nerves royally— and I'd probably never live this visit down if Tina had anything to do with it—he was just a kid with a crush. Hey, we'd all been there at some point, right? "Look, Shane, I really appreciate the help you've given me, but I think you need to go home. Don't you have school or something?"

"Teachers' in-service day." He grinned. "Sweet, right? I love random days off."

"Do your parents know where you are?"

He blinked at me like I'd just asked the stupidest question on earth. "They're at work."

I felt a headache starting to brew between my eyes. "Don't you have friends to go hang out with or malls to loiter at or something?"

"You know, your notes on the case are pretty sparse," Shane said, ignoring me as he pointed to the open file on my screen.

"Gee. Thanks."

"Hey, not that I blame you, babe. I mean, it looks like you're just getting started, right?"

"Sorta," I mumbled, not willing to admit how hard I'd been working already.

"I'm sure once you get into it, you'll have more. You know, once you interview some suspects—"

Been there, done that.

"—find out about the murder weapon—"

Check.

"—go through his phone records—"

"Fat chance of that," I interrupted.

Shane paused. "Why?"

"I'm a reporter, not the police. I can't get a warrant for things like phone records."

Shane's face broke into what could only be described as a wicked grin. "Who needs a warrant?"

I blinked at him, his meaning slow to compute. "Wait—you can hack into the phone company?" I whispered, glancing guiltily over both shoulders.

"Child's play."

"But we can't do that."

"Sure we can." Shane nudged me out of my chair and sat down.

I stood and nervously looked around the newsroom as if there was a neon sign above my head that read *illegal activities about to commence.* Cam was staring at her computer screen, sifting through photos. Tina had gotten her laughter under control and was on the phone. Max looked hung over and preoccupied with his dinosaur computer. No one was paying us any attention.

"Isn't this illegal?" I asked.

Shane shrugged. "Are we hurting anyone?"

"Well, no."

"I mean, we could even be helping someone if it brings a murderer to justice, right?"

While the wording made us sound like some kind of comic book superheroes, he had a point.

"Who's his cell carrier?" Shane asked.

I quickly rattled it off. I only knew because Henry had told me their cell service was spotty on the soundstage when I'd been playing phone tag with him and Bobby while trying to set up the interview.

Shane pulled up the company's website.

"What if we get caught?" I asked. "Can't they trace this kind of thing?"

"You should relax. I can cover my tracks. I'm not an amateur."

"Are you sure? I don't want you to end up in jail."

Shane looked up at me. "Aw, babe! You do care."

Oh brother.

"I care about being slapped with contributing to the delinquency of a *minor*," I said, putting emphasis on that last word in hopes he got the point.

"Look, companies only bring in the police if they lose money. We're not gonna touch any financial records, right? We just want to see who Bobby's been talking to."

Man, the kid could make a good argument. As much as I was nervous about this whole thing, I had to admit I really did want to see who Bobby had been talking to. If his marriage had broken up over an affair, maybe the girlfriend's number would show up. I wasn't sure what motive she could have for wanting to kill Bobby, but seeing as he'd cheesed off just about everyone else in his life, it was possible.

I watched intently as Shane's fingers flew across the keyboard. The screen went black, then blue, then black again. Numbers and letters filled the screen and scrolled by rapidly.

I watched for a few minutes until my eyes started to cross.

"How long is this going to take?" I asked, glancing over my shoulder again. Which, if anyone had been looking, just made me look more guilty than I already felt.

"Patience, babe. This is a highly technical art form."

"I thought it was 'child's play.'"

Shane grinned at me. "Touché. I like a girl who can keep me on my toes."

"Just hurry up, okay?" I urged him, half expecting the internet police to come bursting through the *Informer*'s elevator doors any second.

I watched the numbers scroll for a few more minutes, and then finally several little folders and lines that I assumed were the phone company's files appeared.

"Did you know the Baxters?" I asked as I watched him type in different sequences of numbers and letters, presumably to get the right files open.

"Not really. I think my mom went over to her house once, but just to deliver some mail that we got by mistake. I saw him and his wife from time to time. We never talked or anything. She's kind of snooty, and he was always in a rush and yelling on his phone."

That sounded like Marilyn and Bobby. I crossed my fingers that we'd know just whom he was yelling at on that phone soon.

"You know this guy's number?"

I nodded, grabbing my own phone and scrolling through the contacts.

Shane typed it in, and amazingly, a few seconds later Bobby's records appeared.

"Is this what you need?" he asked with a grin.

"Wow. I'm actually impressed. Can you print that out, or is it too risky?"

"I can print it," he assured me. Then a second later my printer started spitting out page after page of phone records.

Shane did something to my computer that caused a lot of flashing then powered it down. "You should be in the clear. I covered my tracks pretty well, but even if they do find the breach, they'll want to keep it quiet," he assured me.

He knew an awful lot about the company's policies. I silently wondered how many times he'd done this before. Probably better not to ask. I didn't want to be an accessory after the fact.

"Thanks," I said as I gathered the records and put them into a folder.

"So, how about that lunch date?" He smiled up at me, batting his eyelashes.

"How about this?" I flipped my purse strap over my shoulder. "I'll buy you a *friendly* lunch before I drive you home."

He shrugged. "I'll take it."

"But this is not a date. Got it?"

"Not a date. Got it," he confirmed.

We stopped at one of my favorite taco stands, grabbed a box of tacos and a couple of drinks, and then I dropped Shane off back at his house, with a stern warning not to show up unannounced at my home or office anymore. It was getting creepy. I wasn't sure it totally got through, as he just grinned at me and said, "Later, babe." How was it the man I wanted attention from was ignoring me, and the kid I wanted to ignore was crushing on me?

I had a sudden horrible thought as I drove back to the *Informer*. Was I being Felix's Shane? Did Felix see me as an annoying kid? The truth was, he was more than a few years older than I was. I'd never minded, and he hadn't seemed to either, though I knew other people had pointed it out to him on occasion. I did a little mental math and cringed. The truth was Shane and I were closer in age than Felix and me. Ugh. No wonder Felix was losing interest.

I made it back to the office in record time—even slowing down at the overpass for the speed trap, where an unlucky silver truck was the CHP's latest victim. As soon as I got off the elevator, I noticed Tina was back at her desk, yelling into the phone. From what I could hear of her end of the conversation, her swear pig—the piggy bank on her desk that she owed a quarter to for every swear word she uttered at the office—was going to be full by the end of the day. Whomever she was cussing out had her really riled up. I felt bad for the person on the other end of the phone. But I kinda hoped it meant her investigation had hit a roadblock.

Cam was out, and Felix was still gone. Max raised a hand in greeting as I walked by.

When I got to my desk I grabbed the folder holding Bobby's phone records and scanned the first dozen pages. There were calls to numbers I recognized as his manager, a prominent talent agency—presumably his—Henry, and one I discovered was Marilyn's Hollywood Hills place. There were a handful of numbers I didn't recognize, so I decided to call them myself, but they turned out to be to other offices at the studio and a couple of takeout joints.

I was starting to think that this was a huge waste of time, when I reached the next page and spotted another number that I didn't recognize. I scanned the rest of the sheet and spotted several more calls to the same number—most in the week before Bobby died. I grabbed my pink highlighter out of the top right drawer of my desk and started highlighting every call made to and from the number.

I grabbed my phone and dialed it, hoping I'd hit the jackpot and got the mistress.

A cheerful voice on the other end answered, "Keepin' it clean with Sunshine Sanitation. This is Ellen. How can I help you?"

"I'm sorry. I have the wrong number," I said quickly and hung up the phone.

I tossed the highlighter back into the drawer, leaned back in my chair, and stared at the papers in front of me. Well, that was unexpected. Why would Bobby be calling Sunshine Sanitation on his personal phone? Ellen sounded about sixty, so mistress was scratched off my list.

I looked at the list of pink highlighted calls again. Some were short, but most were over five minutes long. Which means Bobby had actually talked with someone at Sunshine, not just had them hang up unceremoniously on him like I had. Had they been cooperating on the story? But if so, why the cold shoulder now when I'd mentioned his name? Had he lied to them about the story? Had he tricked them into talking to him? And why call from his personal number—why not have a research assistant or PA do the dirty work?

I dialed the production office of *Bobby Tells All* again.

"BTA productions. This is Amelia. How can I help you?" came my answer.

"Hi, Amelia. Allie Quick again."

"I'm sorry, Ms. Quick, but Henry's still not in."

"Actually, there was something I was hoping you could help me with," I told her.

"Oh? Well, I'll try."

"It concerns a show that Bobby was working on. 'Takin' out the Trash'?"

"Yes. I know the one."

"I was wondering—who was doing the research for the show?"

"I'm not sure I know what you mean," she said hesitantly.

"I mean, would Bobby have directly contacted Sunshine Sanitation? Would he have been doing research or interviews or anything like that personally?"

Amelia snorted. "Not likely." She paused. "Oh sorry. I didn't mean to speak ill of the dead. It's just that Mr. Baxter had a team who did that sort of thing for him. He'd come up with the idea that they'd do the legwork. Then they'd report back to him and the writers, who'd make a show out of it."

"So he wouldn't have any reason to contact them himself?" I asked, looking down at the marked-up phone records on my desk.

"Not that I can think of," she said.

"Thanks," I told her, absently hanging up the phone. So why had Bobby made multiple calls there? Maybe he was seeing someone at the company? Maybe there was a hot female exec? Or maybe there was more to this trash story than it appeared.

Talking to someone over the phone at the plant was impossible, so I went to plan B. I'd show up at the Sunshine Sanitation office and see how far I could get face to face.

Sunshine Sanitation sat east of L.A., down the 10 freeway in an industrial area of Pomona, in a huge white cement building. Small windows lined the top of the building, and rolling metal doors stood open all around the sides, revealing forklifts and large recycling trucks. The building appeared clean on the outside with a fresh coat of paint, though I could smell the place even with my windows up.

I pulled into a visitor parking lot near the front and made my way toward the sign marked *Office*. The stench coming from the plant hung heavy in the air. Hopefully, the stink wouldn't cling to me after I left. I'd worn one of my favorite teal sundresses, and the thought of chucking it made me tear up a bit. Or maybe that was just the smell.

A bell over the front entrance chimed as I entered the main office. The walls were a sterile white, and the floors were a matching white cement tile. The scent of disinfectant permeated the air, as if someone had just sprayed an entire can of Lysol, and their logo of the giant smiling sun I'd seen on their website was painted on one wall.

I blinked a few times to let my eyes adjust to the light of the office and spotted a portly woman with dark blonde hair and small green eyes behind a large counter with a computer monitor mounted on it.

"Welcome to Sunshine Sanitation. I'm Ellen. How may I help you today?" she asked in the same cheerful tone I'd heard over the phone.

I approached the counter. "Hi, my name is…Tina Bender," I lied. "I'm with the Environmental Protection Agency. We're asking some routine questions of all the waste processing plants in the area."

While I normally hated lying—as I usually got caught—this time it was a necessary evil. I'd already given her my real name and credentials over the phone, and that had gotten me nowhere. I crossed my fingers this tactic at least got me in the door.

Ellen eyed my sundress. "*You're* with the EPA?"

"It's casual Wednesday at the office." I shrugged and did a laugh that came off a little more nervous sounding than I'd hoped. I mentally kicked myself for not thinking of going home to change first.

Ellen clicked on a keyboard hidden under the counter and frowned. "I don't see an inspection scheduled for today."

"No, you wouldn't," I told her. "It's a surprise inspection. You know, to make sure…everything is running smoothly." I suddenly wished I knew a bit more about how a recycling plant actually did run. I just prayed I could fake it.

Ellen's cheerful countenance was quickly morphing to suspicion. "Can I see your credentials, please?"

Right. I should probably have some of those. "Uh, credentials...." I peeked into my purse as if searching for them. "Credentials, credentials....I know they're here somewhere. Let's see...lip gloss, nail file, breath mint, quarters..."

Ellen sighed loudly, crossing both arms over her chest.

I looked up and gave her my best winning smile. "You know, I really just have a couple of quick questions. Tiny ones."

She raised an eyebrow at me. I took it as the best sign I was going to get to forge ahead.

"We heard a rumor that a Bobby Baxter was doing one of his tell-all shows on your facility."

Any sign of Cheerful Ellen disappeared at the mention of Bobby's name, a deep scowl embedding itself on her features. "And?" she challenged.

"And I was wondering if you know what the show was about?"

"No." She spit the word out so quickly that I knew she must be lying.

"No clue, huh?"

She shook her head, her hair bouncing against her cheeks.

"Is there anyone else here who might know?" I asked, looking behind her to a door marked *Employees Only*.

Again with the headshake. "No. Sorry."

"Really? Because I have it on good authority that Bobby called here and spoke with someone. *Several* times," I emphasized.

Her eyes narrowed. "You must be mistaken."

Problem was, I wasn't. The phone company's records didn't lie. This woman, however, I had my doubts about. Either she was hiding something, or she'd been told to stonewall by someone higher up in the company. I had a suspicion it was the latter.

"What is the EPA's interest in this anyway?" Ellen asked, eying my sundress again.

Great question. "We...just want to make sure that you're being properly protected." I cringed even as I said it. It really would have helped my cover if I knew more about the organization I was pretending to be from.

"We're fine." She paused. "Bobby Baxter is dead, and his show won't be airing anymore. There's nothing to tell. Now, if there isn't anything else..." She trailed off, gesturing to the door.

There was plenty else. However, I figured I'd pushed my luck enough for one day. "Thanks a bunch!" I told her, going for overly cheerful.

She didn't reciprocate, continuing her scowl as I left as quickly as I could—trying to avoid her stare that I swear said *liar, liar, pants on fire* as I scurried across the parking lot.

Traffic was going to be insane getting back into L.A. at this hour, so I decide to wait it out and hit a drive-thru In-N-Out Burger instead. As I munched on my burger and fries, I went over my notes again—not just on Sunshine but the entire list I'd amassed on Bobby, from my initial questions to take to the interview to what I'd learned since his death, trying to get a big-picture overview. I felt like I had all the pieces of Bobby's life, but none of them fit together. What I really needed was *Bobby*'s notes. What had he been planning to tell all about in his show on Sunshine Sanitation? Why the personal calls to the plant? Was he onto something big?

The wife had said he kept his laptop at work. I knew from my experience on the set that Bobby had spent a lot of time in his trailer. I wondered if the laptop was still there.

I looked down at my watch. Half past five. But studios didn't necessarily keep regular business hours.

I dialed the number for the production office, but instead of the helpful Amelia, I got a message saying the offices were temporarily closed due to "unforeseen circumstances." I assumed that meant Bobby's death, and production had officially shut down on *Bobby Tells All*.

Which meant there was no one around to put my name on the guardhouse list. Then again, there was also probably no one around to notice me slipping into Bobby Baxter's trailer...

I quickly tossed my trash in the bin and headed back to my car. I was just cranking on the AC when my phone buzzed with a text. I glanced down. Felix.

Been a long day. Drinks?

I bit my lip. Dang it. Why did he have to pick the one time I was busy? I paused, my fingers hovering over the screen.

Part of me wanted to type back *Heck yes!* But I knew if I wanted to get a look at Bobby's things, I was on borrowed time. I wasn't even sure some assistant hadn't cleaned his trailer of personal effects already.

Sorry. Busy tonight. Rain check?

I cringed even as I typed it.

I waited what seemed like an eternity for his one word answer: *sure.*

Why did I suddenly feel like I'd blown it with this relationship?

I tried to shove that thought to the back of my mind as I pulled out of the parking lot and headed toward the 10.

CHAPTER NINE

It was almost dark by the time I hit the main gate at the studios. The night guard was on duty in the shack, a different guy than I'd encountered in my last two visits. Which meant I couldn't rely on him recognizing me and conveniently letting me in. Dang it.

I braked as I approached the shack, thinking quickly.

"'Evening," the guy in the guard uniform said. He was tall, slim, and had a name tag that read *Alfredo*. "Name please?"

"Marilyn Baxter." I said a silent prayer that Marilyn wasn't a regular visitor to the set.

Luck must have finally been with me, as he just nodded and checked his electronic tablet. After a moment of searching, his eyebrow drew into a frown. "Sorry, ma'am. Your name is not on my list tonight."

I huffed out a sigh in my best Mrs. Baxter imitation. "You have *got* to be kidding me. I told my husband's assistant that I was coming by to pick up his personal effects. Are you telling me he didn't call you?"

"Uh…" Alfredo looked a little intimidated, like he wasn't used to irate wives. "I'm sorry, but no one informed me."

"Henry Klein. Call him. In fact, let me call that little no-good weasel and let him know he's fired." I made a big show of rummaging in my purse for my phone.

"Wait, uh…no one needs to get fired."

I paused. "Oh, yes he does!"

"Who is your husband, ma'am?" the guard asked, starting to sweat.

"Bobby Baxter. The recently *deceased* Bobby Baxter." I let out a small sob on the last word, hoping crying wives intimidated him too.

"Oh geez, I'm sorry I didn't recognize you, Mrs. Baxter," Alfredo said, tripping over himself. "I'm really sorry about your husband. We all are."

I nodded, dabbing at my dry eyes. "Thank you."

"Of course you can go right in. Don't worry about the list mix-up. I'll straighten it out with Henry."

I sniffed loudly and nodded again. "You're very kind," I said, quickly putting my car in gear and driving through the gate before he could change his mind.

I parked my golf cart a couple of studios down from Bobby's and slipped my heels off to keep from clacking along the pavement as I kept to the shadows. I didn't pass anyone else, the rest of the nearby productions shut down for the night. The large warehouse doors to studio 28B, where *Bobby Tells All* was filmed, were locked up tight. Quite probably forever, I thought sadly. I wondered what they'd do with the shows they'd already filmed. Would they air as a final tribute to their host?

I looked over both shoulders then slipped around the back of the building where the trailers were kept. It was dark behind the building, the dim lights from the studio's streetlamps not quite reaching the area. I pulled my phone out and flicked on my flashlight app. The three trailers were still lined up neatly, a smattering of potted plants sitting between them to liven up the sparse alleyway. Bobby's trailer still bore his name on the door. I just hoped the contents were still untouched.

I was just about to try the door, when the sound of another golf cart reached my ears. I quickly looked around for a hiding spot and dove behind the wardrobe trailer, crouching onto the ground beside a potted topiary.

The golf cart stopped, and a guard got out. He shined his flashlight in arching beams, and I thought really small thoughts trying to make myself as invisible as I could.

What felt like an eternity later, the guard put his flashlight away, got back into his cart, and drove away.

I breathed a sigh of relief, got back to my feet, and padded to the door of the trailer, ready to pull out the lockpick set that Felix had given me when I'd first started working for him. But when I touched the handle, the door easily pushed open an inch.

I stared at the ajar door for a moment, unsure quite what to do. Why would the door to the trailer be unlocked? Surely the production staff must have secured it after Bobby's death? Or the studio security?

I nibbled my bottom lip for a second then decided I was just being paranoid.

I pressed the door open and stepped inside. I flicked on my flashlight app again and scanned the room. It looked a lot like my grandparents' Winnebago, if they'd hired an interior decorator. A small table and bench seats to my left, a sofa along the wall to my right, and some cupboards and shelves filled with various jars of stage makeup, empty coffee cups, and script pages. None of which looked particularly telling. Just beyond the shelves was a door that probably led to a bedroom. If Bobby had any personal items, like, say, a laptop with incriminating notes on it, my guess is that's where they'd be.

I walked forward and put my hand on the knob...

Then froze as I heard a thump from beyond the door.

Everything in my body told me to get the heck out of there. That something wasn't right. I clicked off my flashlight and turned to go. But my hand had barely left the doorknob when the door burst open and knocked me down. My head hit the floor with a crack that I felt all the way down to my toes. I forced myself to roll over and stand up, moving as quickly as I could toward the trailer's door. Stumbling down the three steps to the ground, I heard footsteps pound behind me.

I moved to run when hands grasped my shoulders and shoved me to the ground. I hit a couple of potted plants, and shards of pottery scattered around me. My entire body ached, and blood trickled down my calf. Turning over onto my back, I hoped to get a look at my attacker. But his face was obscured in the darkness, covered in a ski mask. I had the fleeting thought that I was about to die, and my lip trembled.

Then I heard the sweet sound of the security guard's golf cart again.

My attacker turned toward the direction of the sound, and that's when I saw it. A tattoo on the back of his forearm. It looked like a snake wrapped around a dying tree.

The sound of the guard's cart came closer, and the shadowy attacker dropped his grip on me and took off at a dead run in the opposite direction.

I breathed a sigh of relief that he was gone, but it was short lived. If I was found here, I'd have some explaining to do. I got to my feet and ran the length of the back side of the building. I didn't dare go back to my abandoned golf cart, instead hoofing it the entire way back to the visitor parking lot, keeping to the shadows. I didn't stop running until I reached the safety of my car. The doors locked automatically when I started the ignition. I quickly drove off the studio lot. Two blocks down, I pulled to the curb under a bright streetlight to catch my breath.

My calf was burning. I turned on the overhead light and looked down at my bleeding leg. A piece of broken pottery must have cut me when I'd fallen. I grabbed some napkins out of the glove compartment and held some pressure on the wound to stop the bleeding.

My hands were shaking, the adrenaline rush leaving me weak. Someone else had beaten me to breaking into Bobby's trailer. That left me feeling mixed emotions. On the one hand, it almost confirmed I was right—Bobby had kept something incriminating in his trailer that pointed to his killer. On the other, I'd likely met that killer face to face tonight. That thought sent a whole new round of heebie-jeebies shimmying through me.

Should I call the police? I quickly dismissed that idea. I wasn't keen on the idea of explaining how I'd lied my way into the studio with intentions of stealing a deceased man's personal effects. Besides, the guard in the cart who'd distracted my attacker had probably already realized the trailer was broken into.

I grabbed my phone and dialed Felix instead.

He answered on the third ring. "Allie?"

"Felix, there was a break-in," I said in a rush.

"What? Where?" I heard rustling, as if he was getting up from somewhere comfortable like a bed or couch. Both sounded like heaven to me right now.

"At the studio where *Bobby Tells All* is filmed. He…someone broke into Bobby's trailer and attacked me on the way out."

"*What*?!" I heard more rustling and a door slam. "Are you all right?"

I nodded at my empty car. "Yes." Mostly.

"Did you call the police?" he asked, and I heard the worry in his voice.

"I, um, sort of can't," I hedged.

He let out a deep sigh. "Do I want to know?"

"No."

"Text me your location. I'll be right there." Then he hung up.

CHAPTER TEN

––––––

I doubled back to the studios and parked in an empty space at the curb across the street from the main entrance. Twenty minutes later Felix's old junker of a car pulled up behind me, and a second after that, a big black SUV stopped behind him. I raised an eyebrow. He'd brought friends?

I got out of my car and greeted Felix on the sidewalk. My head still ached, and my calf throbbed as I put pressure on it.

Felix took one look at me and pulled me into a bear hug. I didn't resist. In fact, I had to fight the urge to cry into his big, warm shoulder that was probably the most comforting thing I'd ever experienced. Or at least it felt like it in that moment.

Finally he pulled back, giving me a visual once-over. "Let me see that leg." He knelt down. "It doesn't need stitches, but it's still pretty deep. You're filthy," he said with confusion as he stood back up.

I looked down at myself and cringed. I was covered with potting soil and dirt from the broken flowerpots, plus some greasy stains from the ground outside the studio that I didn't want to try to identify. "It's a long story," I said.

"I've got a first-aid kit in the SUV. I'll grab it," a second voice said.

I looked behind Felix and spotted Calvin Dean. Cal was a private bodyguard that Felix sometimes employed when things got a little hairy at the tabloid. Most celebs had a love-hate relationship with our paper, but once in a while one of them would get threatening, and it was nice peace of mind to know Cal was around. There was a rumor he was seeing Tina, but I didn't hold that against him.

"I'm fine. Really," I protested in vain as Cal jogged back to the SUV.

When Felix and I were alone again, he gave me a hard stare. "Want to tell me what happened?"

"Do I have a choice?" I asked, suddenly feeling very foolish.

"Nope," Felix said.

I sighed as Cal came back with the first-aid kit. Reluctantly, I told them all about my brilliant (insert sarcasm) plan to break into Bobby's trailer and how the bad guy with the tattoo had thwarted that plan.

When I was finished, Cal had neatly bandaged up my leg, and Felix was running his hands through his hair in a frustrated gesture until it stood on end.

"What were you thinking?" he asked. "You could have been killed."

"I was thinking there's a reason Bobby was killed, and I want to find out what it is. You know, so *you* have something to print."

"Don't you dare put this on me, Quick," Felix said, pointing a finger my way.

He was right. That was kind of childish. But I didn't like the accusation in his tone. Maybe it hadn't been my best plan ever, but it wasn't my fault some goon had had the same idea.

"What do you think Bobby had in his trailer?" Cal asked, his demeanor much more calm, almost Zen-like. Then again, I guessed he was used to situations like this.

I shrugged. "His wife said he kept a laptop there. I was hoping to get a look at his notes."

Felix and Cal exchanged a look. Then Cal asked, "Did the guy who attacked you take it?"

"I…" I paused, thinking back. It had been dark. I'd barely been able to make out the shape of the man. "I don't know. It was dark. I did see a tattoo on his wrist that went up the back of his forearm. It was a snake wrapped around a dead tree."

Cal looked across the street at the studio gates. "You said you thought a security guard was already on the scene?"

I nodded. "He spooked the guy with the tattoo off of me."

Felix's jaw seemed to clench a little tighter.

"Well, I guess we could go find out if the laptop is still there," Cal suggested.

I let out a bark of laughter. "Yeah, like the guard is just going to let us saunter in and check."

Cal grinned. "Who's on duty at the shack tonight?" he asked, gesturing to the guardhouse.

"A guy named Alfredo," I answered.

He nodded, smiled, and then stepped off the curb and jogged across the street.

I sent a questioning look to Felix. He shrugged.

We quickly crossed the street to follow Cal and caught up to him just in time to hear the tail end of a conversation with Alfredo.

"...good to see you again too, man," the guard said.

"Hey, say hi to Mona for me, okay?" Cal told him as the security gates opened for us.

"Will do. You gotta come over soon. We'll barbeque."

"Consider it done," Cal said. Then he turned to us and winked before leading the way through the gates.

Felix and I quickly followed.

"Nice to see you again, Mrs. Baxter." Alfredo waved as we scuttled through.

"Mrs. Baxter?" Felix whispered to me.

"It's a long story," I mumbled. Then as a clever (or not-so-clever) conversation changer, I turned to Cal. "You know the guard?"

He nodded. "The security community is small," he said nonchalantly as we all hopped into a golf cart. "Alfredo and I did security together on the last Brad Pitt movie."

"You know Brad Pitt?" I had to admit, I was impressed.

"We're like that." Cal held up two intertwined fingers.

"Where's the *Bobby Tells All* soundstage?" Felix asked. He looked less impressed with Cal's celeb friends than I was.

"To the left," I directed. "28B."

Felix made a left then slowed to a halt a few paces down from Bobby's studio. Three other golf carts were already parked in front of 28B, security guards standing near them. They'd discovered the break-in alright.

"Wait here," Cal told us. "I'll see what I can find out."

That was fine by me. I had no interest in being anywhere near Bobby's trailer again. Just being on the lot again was spooking me more than I liked to admit.

From where we sat, I could just make out Bobby's trailer through the now open warehouse doors. The lights were on inside, and I could see silhouettes of security through the windows. A potted palm lay on its side, the pot shattered and dirt scattered along the ground. I shuddered and tried not to think of my aching calf.

We watched Cal approach one of the security guards standing on the steps of the trailer. They did a complicated handshake that clearly said Cal knew this guy too.

"Glad I brought him along," Felix said beside me.

I nodded. "Thanks for coming."

"Where else would I be?"

I turned to look at him. "I don't know. But you've been awfully *busy* lately," I said, the word coming out more accusatory than I'd hoped.

Felix raised an eyebrow at me. "I do believe *you* were the one who was busy tonight." He waved his hand toward the trailer.

Touché.

I was saved from responding by Cal jogging back toward us.

"Well?" I asked. "Did they find the guy?"

He shook his head. "Unfortunately, no one got a look at the perp." He paused. "Except you, that is."

Gee, lucky me. "And the laptop?" I asked.

"Gone."

I felt my heart sink.

"Sorry," Cal said. "Jameson, that's the head of night security there," he continued, pointing out the man he'd been chatting with on the steps. "He said the back room looked like it had been ransacked. Papers tossed, cupboards ripped open, the whole deal."

"Was anything else taken?" Felix jumped in.

Cal shrugged. "Too early to tell. Jameson said he'd have to get an inventory of what Bobby usually kept in there. But he said the place was cleaned out of any electronic equipment."

"So all of Bobby's notes are gone," I said, feeling the weight of the night suddenly settle on me. I fought hard not to tear up as my head started to pound again.

"Sorry, kid," Cal said, sending a sympathetic look my way.

"Come on. Let's get you home," Felix said, eyeing the bandage on my leg.

I looked down and noticed blood starting to stain the bandage. While I hated leaving empty-handed, there wasn't anything more to find out here anyway. And my head was killing me. I nodded docilely and got back into the golf cart.

We left the studio, and Felix helped me into my car. "Are you sure you'll be all right? Do you want me to drive you home?" he asked through the driver side window.

I bit my lip. I desperately wanted to say yes. After nearly being killed, the comfort of being in Felix's arms sounded like heaven. But while I wasn't sure I was totally alright, pride was stronger. The last thing I wanted was a pity overnight.

I shook my head. "I'm fine."

He didn't look convinced. "Let me at least follow you home. Make sure you get in alright."

"It's late. It's been a long day, and I'm a big girl. I can manage to get home," I told him. I halfway wished I'd shut up and just accept his offer.

He sighed. "If you're sure?"

No. "Yes."

"Okay, I guess I'll see you at the office in the morning."

"Yep!" I said with way more fake perk than the situation called for.

A soon as he stepped back, I hit the gas before I could change my mind. I looked in the rearview mirror. Felix was watching me. I turned the corner and pressed down on the accelerator.

When I got home, I tossed my trashed shoes into the corner, fed Mr. Fluffykins, and trudged to the shower, dropping my filthy clothing in the hallway along the way. The hot water rolled over me. I watched the dirt and grime slide off my body and swirl down the drain. I wished my uncertainty about Felix would wash down the drain along with the stench of the day. If the only way Felix wanted to come up to my place was for a pity party, it was clear he and I were going nowhere and fast.

CHAPTER ELEVEN

———

I woke up feeling like an extra from *The Walking Dead*. The red numbers on my bedside clock read six a.m.

My brain ached like I'd gone twelve rounds with Mike Tyson, and I fought against the urge to pull the blanket over my head and go back to sleep. Mr. Fluffykins made the decision for me. I blinked my eyes open against the pale sunlight streaming in through my bedroom window and groaned. Mr. Fluffykins was standing on my chest, staring at me.

"I supposed you're hungry?" I murmured. My mouth felt like I'd swallowed an entire field of cotton.

He meowed and started kneading my chest with his claws, and I jolted upright. He jumped off the bed and trotted toward the kitchen.

I slung my legs over the side of the bed. My head throbbed, and my calf ached. I reached up and felt the lump on the back of my head. It was smaller but still hurt like heck. Then I checked the bandage on my calf. The cut had stopped bleeding at least. I went into the bathroom and redressed the wound and brushed my teeth.

Afterward, I fed my kitty then dressed and put myself together for the day. Dressing up always made me feel better, so I chose one of my favorite black A-line skirts, a hot pink wrap top, and a pair of hot pink matching heels. My legs had always been my best asset, and I was damned if I was gonna cover them up just because some creep had attacked me.

I added a little flair with some silver bangles, matching hoop earrings, and an oversized pink bag. I went light on the makeup and piled my blonde hair on top of my head in a somewhat messy bun, then wrapped a hot pink silk wrap around the base of the bun and tied it in a cute little bow.

I checked out my reflection in the full-length mirror in the bedroom corner. The bandage on my leg stuck out like a sore thumb, but the rest of the outfit looked great, so I could ignore it. Plus, I was already feeling much better.

I wasn't particularly ready to face Felix, but I had a job to do, so I locked up the apartment and drove to the *Informer*.

As soon as I stepped off of the elevator, I spotted another bouquet of flowers sitting on the corner of my desk. They were hard to miss, as this time there was a bundle of at least a dozen balloons attached to them. I felt myself blush. They had to be from Shane.

I chanced a glance at Felix's office. He was on the phone, but he was staring right at me. His expression was dark and unreadable again. But I could tell for sure it wasn't a very cheery one.

I felt a little bit bad. Felix had interrupted his evening to come rescue me the night before. I took a step toward his office to explain. But before I got any farther, he quickly swiveled his chair so his back was turned on me. Ouch. Cold shoulder much?

Fine. Let him stew in his jealousy for a bit. Maybe a little jealousy would be good for him and in the long run, us...if there even still was an us.

I made my way to my desk and pulled the card out of the flowers. Sure enough, they were from Shane.

I stuck the card back into the bouquet, took a seat, and powered up my computer.

"Secret admirer?"

I looked up to see Tina leaning back in her chair to peek out of her cubicle, her feet on her desk, her black and purple hair hanging down her back, one eyebrow raised at me.

"Something like that," I answered cautiously.

"He's kinda cute. Your new boyfriend." She grinned, showing off a wide row of white teeth.

"Ha. Ha. Very funny, Bender. But I'm not dating a teenager."

"I heard about what happened last night at the studio." This time the grin disappeared, and she looked almost earnest. "Scary stuff. You okay?"

"Yeah. Thanks." Okay, so maybe Tina wasn't all bad all the time.

"Cal said the guy took Bobby's laptop?"

I nodded.

"Any idea what was on it?"

"Not really," I hedged.

"Bummer." She plopped her feet back on the floor. "Well, I'm glad you're okay," she said, ending the conversation as she scooted back into her own cube.

That made two of us. I had spent the night trying to block the attack out of my head as I'd tossed and turned, but now in the bright, safe space of the newsroom, I tried to focus on the details. Clearly whoever had attacked me was after something incriminating in Bobby's office. I couldn't be 100 percent sure it was Bobby's killer, but it was a good bet. I mentally went down my list of suspects.

The wife was immediately out. The person who had attacked me was definitely male. That much I had been able to make out in the dark. Henry maybe? I'd had the impression the guy was bigger than Henry's frame, but that could have been fear taking over. I tried to remember if I'd seen Henry in short sleeves.

I picked up my phone and dialed Henry's number. Straight to voicemail again. I left another one asking him to call me, but I was starting to think that was a lost cause.

I looked at the next name on my list. Someone at Sunshine Sanitation. And "someone" was about as vague as you could get. There had to be hundreds of people employed by the sanitation company.

If I went along with the idea that Bobby was going to expose the company in some big negative way, then he had to have had someone on the inside to feed him that information. A mole. Maybe the guy with the tattoo. Had he been feeding Bobby inside info? But then, why kill Bobby before he could expose it?

And then there was Ritchie Mullins. His size certainly fit the guy who'd attacked me. Had Ritchie had a tattoo? Hard to tell. He'd been wearing long sleeves when I'd seen him at the gym. I thought back to the video of the assault. He'd been in long sleeves then too. Considering the weather report was calling for the upper eighties today, I grabbed my purse and headed for the elevator.

Half an hour later I parked across the street from the Oceanside Gym. I made my way inside with a longing glance at the coffeehouse, and found a different person on duty at the desk, this time a petite brunette.

"Can I help you?" she asked

"I was wondering if Ritchie is working today?" I asked, glancing past her at the already busy gym full of ellipticals and weight machines.

"He is, but he's not in yet." She glanced at the clock. "His first client isn't until 10:30, so he probably won't be in for another twenty minutes. Did you want to wait?"

"Uh, maybe I'll grab a coffee and come back," I told her, my internal caffeine addict not minding a short wait.

I thanked her and left, heading back across the street to the café. The air from the ceiling fans blew down on me and cooled my sun-heated skin as soon as I entered. I ordered an iced caramel macchiato and took a seat by the window.

I sipped and played a couple rounds of Candy Crush on my phone before I finally spotted Ritchie Mullins. He parked a shiny new mustang a few doors down from the gym, then exited…wearing a tank top.

Bingo.

I quickly tossed my cup in the trash and jogged across the street, entering the gym just a few paces behind Ritchie.

"Ritchie Mullins," I said, catching up to him at the reception desk.

He turned from flirting with the brunette, and his smile faded immediately at the sight of me. "You again. The reporter."

I grinned at him, trying to ignore the hostility as I quickly scanned his body for the telltale tattoo. "Yep, it's me. I, uh, just had a couple of follow-up questions." His left arm was clean. He was leaning on the counter with his right, so I couldn't see his forearm.

He shook his head. "I've got no comment." He moved to turn his back to me, further obscuring my view.

"Wait! Uh, I was just, um, wondering how to spell your name."

He turned back around. "What?"

"You know, for my article on how Bobby wronged you by punching an innocent man. I'd, uh, hate to spell your last name wrong. I'm a stickler for details." I shot him a big toothy grin, hoping he didn't notice my gaze flicking to his arm every two seconds. Why wouldn't he quit leaning on the counter?

He paused, seeming to mull this over for a moment, then finally said, "It's Mullins. M-U-L-L-I-N-S."

"You know what? I've got a terrible memory. Could you write that down for me?"

He blinked at me as if not sure he should buy my stupid act. Luckily, in my cute little skirt and heels with my cute little bow in my hair, it wasn't all that hard for me to "play blonde." And Ritchie was no brain surgeon himself.

"Fine," he muttered, reaching across the counter for a pen and Post-it.

With his right arm.

I took a step closer to him, trying to get a good look…and easily saw he was tattoo free.

Crap cakes.

"Here. Now if you'll excuse me, I got a client," Ritchie said, handing me the paper with his name and heading onto the main floor of the gym.

"Thanks," I called after his retreating back.

Thanks for nothing, I amended silently as I shoved the Post-it into my purse and trudged back to my car. Unfortunately, my tattooed assailment was still an unknown.

I got into my car, cranked on the AC, and was just contemplating my next move when my phone rang. I looked down to see Cam's number.

"Hey, Cam, what's up?" I asked.

"Hi, Allie. There's, um, there's someone here at the office to see you."

"Who is it?"

She was fighting to hold in her laughter. "Just get here," she said and hung up.

What on earth? I tossed my phone on the passenger seat, pulled into traffic, and hurried back to the *Informer*.

I stepped off of the elevator. And immediately wanted to turn around and get right back on. What was waiting for me at my desk was not cool.

I peeked over at Cam, who was giggling quietly. I glared at her, and she laughed harder, covering her mouth and turning to face her computer.

Thankfully, as I passed Felix's office, I saw he was absent.

I hurried to my desk and stopped.

"What in the world are you doing here, Shane?"

The kid was standing behind a giant stuffed teddy bear. The thing was as tall as he was, which meant that it was about a foot taller than I, and it was neon pink. It looked like it belonged backstage at a strip club. He poked his head over the big pink bear's shoulder and grinned.

"Do you love it?"

Despite its wild neon color, I hated to admit, I kinda didn't hate it. But I wasn't about to tell him that.

"Shane, I told you already that you have to stop sending these gifts and find a girl your own age," I said as gently as I could.

"You keep playing hard to get, but you'll cave." He smiled.

I shook my head. "I'm a lot older than you are, Shane."

"Says you, babe. That age business is old news nowadays. You'll come around," he said, undeterred.

"Shane—

"I got to get going. I got an appointment with my tutor in about fifteen minutes. Call me if you need any more help." He leaned the bear back against my desk, grinned at me, then hurried out of the office.

"You sure he's not your boyfriend?" Tina peeked around her cubicle wall, laughing.

"Welcome to my world," I grumped and reached out and patted the bear.

"No thanks. I like my men a little…older." Tina laughed and turned back to her computer.

I glanced to Felix's empty office and frowned.
"So do I."

CHAPTER TWELVE

———

I was trying to shove the enormous teddy bear into the passenger side of my Bug when my phone rang. I crammed Mr. Bear's legs into the car and slammed the door shut before they could pop back out. I took a second to catch my breath then pulled the phone from my purse and answered.

"Allie Quick?"

"Yes," I confirmed.

"It's Amelia. From BTA productions."

"Oh, right, yes. How are you?" I asked, only slightly out of breath. That bear was much heavier than it looked. "I, uh, thought the offices were closed?"

"They are," she answered quickly. "We're just clearing some things out today. But you asked me to let you know when Henry was back in?"

"Yes. Is he back?"

"He is. I just saw him head into his office a few minutes ago."

"Thanks, Amelia. I'm on my way." I paused. "Uh, would you mind putting my name on the guard's list?"

"Sure thing," she said in her always cheerful voice.

I ended the call and jumped into my car. If Henry wouldn't return my calls, I was just going to have to ambush him. I made a beeline for the studio in hopes of catching him before he left.

I made the drive in record time and gave my name to the guard at the gate (who thankfully was *not* Alfredo), and he directed me to the visitors' parking area. I hopped into the closest golf cart and steered in the direction the guard had given me for the BTA production offices. I had to pass studio 28B on the way, and I gave a quick scan of the area. The studio was locked up tight again, but today there was a guard posted outside the doors. They clearly weren't taking any more chances on break-ins.

I pulled up in front of the small, cottage-like building on the edge of the studio lot just in time to see Henry exit with a cup of coffee and a bundle of file folders in hand.

I stopped the cart, slung my purse over my shoulder, and hurried toward Henry before he could get away.

He saw me coming and smiled, but it didn't quite reach his eyes. "Ms. Quick, I'm surprised to see you here." He took a sip of his coffee.

I gave a quick glance at his bare forearms, revealed by his short sleeve polo shirt. Neither was tattooed. Well, so much for that theory. "I've been trying to get hold of you," I told him. "I left you a few voicemails."

His smile wavered. "Sorry. I've been taking some personal time."

I nodded. "Understandable. It's got to be hard when your boss is murdered."

He flinched at the words. "Yes, well, I'm on my way to a meeting." He held up the folders in his hand.

"I won't keep you," I promised. "I just had a couple more questions about your relationship with Bobby."

He shook his head. "I don't know what else I can say. I've told you everything there is to tell."

I propped my hand on my hip and raised an eyebrow. "Except you left out the part where you were angry at Bobby because he was blocking your show from airing."

He frowned. "Who told you that?"

"A source."

His eyes narrowed. "Okay, yes, I was upset that the network had decided not to pick up my show. But that was their decision, not Bobby's."

I suddenly wondered if Henry was actually ignorant about the fact Bobby had killed his show or if he was just hoping *I* was.

"Bobby had a big hand in swaying their minds, though, didn't he?"

Henry shrugged and sipped his coffee.

"In fact, he basically said it was his show or yours."

"Did you say you had a question for me?" he asked, neither confirming nor denying my accusations.

Okay, if he wanted to play it that way… "Yes, I do. Where were you the night that Bobby was killed?"

His expression turned stony, his jaw clenching. "Home. Asleep."

"Alone?"

"Yes."

"That's not a great alibi."

"I wasn't aware I needed one," he said, his tone hard.

"Well, you do have ample motive to want Bobby out of the way."

He shook his head. "Not true. Yes, I was angry that Bobby was holding my career hostage. But I didn't kill him over it. Look, my agent was set to launch a lawsuit against Bobby for burying the show. Why would I kill him if I thought I would be getting a major payout?"

"What kind of payout are we talking about here?" I asked.

Henry stepped closer and lowered his voice. "Hundreds of thousands in restitution, according to my agent and the lawyers."

He was right. No one would want to lose that kind of money. If his lawyers really thought they could win.

"Did Bobby know you were going to sue him?"

Henry shrugged. "I certainly didn't tell him. Not that it matters now. With him gone, I get squat. So print what you want, but I didn't kill Bobby." Then he sipped at his coffee again and walked away.

I made my way back to the golf cart and steered back in the direction of my car, feeling another theory shot down. If Henry had been expecting to make hundreds of thousands of dollars from his lawsuit against Bobby, he had no reason to want Bobby dead. Heck, if he won, he might even be able to get the green light on his project after all. His alibi might have been crap, but his motive suddenly looked a lot slimmer.

I was halfway back to the *Informer* when a text popped up on my phone from Max.

Beading of Bobby's villain day. Four on sock.

I blinked, staring at the readout. What the—?

I pulled over to the side of the road at the next light and texted back. *What?*

Feeding of bobbies will toothsay. For the clock.

I stifled a snort of laughter. I was impressed that Max was attempting to text, when I was pretty sure he still preferred a rotary to a cell phone, but he clearly hadn't gotten the hang of it yet. I dialed the *Informer*'s number and keyed in his extension.

"Max Beacon?" came his grizzled voice through my car speakers.

"Hey, Max, it's Allie. I got your text. Sort of. It was a little…unclear."

"Damned contraption. Felix told me all I had to do was talk into this smartphone thing, and it would send a message. But it never understands me. More like an idiot phone if you ask me."

I didn't bother stifling the laugh this time. "What was it you meant to say?"

"Well, I was trying to tell you that I got a tip they're reading Bobby's will today. Four o'clock."

I glanced at my dash clock. It was 3:45. "Any idea where?"

"His lawyer's office. I could text you the address."

"Uh, maybe you better just tell me," I said, reaching for a pen from my purse. I wrote the address Max rattled off on a Coffee Bean napkin and quickly thanked him before flipping a U-turn and heading toward the lawyer's Burbank offices.

It was ten past four by the time I got there, and I quickly parked in the adjacent garage before heading toward the two-story building. After a quick check of the directory, it looked like Abraham, Schmidt & Associates took up the entire first floor. I bit my lip, wondering what the chances were I could just walk in and ask how the reading was going. Probably slim to anorexic. I quickly walked the perimeter of the building, looking for any low windows or open back doors. Blinds covered the four windows on the side. The back of the building butted up against a small alleyway, rimmed in a chain link fence. Not the most scenic of views, but I hoped maybe the inhabitants wouldn't be as concerned about privacy and keep a blind or two open. At least enough so that I could make out which part of the building held Marilyn Baxter and company.

Only what I found as I rounded the back of the building wasn't a view of the trophy wife. It was a nosey, purple haired reporter crouched beneath a covered window.

I thought a really dirty word as I approached my competition.

Tina looked up, and I could see the same word mirrored in her thoughts. "Allie."

"Tina," I responded in kind.

"I see you got Max's text too," she said.

"Such as it were," I mumbled.

I saw a ghost of grin tug at Tina's mouth. Then she pulled at my sleeve, dragging me down to a crouch beside her.

"They'll see you." She gestured up at the window above us.

"Is that the room they're reading the will in?" I whispered back.

Tina nodded. "I got a glimpse of the wife before the legal secretary closed the blinds."

I glanced up. It looked just like all the other windows. For once, I was grateful Tina had gotten there before me. However, with both window and blinds shut tightly, there wasn't much we were going to get from the knowledge. "Oh, to be a fly on the wall," I murmured.

Tina grinned beside me. "I kinda am."

I raised an eyebrow at her, for the first time noticing that she had an earbud lodged into her left ear. "Do tell, Bender?"

She shrugged, still grinning. "Let's just say, I might have *borrowed* a little something from Cal's surveillance stash."

I blinked at her. "You are brilliant, girl."

Tina turned a shocked face my way. "Was that a compliment?"

I felt my cheeks heat. She was right. I couldn't think of another time I'd ever said anything nice to Tina. "Hey, I call it like I see it."

Her expression softened, and for a moment something eerily like camaraderie passed between us.

Just for a moment.

"Yeah, well, glad *one* of us can get the scoop." She smirked.

I rolled my eyes. "Come on. What are they saying?"

She shot me a reluctant look. Maybe it was the out-of-character compliment, but finally she removed the earbud and held it between us instead. We both leaned in, getting as close to it as possible without whacking our heads together.

"...portfolio at Schneider investments to be divided equally among the heirs heretofore mentioned," I heard a deep male voice read. Presumably Bobby's lawyer. I heard someone clear their throat in the room and papers rustling. The quality of the audio was pretty darn good. I could swear I even heard Mrs. Baxter sigh as the lawyer went on to list all of Bobby's bank accounts individually in exhaustive detail.

"How did you get the bug in there?" I whispered to Tina.

That big grin reappeared. "Turns out a member of the evening cleaning crew is a big fan of Ellen DeGeneres. I got her two tickets to a taping of *Ellen* next week, and she hooked me up."

"Nice," I said, meaning it. I filed that trick away for later. "So that's how you knew about the prenup too?"

Tina nodded. "Dating a security expert comes in handy."

So it seemed. I wondered what dating a tabloid editor came in handy for? That was, if we were even still dating at this point.

That disconcerting thought was interrupted as I heard the lawyer finally get to the good stuff.

"...and to my wife, Marilyn, I leave the rest of my assets and real property, totaling the estimated current value of..."

Tina and I both leaned in until our temples were touching.

"...just under thirteen million dollars."

I almost swallowed my tongue. I looked over at Tina and saw the same thought mirrored in her eyes.

No matter how Mrs. Baxter had tried to downplay her husband's celebrity status, he'd clearly been raking in celebrity bucks. Bucks she wouldn't have seen a dime of had Bobby divorced her. Giving her thirteen million reasons to want her husband dead.

* * *

I left Tina still listening to the details of Bobby's will as I made my way back to the office. I figured I'd heard the best parts, and I was eager to jump on them before Tina had the chance. I slowed only as I approached our friendly neighborhood CHP's speed trap then made my way up to my desk, where I added this latest juicy detail to my notes on the story. Then I went searching for anything I could find to try to corroborate that Bobby had been cheating on his wife, as his housekeeper had implied. I went over his phone records again, double checking each number. I did an exhaustive search of his social media accounts, searching for any overly-friendly encounters with female fans. And I looked back over the cast and crew list for the show, checking each female member in detail, looking for a hot receptionist or young assistant. Unfortunately, nothing yielded any results. If Bobby had been seeing someone on the side, he'd been incredibly careful to cover his tracks.

"Hey, Allie." Cam took a seat on the corner of my desk just as I was about to give up for the day.

"Hey back," I said, grateful for the distraction as I rubbed my eyes.

"Trace is still on set filming that new action movie he landed, and I don't feel like having dinner alone. Do you want to grab a bite to eat? If you're not too busy, that is." She motioned to my screen.

I glanced at Felix, who was studiously ignoring me, and then nodded. "Sure. Just let me grab my purse. Oh—" I stood to take a step then stopped. "Can we take your car? I'm still driving around with a big pink teddy bear in the front seat of mine."

Cam laughed. "Sure thing."

I followed Cam to the elevator, not looking in Felix's direction as I passed his office. I needed a break from everything. The questions about our relationship included.

A girls-only dinner with Cam sounded like just what the doctor had ordered.

CHAPTER THIRTEEN

———

Cam and I decided that a fancy dinner wasn't what either of us was in the mood for and stopped at a mom-and-pop Mexican place a few blocks down. We both ordered a three cheese and chicken quesadilla and a bottle of water. All of that cheesy goodness would go straight to my thighs, but at the moment I couldn't care less.

We took our meal to a booth near the back. Almost as soon as we sat down, Cam busted out with, "So what's the deal with you and Felix?"

I almost choked on my water. I grabbed a napkin and patted my lips. Cam had never asked about my relationship with Felix before. In fact, no one at the office ever mentioned it. I was sure everyone knew we had something going on, but no one ever commented on it.

"What do you mean?" I asked as nonchalantly as possible because, honestly, I didn't have an answer for her. I had no idea what the deal was with me and Felix.

"I mean, you two obviously have a thing—" She flicked a hand in the air. "—but it feels like there's this tension there lately."

Damned. Even Cam could tell?

I let out a pent-up sigh and shook my head. "Honestly? I don't know what's going on between us. I thought we were a thing, but now I'm kinda worried we were just a fling."

"Ouch," Cam said, taking a bite of her quesadilla. "Did he say that?"

"No, but I'd swear he's been avoiding me lately. Plus…" I trailed off, not sure how personal I wanted to get with Cam. While I liked her fine, she was a coworker, and this was her boss we were talking about.

"Plus what?" she asked, chewing thoughtfully.

I sighed again. "Well, there's just this other thing between us."

"Other thing?"

I leaned back against the red vinyl back of the booth. "He kinda won't stay over at my place."

"He won't stay over? As in—" She held up her hands and made air quotes. "—*stay over*?"

I rolled my eyes. "Exactly."

"Why? Does he have *issues* in that department?" She held up a straight index finger then let it slowly droop down.

"No! No, God, no. I mean…no. He's…we're good there." I felt my cheeks grow fierier than the hot sauce packets on the table. Maybe it wasn't such a good idea to discuss this with Cam.

She shrugged. "Well, maybe he just wants to take things slowly."

"Maybe," I mumbled, sipping my water.

"Have you talked to him about it?"

"No." I shook my head wearily. "I don't even know where I'd begin."

"That's a tough one," Cam said and recapped her water bottle. "Well, you're going to have to face him sooner or later. I mean, you do work for him."

I groaned. "For now."

Cam frowned. "What's that supposed to mean?"

I shook my head. "Oh, nothing. It's just the article I'm supposed to be writing about Bobby Baxter. I have a bad feeling Tina's gonna scoop me, and I'll have nothing to show for the last week of work. I'm not exactly in the running for employee of the month at the moment."

Cam leaned her elbows on the table. "Tell me what you have so far. Maybe a fresh perspective would help?"

I hesitated a moment, knowing that Cam and Tina were friends. Should I trust her? On the other hand, it wasn't like I had a whole lot to go on anyway.

I wiped my lips on my napkin and gave Cam the rundown on my extremely short list of suspects, my conversations with them, and lastly the guy who attacked me at Bobby's trailer.

"Whoa," she breathed and leaned back against her seat. "Scary encounter. And you didn't get a look at his face?"

I shook my head. "No, it was dark, and he was wearing one of those thick black ski masks. All I saw was that he had a tattoo on his forearm. It was a dead tree with a snake wrapped around it. For all the good that's done me."

"Actually..." Cam leaned forward. "I think that might be a good lead."

I shook my head. "None of my other suspects have tattoos."

Cam tapped a fingernail on the Formica tabletop. "If you can find out who did the tattoo, the tattoo artist might be able to tell you who it was for. If so, that would lead you to your attacker and possibly Bobby's killer."

I felt a small glimmer of hope. "That's not a bad idea. I never thought to track down the tattoo artist." I paused. "But do you know how many tattoo shops there are in L.A.? It's like trying to find a needle in a stack of needles."

Cam grinned. "I know a guy. He's been in the business forever. If the tattoo is unique enough, he might be able to help you track down the artist."

"You think?" I asked, skeptical.

"Sure. Every artist has their own signature and style. I'm sure he could at least point you in the right direction. I'll give him a call and tell him what you're looking for."

It still felt like a long shot, but it was the only lead I had at the moment, so I thanked her anyway.

"No sweat," she told me with a grin. Then she checked the readout on her phone. "Okay, I have to get going. I'm supposed to get some shots of Bradley Cooper's birthday party tonight. He's throwing a big pool bash in Beverly Hills, and there's an extremely good chance some will end up drunk and in their birthday suits." She waggled her eyebrows.

"Ooh, I wouldn't want to miss that either." I grinned to match hers.

Cam stood and grabbed her bag. "You can tag along if you want," she offered.

"Squatting behind a bush for who knows how many hours until you get the perfect shot? No thanks. I'll pass." I laughed.

"Spoilsport," she teased. "Come on. I'll drop you back off at your car."

We tossed our trash in the nearest bin and left the restaurant.

Cam pulled to a stop behind my car, and I got out. "Thanks for the ride and the company," I said.

"Anytime," she called as she left.

I got into my car, frowned over at my enormous furry pink passenger, and drove home.

Mr. Bear was a pain in the butt to drag up the stairs, but I managed to make it to the top without falling. As soon as I approached my apartment, I saw another bouquet of flowers sitting beside the door. I picked them up, juggled them, my keys, and the bear, and let myself inside. I dropped the huge bear in the corner and placed the flowers on the living room table without bothering to read the card. I already knew who they were from. I just hoped his allowance ran out soon. This was getting ridiculous.

I fed Mr. Fluffykins, who was snoring away on the kitchen table, grabbed a hot shower, and then settled into the bed, alone. I was exhausted, but at least I had a plan.

* * *

When I woke up the next morning, I hit the ground running.

In a pale peach spaghetti-strap top with a crisscross back, white pencil skirt, and a pair of nude heels, I walked into a tattoo shop on Ventura, the Silver Fox. Cam had sent me a text bright and early that morning saying that her friend had, in fact, been able to find someone who recognized the tattoo description. Hope fluttered in my belly as the little bell over the door chimed when I entered.

I wasn't sure what I was expecting, but the shop was like walking into a biker bar and a fine art gallery all in one. The walls were covered in bits of small artwork and paintings in all subject matter. The lighting was brilliant, and several metal, industrial-looking fans lined the ceiling between black wooden rafters. Beneath my feet, the floor was a deep dark, rich wood, and the air held the scent of disinfectant and a faintly woodsy incense.

"Hey, I'm Sky. Can I help you?"

I turned to see a tall tattooed woman with flame red hair, a nose ring, and a vintage Ramones T-shirt tied at the waist approaching me.

"I hope so. My name is Allie Quick." I introduced myself and pulled a business card out of my clutch. "I'm a reporter for the *L.A. Informer*. I'm looking for Brody," I told her, giving the name Cam had texted me.

She nodded. "Sure. He's in the back. Follow me."

I followed Sky through a beaded curtain with a pattern of the Mona Lisa printed on it and into the back. The smell of disinfectant was strong here, mixing with the buzz of a tattoo machine. There were only two tattoo stations. The currently empty one I assumed was Sky's. She led me toward the second station where a rather large, tattooed man was busy inking the back of a smaller man wearing leather pants and a bandana on his head.

"Hey, Brodie. This is Allie." She hiked her thumb in my direction. "She's a reporter."

"My friend Cam said you might be able to help me," I explained.

The man she called Brodie looked up at me and stopped his machine. His eyes were a deep chocolate brown, his head was shaved, and he had a thick brown beard threaded with gray. He leaned his muscular form back in his chair, squirted some liquid on the man's back, and wiped it with a paper towel.

"Right, she mentioned something about you being attacked?" he asked in a deep baritone voice.

I nodded. "The only look I got of the guy was his tattoo."

"Can you describe it again?" he asked.

"It was a dead tree with a snake wrapped around it. It was on the guy's forearm," I explained.

"Black and white or color?"

"Black and white," I answered.

Brodie nodded. "I think I remember that one. Just let me finish up here." He waved toward the massive tiger tattoo he was currently working on. "In the meantime, Sky could probably work you in if you want a little something-something." He grinned.

"Thanks, but I'll just wait." I thought I felt Sky and Brodie exchange a look, but neither said anything. Sky led me back out to a chair in the lobby, where I sat and pursued the collection of magazines showing tattoos from around the world. While I had to admit some were really beautiful, I lacked the kind of commitment needed to put something permanent on my body. Fleetingly, I wondered what Felix thought of tattoos— sexy? Stylish? Or too trendy? Not that it mattered. I had a bad feeling he wouldn't be getting any views of my body again anytime soon.

Half an hour later, the man with the bandana was done, and Brodie came out wiping his hands on a rag. "I have a book with the stencils of tattoos I've done," he told me, reaching behind the reception desk. He pulled out a large black binder, sat the book on his lap, and thumbed through a few pages. He then turned the book around so that I could see the image he'd stopped on.

"Is this the tattoo you're looking for?"

The image I was looking at was the same one on my attacker.

"Yes. That's it! Do you happen to remember who you put it on?" I tried to control my excitement.

He shook his head. "Sorry. I don't remember the guy's name. He paid in cash."

Great. Another dead end.

"But I remember talking to the guy. He was awfully chatty."

Okay, maybe not totally dead… "Could you describe him?" I asked, pulling a notepad and pen from my purse.

"Tall. Dark hair. Big guy. Looked like he worked out. Kinda rough around the edges, if you know what I mean."

I might have described Brodie the same way, but I didn't mention it. "Did he talk about anything personal? Like where he was from, what he did for a living?"

Brodie rubbed his beard. "The guy was talking about this new job he just landed. He said he was pretty happy about it since not a lot of places hire former felons."

Eeek. So his theft at Bobby's trailer wasn't his first time breaking the law. "Did he say where this job was?"

"Oh yeah. He said he was going to be driving a truck for a sanitation plant. Sunbeam Sanitation? Sunrise Sanitation..." He trailed off, snapping his fingers, trying to remember the company name.

"Sunshine Sanitation?" I provided, feeling my heart leap into my throat.

"Yes! That's it." He slapped his knee. "Sunshine Sanitation. Weird name for a trash company, right?"

I nodded, but my mind was reeling. Someone at Sunshine had wanted Bobby's notes badly enough to break into his trailer...and they hadn't cared who they'd hurt in the process. Was my tattooed attacker that "someone," or had he been simply the hired goon? And had he been hired to kill Bobby as well?

I shoved the pen and paper back into my purse, tossed the strap over my shoulder, and thanked Brodie before handing him a business card. "Call me if you see him again or remember anything else, please."

He nodded and took the card as I hurried out of the shop. Then I jumped into my car and sped back to the *Informer*.

Someone at Sunshine Sanitation was now sitting firmly at the top of my murder suspects list.

All I had to do was figure out who that someone was.

CHAPTER FOURTEEN

───────

My first instinct about Tattoo Guy was that he was muscle for hire. He had a criminal record already, which made him a prime target for someone looking to get Bobby's laptop for a fee. If Bobby had something bad on Sunshine Sanitation, the people it was most likely to affect were at the top of the company's food chain. Unfortunately, when I got back to the office and did a little digging into their corporate officers, I realized that encompassed a lot of people. Not to mention their board of director and major shareholders.

What I needed was a clear link between Bobby and someone at Sunshine who I could put a name to. His phone records had only listed the main company number. But if he'd called them…maybe he'd emailed them too. Of course any record of that would have been on Bobby's stolen laptop. Or stored in Sunshine Sanitation's mainframe.

If I could get into their computer system, I could snoop around and see if there was any written correspondence between Bobby and an executive at the company. What I needed to do was hack into their computers and go through the higher-ups' email accounts. The only problem with that was that I had no idea how to hack into anything. I couldn't even follow those "life hacks" that people post on Facebook all the time and that make everyday chores easier.

As much as I didn't want to do it, I knew I needed backup on this one.

I picked up my phone and reluctantly called Shane. While the kid's crush on me was out of control, and I was certain that the last thing his parents would want was for him to be hacking into a recycling plant's system with an older woman, he was currently my best bet.

Before I could change my mind, I dialed his number.

"Babe! You called." Shane sounded excited enough to make me feel guilty.

"This isn't the kind of call you think it is," I quickly hedged. "I, uh, need your help with something."

"With what?" he asked.

"Something big, illegal, and possibly dangerous if we don't play our cards right. I feel terrible for asking you because you're just a kid, but I really need your help."

"Hey." Shane sounded affronted. "Watch it with that kid business. I'll have you know that I'm seventeen and three quarters."

Yeah, counting the quarters was not helping his case.

"Sorry," I said quickly. "Can you help me?"

"Sure. Whatever you need, babe."

"I'll pick you up at seven o'clock. And, uh, can you bring a laptop with you?"

"Sure thing. I'll be waiting," he said, and I disconnected the call.

* * *

I ate lunch at my desk and spent the rest of the afternoon poring through the bios of the corporate officers of Sunshine Sanitation. By the time six o' clock rolled around, I was bored stiff and anxious all at the same time.

I grabbed my purse, powered down my computer, and turned to go.

I didn't get far however, as Felix beckoned me into his office with a crooked finger as I passed by.

I reluctantly obeyed, pausing in his doorway. "You called?" I asked.

"I was hoping for an update on the Baxter story," he said, looking down at a file in his hands instead of meeting my eyes.

"I'm still working on it."

"You've been working on it for a few days now."

I bit my lip. Yeah, I was aware. "It's a murder case. I'm not Columbo. It takes a while."

He glanced up. "I'm not asking you to *solve* a murder. I'm asking for a story. Something to print."

"Yeah, but wouldn't printing the truth about Bobby's death be sweet?" I smiled, going for charming.

He frowned. "Tina said she's turning something in by the end of the week."

I closed my eyes and thought a really dirty word. "I'll have a killer story to you before then." I paused. "No pun intended."

The corner of his mouth hitched up a bit. "You know, I'm happy to go over your notes with you. Maybe over those rain-checked drinks?"

I sunk my teeth into my lower lip again. "Uh, tonight?" He nodded.

"Actually, I would love to, but I kinda have plans."

"Plans." His smile faded, his eyes going back to the file folder in his hands.

"Yeah. Kind of important ones, actually."

Still not looking at me, he asked, "They wouldn't be with the fellow who sent you the roses, would they?"

Oh geez. This again? "Yes, but it's not what you think. Shane is just—"

"It's none of my business, Allie," he said, cutting me off, his voice terse.

I rolled my eyes. "He's a kid, okay! Seriously, there is nothing going on. He's helping me with the story. You know, the one *you* want."

"Fine. Enjoy your evening." He turned his back to me.

"Felix—"

"I expect the story by noon Friday, or I go with Tina's," he told the wall behind him.

I shut my mouth with a click. Ouch. Low blow.

"Fine," I shot back, matching his clipped tone. Then I spun around and left before he could throw any more threats my way.

I fumed all the way down to my car and moved on to cursing by the time I hit the freeway. It was one thing to be jealous or to be busy. And if he was losing interest in me, if I really was just a fleeting fling to him, well, I could get over that.

Eventually. But it was crossing a line to bring Tina into it. Oh, he was going to get his story all right. It was going to be the best damned story he'd ever seen!

Traffic was a nightmare, but I pulled up outside Shane's house two minutes before seven o'clock.

He was waiting on the curb, a black backpack covered in skateboard stickers next to him. I swallowed down a healthy dose of guilt and unlocked the passenger side door.

Shane hopped in and tossed his backpack in the miniscule backseat before I pulled away from the curb.

"So what's on tonight's agenda?" he asked cheerfully and popped a piece of cinnamon gum into his mouth. He offered me a piece.

"No thanks," I said. "First, when do you have to be home?"

Shane rolled his eyes. "Didn't I tell you I'm almost eighteen? I can stay out as late as I want."

I wondered if his parents agreed with that logic. "You sure?"

He nodded. "Mom's busy with her book club tonight, and Dad is on a business trip in China."

"Okay. Good." I nodded. "Let's get something to eat, and I'll explain."

I weaved my way through traffic and pulled in at an Arby's with free Wi-Fi. I figured it made for a slightly more anonymous network than the office to do our hacking from. Plus, there'd be no chance I'd run into anyone who knew me at an Arby's. We both grabbed beef and cheddar sandwiches, curly fries, and sodas and slid into a corner booth to eat.

"So what's this secret mission?" Shane asked as he unwrapped his sandwich and took a bite.

I quickly filled him in on the attack at the studios, the guy with the tattoo, and the connection to Sunshine Sanitation.

"So what do you need me for?"

"I need you to hack into Sunshine Sanitation."

His eyes lit up. "Sweet!"

He was way too excited about this. There went that guilt again. "I need you to get into the company's computer system and find any emails that might have been sent to or from Bobby. Can you do that?"

He shrugged. "I don't see why not." He wadded up his now empty sandwich wrapper and tossed it on the tray. I'd barely made a dent in my meal. Then again, I didn't have a teenager's metabolism either.

"What do you think is in the emails?" Shane asked, pulling a slim silver laptop out of his backpack.

"I have a feeling someone at Sunshine was involved in Bobby's death."

His eyes went wide. "Dude."

"I know," I agreed. "The problem is, it's a big company, and I don't know who."

"So you're looking for some email that says 'I'm gonna kill you, Baxter.'"

"Something like that," I mumbled. When he put it like that, it did sound farfetched.

I sipped at my soda as I watched Shane go to work, his fingers flying over the keyboard. His features were hunkered down in concentration, the tip of his tongue protruding from the corner of his mouth. We sat in silence like that for a while, me nibbling fries and him click-clacking away like a mad man.

After a few minutes the look of concentration turned into a frown. "For a garbage place, these guys have a lot of security."

"Does that mean you can't do it?" I asked, hearing a whine of desperation in my voice.

He blew out a long breath. "Not from here."

"What does that mean?" I asked.

"It means I need to have access to their system."

I pursed my lips. "So we need to be in range of their Wi-Fi?"

Shane shook his head. "Doubtful. With the amount of security these guys have in place, I'm thinking it's gonna be pretty hard to tap into their Wi-Fi from outside. What we need is access to the system from inside."

"Wait—*inside*?" I set my drink down on the table with a thunk. "Like, in their offices?"

Shane nodded. "I mean, I could maybe get through the external security they have in place if I worked on it, but it could take a couple of days."

I didn't have days. "But if you could get inside?" I asked, hating that I was actually contemplating this.

He shrugged. "I'd have to see what I'm dealing with there, but I think I could swing it."

I bit my lip. I fiddled with my straw. I prayed I wasn't making a decision that would land an innocent kid in jail. How long would a seventeen-and-three quarters-year-old kid really have to serve? I mean, he *was* a minor. Chances were they'd let him go with a warning, right? I'd be the one they'd make an example of. I shuddered, picturing how an orange jumpsuit would totally clash with my hair.

"Fine. Let's go to Sunshine."

CHAPTER FIFTEEN

———

We made a quick stop at my place for a couple of supplies. I wasn't entirely sure what I'd need for an evening of breaking and entering, but I figured at least changing out of my heels was a good idea. I opted for a pair of black skinny jeans, a black formfitting T-shirt, and a pair of black knee-high boots that Shane said made me look like Batgirl. I decided to take it as a compliment.

I glanced at Shane's outfit. He was in dark jeans and a black T-shirt with some skateboard company's logo on it. Once he pulled a black beanie from his back pocket to cover his red hair, he looked the part of a B&E artist to a tee. Huh. I guessed there was little difference between regular teen style and criminal attire.

It was well after dark by the time we turned onto the bumpy road leading to the sanitation plant. The industrial area was nearly vacant this late at night, and I thanked God for small favors. The security lights of the plant became visible around the final curve in the road. I drove closer then pulled the car off the side of the road and rolled to a stop.

"Why are we stopping out here?" Shane asked.

"They probably have security cameras installed somewhere. Parking away from the plant will keep the cameras from getting my license plate if we were to happen to get caught," I explained.

"Good thinking, babe!"

"You know, I really appreciate you doing this for me, but I think you need to chill with the 'babe' thing, Shane."

He ignored me, his eyes focused on the looming recycling plant. "If they have cameras, won't they see our faces while we're roaming around in there?"

"Got it covered." I reached behind my seat then pulled out two Halloween masks I'd grabbed from my place.

I held Shane's mask out to him. He looked at me like I'd handed him an insult.

"You have got to be kidding me? There's no way I'm wearing that thing," he protested and held his hands up like I was trying to hand him a snake.

"Why? It's just a mask," I argued. "Take it." I pushed it toward him.

"It's a freaking Hello Kitty mask. You expect me to break into a company wearing a Hello Kitty mask? You must be off your rocker. The only thing worse than being caught while committing a crime is being a guy caught committing a crime wearing a kitten mask." He shook his head.

"Good grief." I rolled my eyes and slipped my own mask on.

He blinked at me.

"What?" I asked behind the plastic face of Wonder Woman.

"I guess there are worse things than Hello Kitty," he mumbled.

"Let's just get this over with."

We started toward the building at a quick clip, both of us self-consciously scanning the area for any night watchmen. None were in sight. The parking lot was void of cars, and the plant sat eerily quiet. We reached the empty lot and stopped. I looked around the exterior of the building.

"I don't see any security cameras," I said, scanning the roof of the building. Maybe Sunshine wasn't too worried about people stealing their trash.

"Neither do I," Shane agreed. "But how do we get in? Are you going to pick the lock or something?"

"Normally I would," I answered honestly. "But if this place has an alarm system, I don't want to set it off."

"Okay, so how are we going to get in?" Shane asked.

I glanced at the building. There was the front office I'd entered before and the large warehouses behind it, housing the main building. The doors leading into the main building were the metal rolling kind, like on a garage. Entering through one of those would be noisy, not to mention they were big enough that I wasn't sure Shane and I could lift them on our own.

Then it hit me.

"Follow me," I said.

I hurried across the parking lot to the farthest side of the building, Shane on my heels, then circled around to the back. A large red door with a handle at the top sat squarely in the middle of the building's back wall. Beneath it was the biggest dumpster I'd ever seen.

"Is that what I think it is?" Shane asked.

"It's the garbage chute."

"And you expect us to…oh, hell no." He held up his hands. "Do you smell that thing? The stench coming off of that dumpster is rank enough to gag a bag of maggots."

At the mention of maggots, my skin began to crawl, and I couldn't even attempt to stop the shiver that went through my body. Gross. Gross. Gross. "Look, it's not my favorite option either," I told him. Especially not in my leather boots. "But it's the best one we have."

He shook his head. "Look, you know I'd do anything for you, babe—"

"Please stop calling me that."

"—but this? This is beyond. It's *trash*."

"It's recycling. It's clean trash," I tried to argue.

Shane shot me a look that said even a seventeen-and-three-quarters kid could tell I was full of it.

I put on my best adult expression even though Shane couldn't possibly see it from behind my mask. "Oh, come on. Don't be a baby."

"Don't be a baby?" He lifted his mask and raised an eyebrow at me. "Don't think I didn't see that full-body shiver-slash-bug-dance you just did there."

"Put your mask back on," I hissed, looking around for cameras again. Just because I didn't see any didn't mean they weren't there.

He did, but not before shooting me another dirty look.

"Look, if there was another way in, I'd take it. But this is what we have. So be a man, and give me a boost." I waved him closer to me.

"I must be crazy. No, *you* must be crazy," he grumbled to himself. But he complied, kneeling down and lacing his fingers.

I put my foot into his hand, careful not to stab his palms with my pointy heel, then grabbed the top of the dumpster and felt Shane heft me up. A moment later, Shane hopped into the dumpster and landed on his feet on top of the bags. He worked his way to the door then hopped up, grabbed the handle, and easily pulled it down. It opened with a loud screech.

We both froze, listening to see if anyone was coming to investigate the sound. After a few seconds of silence, I felt my muscles relax again. Pulling my phone from my pocket, I hit my flashlight app and shined the light up the chute.

I didn't know what exactly was coating the chute's walls, but it was beyond disgusting.

Shane must have seen my dry heave, as he said, "This was your idea, babe."

"Don't remind me," I grumped. Luckily, as gross as it looked, the angle wasn't too steep, and it was plenty big enough to accommodate a person. I lifted my knee and hoisted myself up onto the chute. It was slick and sticky at the same time. I could practically feel the nasty stench latching on to my skin. I'd have to shower for a week straight to rid myself of the smell.

I heard Shane climb into the chute behind me. The door was spring loaded, so as soon as he crawled off of it, it slammed shut with a bang. I willed myself to take shallow breaths and quickly crawled forward. A few feet later, we hit the opening, and I looked out with my light, noting that there were several small security lights mounted at the floor against the walls of the warehouse. They didn't provide a huge amount of light, but it was enough to maneuver around the building, so I shut off my phone. I swung my legs out of the opening and dropped the short distance to the floor. Shane followed a second later, and we both looked around.

"There's no one here," he noted. "Funny, I thought there'd be some sort of security guard or something."

I shook my head. "Well, this is a recycling plant. Why would someone break in?"

"Besides us?" he asked.

I ignored his snarky comment and crept through the building, sticking as close to the wall as possible. We passed several conveyor belts and large machines that I knew were used for sorting recyclable products. The smell of bleach and strong chemicals permeated the air, and I had the fleeting thought that we might need more protection from the air than our plastic masks provided. Those chemicals couldn't be good for someone to breathe.

Along the far wall were rows and rows of gallon jugs and five-gallon buckets. Below that was a row of blue barrels. We crept closer, and I pulled out my light and shined it on the containers. All were labeled *Caution: Hazardous Material*.

"I didn't know so many chemicals were used in recycling," Shane whispered, leaning down beside me to look at the barrels.

I thought back to what I'd seen in their books. I had no idea how those amounts of chemicals processed equated to the barrels I was seeing here. "They're using less now than they were before. Supposedly," I added, taking a couple of quick photos. I wasn't sure what they could prove, but at the very least Cam could run them with my story if it turned out Sunshine was responsible for Bobby's death.

"What was that?" Shane asked and stood up straight, looking around.

"Did you hear something?" I asked, adrenaline shooting through me as I stood too.

He remained quiet for a little longer then shook his head. "I thought I did. Footsteps maybe, but I don't hear it now."

"Come on," I tugged on his sleeve. "Let's get this over with and get out of here."

We moved quickly toward the rear of the building. The clack of my boot heels on the cement floor echoed like gunshots, but there was no way on earth I was taking them off and walking around the place barefoot.

"Does that say offices?" Shane asked and motioned toward one of the red doors we were approaching.

I brought my light up and shined it on the silver lettering on the door. "Yeah, it does."

Shane tried to twist the knob. "It's locked. Now what?"

I knelt down and looked at the knob. It was a cheap one and easily picked.

"Do you have your wallet on you?"

Shane nodded and pulled his wallet out of his back pocket and handed it to me.

I opened it, pulled out his license, and wiggled it between the door and frame. A moment later the door popped open.

"You're awesome." Shane grinned as I handed his license back to him.

"I'm glad someone thinks so."

We hurried inside the small corridor and closed the door behind us.

A half dozen doors led off the main corridor, all with silver nameplates attached. Thanks to my research that afternoon, I was familiar with them all. We silently moved along the corridor until we came to the third one on the left: Alvin Daily.

I tried the door, which, thankfully, opened easily.

The chief operating officer's office was small but tidy and filled with plush enough furnishing that I figured Sunshine Sanitation was doing alright. A large cherry desk sat near a window overlooking the warehouse floor, a tall leather chair behind it. Bookshelves and glass display cases lined the walls, and the Persian rug was soft and muffled our steps as we entered.

Shane circled the desk and took a seat in the chair, immediately turning to the computer and lifting his mask over his head. The whir of it starting up was soft, but in the silence it sounded like a car engine running. I peered out of the mini blinds and scanned the building's main floor. All was quiet. Eerily quiet. I couldn't shake the feeling that we were being watched. I looked out the window for a few more minutes then let the blinds slide shut and turned back to Shane.

"Can you get in?"

"No sweat," he answered, never looking up.

I went around the desk and watched him over his shoulder. His fingers whizzed across the keyboard, and letters and numbers danced across the screen as windows opened and closed.

"They've focused all their security on external attacks. Their internal firewall is complete crap. A kindergartner could get into their system," he said with a shake of his head.

I didn't mention that I had, in fact, completed kindergarten, and I only understood half of what he was saying. "So you can access their emails?"

"In a minute," he said, still typing furiously. I anxiously chewed my lip as I watched him switch to a new screen that looked a lot like my Gmail inbox at home. Only fancier and with a lot of sunny logos pasted all over.

"Is that it?" I asked. "Can you find any emails to or from Bobby Baxter?"

Shane nodded. "I can look. But it's going to take me a while. I need to access the main server and do a search." He paused, looking up at me. "Which could be a bit tricky if whoever sent them then deleted them."

My heart sunk. Of course they would delete incriminating emails. Why had I thought they'd just be sitting neatly in someone's inbox? I suddenly felt as blonde as I looked. "Does that mean we can't read them?" I asked, thinking this whole thing might have been for nothing.

"Not necessarily," Shane said, still typing. "Delete isn't the same as erase. It basically just tells the system to archive it from sight. But most systems have some sort of backup that stores old data for a certain amount of time, even after it's deleted. So it might be a little harder to find, but that doesn't mean it's gone."

I held my breath, hoping he was right. And that he really was as good as he said he was.

I stayed quiet while Shane worked his magic, vacillating between checking the windows and checking the time. We'd been in the building fifteen minutes already. Every passing second felt like we were that much closer to getting caught.

"Could you quit checking the window?" Shane asked. "You're making me nervous."

"Sorry," I mumbled, wiping my sweaty palm on my jeans. I took a couple of steps away, aimlessly pacing the office. Company pictures and awards lined the walls. I stepped closer to them and held my flashlight up to get a better look. Smiling faces stared back at me. I recognized a few from my afternoon of company browsing. The CEO and CFO at some fundraiser. Various members of the board at a ribbon cutting. Mr. Daily and a younger, blonde woman I took as his wife, on the company yacht. Daily on the warehouse floor with his arm around a couple of guys in Sunshine Sanitation uniforms.

I paused and lifted my mask.

"No way," I said out loud. I grabbed the picture from the wall and held my flashlight closer as I stared at the faces of the two guys in uniform. One of them I recognized all too well. Ritchie Mullins.

"What?" Shane piped up from behind the desk.

"Nothing," I mumbled, quickly putting the picture back as my mind reeled. Ritchie hadn't mentioned anything about a second job. And it wasn't on his social media profile. Was it something he'd wanted to keep quiet? Had Ritchie been the inside guy Bobby had been speaking to? An informant giving Bobby dirt on the company for the show? But if so, why had Bobby punched him? And how had that led to his death?

"Uh-oh." Shane sat back.

My heart leapt into my throat. "Uh-oh?"

He turned to me and grinned. "I think I found something."

I let out an audible sigh of relief. "God, don't do that to me." I put a hand to my chest. "You almost gave me a heart attack."

"Sorry," he said sheepishly. Though I noticed his eyes had gone to my chest.

I hiked up my shirt, covering my cleavage. "What did you find?"

He turned (reluctantly) back to the screen. "Well, I'm in the system, and I've got at least three emails that have the name 'Baxter' attached to them."

I hurried over to look at the screen. "What do they say?" I asked eagerly.

Shane shrugged. "I don't know."

"What do you mean you don't know?" I whined.

"I mean, I can see they exist. It's gonna take a few more minutes for me to recover the data and see what the actual contents are."

I groaned, looking down at my phone again. "Hurry, would you?"

"Hey, art can't be rushed—" Shane started.

But he stopped midsentence.

We both froze at the sound of a door opening softly nearby.

My eyes met Shane's, the panic I felt mirrored there.

"We need to go," I said. "Now." I shoved Shane's mask back on, doing the same to my own.

Shane nodded and shut the windows he'd been working in. We both tiptoed to the door. I cracked it open and peered out at the corridor.

"Anything?" Shane whispered.

I shook my head. "No."

I took my boots off and shuddered at the thought of what I might be stepping in on the bare floor. But if someone other than us was in the building, they'd definitely hear the clack of my heels as we ran back to the garbage chute. I tamped down the urge to gag at the feel of the grimy floor beneath my feet as we slowly pushed through the door to the warehouse and felt our way along the dimly lit walls.

We reached the chute opening without incident. Once there, Shane hefted me up into the stinky corridor, and a moment later I was sliding down the chute much faster than I'd climbed up it. I landed in the dumpster with a thud. Something cold and moist squished beneath me again, but I ignored it. I struggled to get to my feet, but it was useless, as a second later Shane flew out of the chute and landed right on top of me, knocking the breath out of my lungs.

"Sorry, Allie," he apologized in a rush.

All I could do was grunt in response as he tugged me into a standing position.

Shane jumped over the rim of the dumpster, landing on his feet on the pavement.

Just as I heard someone opening the chute door from inside the warehouse.

Crap. We'd been made.

I quickly jumped down, landing hard on my bare feet. Then we took off running as fast as we could across the parking lot and down the road toward where I'd parked the car. My feet protested with every step on the hard gravel, but I didn't dare waste time putting my boots back on. My Bug came into view, and while the sight of my car was a huge relief, I wasn't about to celebrate a victory until we were far away from Sunshine Sanitation and whoever was chasing us.

Shane slid across the hood of the car Dukes of Hazzard meets Hello Kitty style and jumped inside the passenger door. I followed suit and started the ignition, whipped a U in the road, and floored the accelerator. We shot down the road, leaving a trail of dust behind us as we sped away from Sunshine Sanitation and toward safety.

We pulled off our masks and tossed them over our seats into the back, but neither one of us spoke until we reached the freeway. My eyes ping-ponged between the road and the rearview mirror, half expecting to see a vehicle chasing us at top speed. But all I saw was the normal L.A. traffic.

"Are we being followed?" Shane asked. If I didn't know better, I'd say there was a note of excitement in his voice.

I shook my head.

Shane was quiet for a moment. Then he started laughing. "Oh, dude, that was close. What a rush!"

I wished I could say the same. I had a feeling it would take me a week to calm my frayed nerves back to normal.

"I'm sorry I put you in all that danger for nothing," I told him, sincerely meaning it. While I'd always known the plan had had a hint of harebrained in it, being actually chased through the warehouse had brought the reality of how illegal we'd been acting crashing home.

"I'm not." He grinned, really looking like he was enjoying this. "And it wasn't totally for nothing. I mean, we know you were right," Shane pointed out. "Someone at Sunshine *was* emailing with Bobby."

"Yeah, but we don't know what they said."

Shane shrugged. "True."

"And we don't know who that someone was."

Shane's grin widened. "I do."

I did a double take. "Excuse me?"

He shrugged again, looking way too pleased with himself. "I said I couldn't read the emails. I didn't say I couldn't see who they were addressed to."

I punched him in the arm. "Spill it," I commanded. "Was it Ritchie Mullins?"

Shane frowned. "No. Who's Ritchie Mullins?"

I shook my head. "No one. Never mind," I mumbled, only mildly disappointed. "So who was Bobby emailing?"

"Some guy named Sal Bukowski."

I perked up. The name didn't ring any bells, but the initials sure did—SB. I tried to think back over the names I'd seen in the company's roster, but I couldn't remember a Sal. Though, I'd gone through a lot of names and profiles that day. It was possible I'd skimmed over him.

"So, what's our next step?" Shane asked, pulling me out of my thoughts.

"*My* next step is a hot shower and a gallon of scented body wash to get rid of this smell," I told him.

Shane's eyes glazed over, and I feared he was picturing me showering.

"And *your* next step," I said, hopefully harshly enough to knock the image out of his head, "is to go home and forget I ever dragged you along on this trip."

"Fat chance of that, babe. This was the most fun I've had all year."

"We've really got to talk about this 'babe' thing. It's not cool."

Shane just grinned at me.

"Seriously. I've got a boyfriend." Maybe. "And he's sure not happy about the flowers and teddy bears and stuff."

"A little friendly competition never hurt anyone," Shane replied, still grinning.

I shook my head. "No. It's not a competition. No competition, Shane."

"Whatever you say, babe."

I gritted my teeth, reminding myself he was just a child. It wouldn't be right to hit a child.

We rode the rest of the way in semi-silence—me contemplating just who Sal Bukowski might be and what his connection to Bobby was, and Shane loudly chewing on a fresh stick of cinnamon gum. When we pulled up to Shane's house, he got out and tossed his backpack over his shoulder.

"Thanks for the awesome date, babe!" Shane said.

"That was so *not* a date. It was…" Trespassing? Breaking and entering? Illegal hacking? "…work," I finished lamely.

"Right." He winked at me.

I rolled my eyes. "Get some sleep. And call me if you need anything," I added. Even though he was perfectly old enough to be home alone, I felt a little responsible for him after the sketchy escapade we'd just pulled off.

"You know I will," he said with a grin before he stepped away from the car.

I was afraid of that. I turned the car around in the middle of the street and drove home.

As soon as I opened the door and stepped inside my apartment, Mr. Fluffykins took one sniff of me and sprinted to the bedroom.

"It's good to see you too," I called out.

I couldn't blame him. I smelled like an outhouse in the summertime.

I dropped my poor boots beside the door, my purse on the sofa, and then trudged the short distance to the bathroom. Mr. Fluffykins was hiding beneath the blankets on the bed. I looked down at my clothing now that I could see myself in decent lighting, and cringed. My clothes were ruined. I pulled them off and reluctantly tossed them into the trash. I tied the bag shut to keep the stench from permeating the clean air in my apartment.

An hour and three shampoos under nearly scalding hot water later, I stepped out of the shower feeling a little better and a lot less stinky. I grasped an end of my hair and brought it to my nose. I couldn't tell if the stink was burnt into my nose or if my hair still held a subtle aroma of garbage plant. I hoped it was the former. I so did not want to explain to Felix in the morning why I reeked of Sunshine Sanitation.

CHAPTER SIXTEEN

———

First thing the next morning I was hard at work at my desk with my best friend, Google, running down every bit of information the internet held on Sal Bukowski. Thanks to three more shampoos that morning and a healthy dose of English Garden body mist, I'd left the stench of the past evening behind me. Even if I did smell just a tad like a Glade PlugIn now.

Luckily, Felix had come nowhere near close enough to smell me this morning. A curt nod of his head through the glass wall of his office was all I'd received as I'd come in fifteen minutes early and plunked myself down at my desk. Apparently I was getting the silent treatment. I tried to pretend it didn't bother me and focused instead on the case at hand.

Sal Bukowski hadn't turned up in my research on company officers the day before because he wasn't technically an officer of Sunshine Sanitation. He was listed in their directory simply as a "consultant." As hard as I tried to find out what he consulted with them on, that info seemed to be nonexistent. As was any social media presence or personal info. Sal had a surprisingly small digital footprint. Which, in itself, was a tiny red flag.

Had Sal been consulting on something underhanded at Sunshine? Maybe illegally dumping chemicals? Had Bobby found out, and Sal bumped him off? It was a fun theory, but I had nothing to back it up. I also had no idea how Ritchie Mullins fit into all of this. Or even if he did. I guessed it *could* be just coincidence that he happened to work for Sunshine Sanitation. I mean, a facility that large had to employ hundreds of people.

"What is that smell?" I looked up to find Tina hovering over my shoulder, a bundle of papers in her hand and a look of disgust on her face.

I felt my cheeks heat. "Nothing. I don't know what you're talking about."

"It smells like someone spilled perfume or something." She looked down at the rug, checking for stains.

"I don't smell anything," I lied.

Tina shot me a *yeah, right* look.

"Did you want something?" I asked, quickly minimizing my search window before she could get a look at what I was doing. No way was I going to let her sneak a peek at the name I'd worked so hard to get last night. Even if it wasn't turning up any smoking guns.

Tina crossed her arms over her chest. "Yeah. Felix told me I had to share the autopsy reports with you." She looked like she wasn't happy about it either.

I, on the other hand, felt a little glow of warmth in my belly. Felix might be giving me the silent treatment, but at least he wasn't totally leaving me out in the cold. "What did they say?"

"Read 'em yourself." She handed the papers to me.

"Thanks," I said, meaning it.

She shrugged. "Nothing new in there." She paused. "At least nothing *I* didn't already know."

With that subtle dig, she walked back to her desk.

I quickly scanned the first couple of pages, trying to read between the medical jargon. Pretty standard as far as I could tell. As had been obvious at the scene, Bobby had died of a single gunshot wound to the head. Postmortem indicated that he'd had a slightly enlarged liver, had broken his wrist sometime in the last ten years, had eaten pasta and red wine as his last meal, and was otherwise a fairly healthy thirty-six-year-old male. Tina was right. Nothing particularly interesting in the pages.

Feeling another dead end brewing, I quickly scanned the rest of the papers. The only interesting fact I found was that Bobby Baxter's name on the official documents was listed as Robert Baxter Smedfield. Apparently he'd dropped the "Smedfield" for Hollywood purposes. I didn't blame him. Robert Smedfield didn't have half the appeal as Bobby Baxter.

I tapped my pen on the top of my desk, taking in that info. If Bobby was really Robert Smedfield, did that mean that his wife was really legally Marilyn Smedfield?

I typed her name into my search engine. Amazingly, several hits came up. Including one in the Internet Movie Database. I blinked at the screen, clicking the link and seeing an image of a slightly younger version of Marilyn dressed in a bikini, wielding an ax, on a movie poster for *Bad Babes in Boston II.* Apparently Marilyn Smedfield had enjoyed a short-lived career as a B-movie actress when she'd first married Bobby.

I thought back to our conversation by her hotel pool the other day. I'd thought her grief had seemed genuine enough then, but knowing now that she was an actress… I glanced at her list of credits again. In addition to two *Bad Babes* films, she'd also had walk-on roles in a couple of TV cop dramas and had shot a sitcom pilot. Not exactly Shakespeare, but that didn't mean she couldn't easily fake a few tears.

I pulled out my phone and texted Shane. *Has Mrs. Baxter come home yet?*

I aimlessly browsed IMDb as I waited for his response. Five minutes later it buzzed in.

Don't know. Sorry. In trig class now.

I glanced at the time. Just past noon. I did a quick search for the number of the Grand Hotel and Spa, and a few seconds later was connected with the front desk.

"Grand Hotel, how many I direct your call?"

"Could you please connect me with Marilyn…Smedfield's room?" I asked, mentally crossing my fingers. If she was avoiding the paparazzi, maybe she'd checked in with her real name.

"I'm so sorry, but it looks like Ms. Smedfield checked out this morning."

"Thanks," I said then quickly hung up, grabbed my purse, and headed for the elevator.

I stopped only long enough to hit a drive-thru taco place before winding my way up the hill to Marilyn's.

The iron gates to her drive were closed, but I noticed that her BMW was parked out front. The grieving widow was home.

I drove to the end of the block then flipped a U-turn and parked on the other side of the street in front of Shane's house. I popped open my glove box and took out a pair of binoculars, training them on the windows of the Baxter house. I wasn't sure what I expected to see, but I had a feeling that Marilyn wasn't going to just let me in for a chat.

Through an upstairs window, I spied the housekeeper, Marta, making a bed, fluffing pillows and shaking out sheets. Downstairs it appeared the front rooms were a living room and some sort of office with bookshelves lining the back walls. Both were empty. Finally I spotted Marilyn through an upstairs window. She looked like she was in a bathroom, putting on makeup. Maybe going out? Maybe to celebrate her newly single and filthy rich status?

Yes, I was totally reaching. But the more I thought about it, the more I wasn't totally buying her grieving widow routine.

I watched Marilyn apply copious different makeup layers for a few more minutes before my arms got tired, and I dropped the binoculars. I finished the last of my tacos, wadded up the papers, and popped a breath mint before picking up my binoculars again. Marilyn had left the bathroom. Crap. I quickly scanned the other house windows, hoping to get a glimpse of her. The car was still in the driveway. It wasn't like she could have left.

I was still trying to track the elusive Mrs. Baxter when another car rolled down the street next to me. I felt my heart rate pick up when it stopped at Mrs. Baxter's gates. I whipped my binoculars toward it, trying to make out the occupant.

It was a plain beige SUV—nothing terribly notable about it. I caught a peek at the driver as he leaned out the window to talk into the security microphone mounted at the gate. Male, maybe late twenties. Dark hair in a stylish, close-cropped look, nice sturdy jawline dusted with just enough stubble to be sexy. He was wearing sunglasses, so it was impossible to see his eyes, but when he leaned one tanned arm out the window, I got a glimpse of his impressive triceps. I felt my hopes pick up. Was this the hottie all that makeup had been for?

After a couple of seconds the gates opened, and Hottie drove through, pulling his car in behind Marilyn's in the drive. I zoomed in on him as he got out of the car and walked around to the back and opened the tailgate…

And pulled out a pool net and a toolbox full of chemicals.

Right. Not a hot liaison—just the pool boy.

I let out a breath of frustration as I watched him walk around the side of the house, tools of his trade in hand, and got a clear view of his T-shirt, which read: *Davies Pool Maintenance.* I scanned the binoculars back up at the house and spotted Mrs. Baxter in the study window now, chatting on the phone with someone as she sat behind a desk. Clearly she had about as much interest in her pool boy as Felix did in me lately.

I was beginning to think I'd just wasted an entire afternoon for nothing, when my phone rang, making me jump in the silence of my car. I dropped the binoculars and glanced at the readout. Shane.

Even though I knew he was at school, I guiltily glanced up at his house as if he could somehow sense I was there. "Hello?" I answered.

"Hey, it's me."

I cringed that he thought we were on an "it's me" phone basis already. "Hi, Shane."

"I've got some info for you on that name we found last night."

I sat up straighter in my seat. "You did? How?" I'd spent all morning trying to find something on Sal Bukowski, and all I knew was that he didn't tweet, friend, or snapchat.

"DA's office records."

"How did you—" I stopped midsentence, feeling guilt wash over me. "You hacked into the district attorney's office!?" Instinctively I lowered my voice and looked over both shoulders, as if the DA could somehow have my car bugged.

"No! Geez," Shane huffed into the phone.

I let out a sigh of relief.

"One of my buddies did it for me."

Ugh. "I don't think we should be talking about this on the phone."

Shane chuckled. "Seriously? You are, like, paranoid."

"I am, *like*, not into going to jail."

"Relax. I told you *I* didn't do anything illegal. Hackensack09 did."

"That's your buddy's name?"

"Online handle."

"Clever. Hackensack because he's a hacker."

There was silence on the other end then: "Uh, he lives in New Jersey."

I shook my head. "Whatever. What did this Hackensack guy find out?"

"How about this? Pick me up from school, and I'll tell you all about it."

As reluctant as I was to spend more time with Shane and encourage any sort of crush he had brewing, I really did want to know what his hacker friend had found. "Text me the address," I told him, shoving my binoculars into the glove box and starting my engine.

Half an hour later we were at a coffee shop across the street from Washington High School. I was thoroughly enjoying a blueberry scone and an afternoon latte pick-me-up, and Shane was slurping a strawberry smoothie as he let me scroll through a list of documents his buddy had "borrowed" from the DA's office records on Sal Bukowski.

"Wow," I couldn't help letting out. I was beginning to see why Sal had almost no internet presence. At least half of the documents I was reading had black sharpie over the words, redacted information. Though, enough of the gist came through in the list of charges that had been brought against the guy and subsequently dropped. Bribery, extortion, money laundering. "This guy has his fingers in everything." I shook my head and looked at Shane.

"That's what Hackensack09 said," he told me with a noisy slurp. "Read the next one. Bukowski was accused of trying to bribe a court clerk about five years ago, right before his charges of bribery were suddenly dropped."

"The result of another bribe?"

"Ironic, right?" Shane grinned at me, showing off a couple of strawberry seeds stuck in his front teeth.

"Very," I mumbled, pointing to his incisors.

He grabbed a napkin and wiped.

"I'm guessing that's how he kept this all out of the press too. More bribes?"

Shane shrugged. "Maybe. Maybe it just didn't register on anyone's radar. I mean, most of what he's accused of is pretty low-level stuff. Five, ten years max sentences. And nothing ever stuck."

"Convenient, that, right?"

Shane nodded. "That's what Hackensak09 thought, too." He scrolled to the next document. "Check this out. He owned a recycling plant in New York around the same time he was accused of bribery. After the charges were dropped, he sold it and moved to L.A., where he started consulting for Sunshine Sanitation."

"Interesting timing, but maybe he just wanted a fresh start," I said, playing devil's advocate.

Shane shook his head. "Okay, but a year ago, right after Sal came on board at Sunshine, a union rep mysteriously disappeared after paying a visit to the plant." He flipped to another page, shoving the phone in my direction.

I raised an eyebrow at him. "Disappeared? How?"

"I don't know. No one does. He was last seen leaving the plant. He never made it home, and no one's seen him since. His wife filed a missing person's report, but there's been no sign of him since before he left the sanitation plant."

"That's quite a coincidence," I said quietly.

"If you believe in that sort of thing," Shane added, slurping again.

Thanks to Felix, I didn't.

"Okay, it seems pretty clear that this Bukowski character is as shady as it gets."

"Total shade," Shane agreed, nodding. "Do you think Bukowski killed Baxter?"

"I don't know." I shrugged. "He's obviously a rotten guy, but the only connection we have between the two is some emails we haven't read."

Shane looked sheepish. "Sorry. I wish I could have gotten into them for you."

I waved it off. "You've done more than enough," I told him, gesturing to the "borrowed" documents on his phone. "Speaking of which—no more hacking, okay?"

Shane's eyebrows drew together in a frown. "I thought all this was helpful."

I nodded. "It is. And I honestly appreciate it. But it's also dangerous and illegal, and I don't want you to get into trouble."

His frown slowly smoothed out into a smile. A really big one. "Awe, babe, you do care about me."

Oh brother. "I care about not contributing to the delinquency of a minor."

"A minor for only three more months." He waggled his eyebrows suggestively at me.

"Okay, time to get you home, kiddo," I said, maybe a little too loudly.

If he noticed the dig at his age, he didn't comment. Instead he just stuck with the goofy grin the entire way back up to the Hollywood Hills.

By the time I got back to the office, the sun was setting, and the sky was a dusky purple, the smog layer creating a brilliant display of colors along the freeway-dotted horizon.

The office was empty with the exception of Max typing away in his cubicle, the sole sound kind of lonely in the big room. Everyone else seemed to have gone for the day, including Felix, whose office was dark and empty, sitting in the middle of the room like a glass-walled reminder that he hadn't said a single word to me all day. I shoved that thought down. I'd worry about that later. Right now, I was on a deadline.

I sat at my computer, eager to type up my notes on Shane's findings while they were fresh in my mind. At the very least, the fact that Bobby had been communicating with a guy like Sal right before his death was enough to wet the tabloid reading audience's appetites and fuel their gossip loving imaginations. Of course, I had no real conclusions or proof of anything, so I had no idea if the story would even make it through the legal department. After we'd been sued last year over a story one of the junior reporters had done with a less-than-reliable source, Felix now insisted we send everything through legal to scan for anything that could lose us money in a slander lawsuit. Since my source was an anonymous hacker in New Jersey, I wasn't 100 percent sure this would stand up.

I bit my lip, dying to know what story Tina was planning to hand in on Friday. Did she have solid sources? I glanced over at her empty desk.

Maybe if I just took one little peek…

I couldn't help myself. I quickly snuck over to her cubicle and powered up her computer. A few seconds later a screen requiring a password popped up. Dang it. I bit my lip, glancing around her desk for any clues. Pen holder covered in pink skulls, pad of neon colored Post-its, mouse pad with a retro Lucky Charms ad emblazed on it, her swear pig. My eyes lingered on the swear pig. If I knew Tina's rebellious streak…

I typed in Tina's favorite swear word, one that I'd heard her utter out of frustration more than once to the tune of twenty-five cents a pop. The screen changed, immediately granting me access to all of Tina's files.

This was almost too easy.

I glanced over my shoulder again, but all I saw was the empty office—Max's slow hunt-and-peck typing the only sound.

I quickly grabbed her mouse and began scanning for any files that looked like they related to the Baxter case. I had to admit, Tina's filing system was nothing like mine, and it took me a bit to get her naming system. She used a lot of initials and weird nicknames that had no meaning to me. I took a different approach and scanned for the most recently viewed files. I quickly opened the top one, labeled *assgreenlightvariety*— praying it wasn't anything like the name sounded.

Ready to look away lest I see pale green derrieres, I did a quick scan of the screen. It was not, in fact, some weird alien porno, but that day's copy of *Variety* magazine. Wondering what it had to do with Bobby, I scanned over the first few articles. Something about the Oscar nominations, some top grossing films, a prominent agent who passed away from a stroke. Nothing seemed relevant.

Until I got to the third page.

My eyes honed in on the name Henry Klein. I suddenly understood the first part of her labeling…"ass" as in assistant. A small blurb indicated that his new show *History Untold* had just gotten the green light from the network and would begin filming the first eight episodes next month.

I raised an eyebrow at the screen. Henry had told me he was worse off with Bobby dead—not only unemployed but also out the money he'd stand to make suing him. He'd failed to mention that with Bobby gone, the network was once again interested in his show. Had that been the meeting he'd been rushing off to the other day? Henry had moved up in the world at an astronomical pace since Bobby had died. Which made me wonder once again—had Henry had anything to do with his employer's death? If anyone knew where and how to find Bobby—and where he might keep his gun—and was trusted enough not to arouse the star's suspicions, it was his meek personal assistant. Maybe the whole Sunshine Sanitation thing was just a coincidence.

"Well, I'm going to call it a day."

I jumped about a mile at the sound of Max's voice behind me. I quickly spun around, covering the screen of Tina's computer with my body.

"I'm right behind you!" I said, with maybe a little more faux-innocent perk than the situation called for.

Max shot me a funny look. "You lose something at Tina's desk?"

"What? Oh, uh, right." I racked my brain, trying to think fast. "Yeah, Tina asked me to, uh, print something out for her."

"She did." Only it didn't sound like a question. It sounded like he didn't believe me. Smart man.

"Yep! That's right!" Wow, I needed to dial down the perk about a hundred notches. I took a deep breath, hoping he couldn't read my guilt.

"Huh." He gave me a hard look but then finally shrugged. "Okay, well, have a good night."

"You too!" I gave him a big toothy grin and a wave.

I didn't stop holding my breath until he was in the elevators, rattling as they made their way back down to the ground level.

I quickly powered down Tina's computer and did the same to my own.

The office was eerily quiet. It was actually the first time I'd ever been completely alone at the *Informer*, and it was a bit creepy. Nothing but silence surrounded me in the one place that was usually chaotic.

The wheels on my desk chair squeaked as I spun around and grabbed my purse and fished out my keys. I flicked off the lights on the panel beside the door to Felix's office and then rode the elevator down to the lobby. Once outside I locked the building's main doors.

My keys jangled as I pulled out my car fob and beeped my door unlocked. I was just about to open the door when I heard a muffled sound behind me.

I whipped my head around to see what it was…

Too late. Something hard slammed into me from behind.

CHAPTER SEVENTEEN

―――――

I hit the side of my car, and the air in my lungs left me in a painful whoosh. I flipped around to see who or what had rammed into me, but as soon as I did, a black leather gloved fist plowed into the side of my face. Stars danced before my eyes as I slammed onto the ground, fighting the darkness that was trying to overtake me.

I blinked, trying to make out the figure looming menacingly over me, but all I saw was head-to-toe black. My vision was blurry, like I had opened my eyes underwater.

"Hey! What's going on? Get away from her!"

I heard the words being shouted from a distance but couldn't quite latch on to them. Everything sounded fuzzy. The black figure paused, and I caught a glimpse of flesh between all the black clothing…just enough to see a familiar snake tattoo.

Then he vanished, and footsteps—at least I thought I heard footsteps—pounded toward me.

A split second later someone knelt down beside me.

"Hey, are you alright?" I felt someone lifting my head, checking for a pulse. "Call 9-1-1."

I tried to open my mouth to tell him I was okay, but the darkness I'd been fighting finally won, and I closed my eyes.

* * *

There were few things in the world that I hated. *Hospitals* was one of them. Answering the same question more than once was another.

"And you didn't see your attacker's face?" a uniformed police officer asked again for the third time. He was tall, bald, and looked like he'd rather be anywhere else.

"No. It was all dark. I think he was wearing a mask," I answered again and did my best not to roll my eyes. I knew the cop was only trying to do his job, but I wanted nothing more than to get out of there, go home, and crash in my soft bed. I was so over this day.

"And he didn't take your purse?"

I shook my head, instantly regretting it as pounding erupted.

"Or anything else?"

"I told you. Those kids scared him away." Once I'd come to, I'd been informed that two teenagers practicing their skateboarding kicks in the parking lot next door had seen the attack take place and come to my rescue, calling the police. I'd made a mental note to find out their names and send them a big thank-you gift basket for possibly saving my life.

I shivered at that thought. Like I'd told Officer Asks-a-Lot several times, I had no idea what the guy in black had been after. I also had no idea how far he might have gone if those kids hadn't interrupted him. Had he meant to mug me? Carjack me? Or worse. My mind immediately went to the snake tattoo. I had a bad feeling this attack hadn't been completely random. Was someone afraid I was getting close to the truth? I sincerely wished they'd clue me in, because I felt like I was still miles away from knowing who'd killed Bobby.

"Anything else you can tell me about the attack?" the officer asked, clearly out of official questions.

I *could* have told him I'd seen the same guy before, breaking into Bobby Baxter's trailer, but then I'd have to tell him how I'd come to be there myself…which was a little more self-incriminating than I felt like being in the presence of a police officer. "No. Sorry."

He sighed. "Alright. Call me if you think of anything. And, uh, we'll be in touch if anything new comes up," he added lamely. Though I was pretty sure we both knew this interview was the extent of the investigating he'd be doing. Random attack, nothing taken, late at night, no description. I hadn't given him a whole lot to go on.

He handed me his card and left.

Half an hour later, a harried looking doctor gave me the okay to leave, though he suggested taking it easy for a couple of days. I agreed. A couple days on my couch binge watching some *Real Housewives* sounded like heaven right now. I was just slipping my shoes back on when a familiar face appeared in the doorway.

"Good God, Allie, what happened?" Felix frowned at me, his eyes doing the same sort of clinical scan of my body that the admitting nurse had done. I hadn't yet seen a mirror, but it must not be pretty, because his frown deepened when he got to my face.

"I had a run-in with someone who obviously isn't a fan." I was doing my best to make light of the situation, but I wasn't sure Felix was buying it.

He took a step toward me, brushing the hair out of my face. The gesture was so gentle and caring I almost lost my composure, wanting to sob my fears away into his adorably misbuttoned shirt. "Are you okay?" he asked softly.

I nodded, not trusting my voice. Ouch. Moving my head still hurt.

"What happened?"

I took a shaky breath and told him about the attack, doing my best to skim over the parts that made my heart race with the feelings of helplessness again. He listened silently, but the frown was looking like a canyon between his eyebrows by the time I was done.

"I don't like this," he said.

"That makes two of us."

"No, I mean I don't like that it happened in our parking lot. That the *Informer* was targeted." He paused. "That *you* were targeted."

I grabbed my purse from the bedside table and hoisted it onto my shoulder. "We don't know that I was," I hedged. "It could have been a random attack. Maybe he wanted my car."

Felix raised one eyebrow at me.

"What? My car is awesome." But he had a point. A hardened criminal probably wasn't in the market for a cute little Bug with daisy decals on it. "How did you know I was here?" I asked, changing the subject as I slid off the bed.

"The police called me to inform me there was an attack on the premises." He frowned. "You sure you're okay?"

I steadied myself with a hand on the side of the bed. I had to admit, the headache was making the room sway a little. "I'm fine. Nothing an ice pack and some *Real Housewives* can't fix."

Felix gave me a funny look, like he only understood part of that sentence, but he didn't ask as he put a hand at my elbow to steady me. "I'll take you home."

I might have protested, but at that moment I didn't think I had it in me to call a cab, let alone drive myself home. Plus, my car was still at the *Informer*. Instead, I just nodded and let him lead me through the hospital corridors and out to his junker, parked haphazardly in a spot near the emergency room entrance.

The ride back to my place was quiet but went by quickly. Felix helped me up the stairs and into the apartment. As soon as we stepped inside, Mr. Fluffykins wound his way around Felix's legs and meowed up at him.

"He's hungry," I said and started toward the kitchen.

"I got it." Felix gently grabbed my arm. "You just sit down."

I didn't argue. I sank onto the sofa, closing my eyes and leaning my head back against the soft cushions while Felix took care of my cat.

A few minutes later I felt Felix sit beside me on the sofa.

"So maybe now you want to tell me what really happened."

I peeked an eye open and looked at him. "What do you mean?"

"I mean, tell me the attack on you has nothing to do with the Baxter story."

"The attack has nothing to do with the Baxter story." I repeated what he wanted to hear.

"Bloody—Allie. I'm serious." He shoved his hand through his shaggy blond hair. "This is the second time I've found you bruised and battered this week. It's not a habit I'm enjoying."

"And you think I am?" I asked, feeling just a bit attacked for the second time at his tone of voice. "It's not like I'm inviting bad guys to use me as a sparring partner, you know."

"Aren't you?"

I narrowed my eyes at him. Which hurt a lot more than it should have. I think my left eye was swelling. I really needed a mirror to assess the damage. "What's that supposed to mean?"

"It means you're doing a really great job of upsetting all the wrong people."

"I'm a reporter. That's kinda my job."

"Your job is to write an enticing piece that makes busy moms stop and buy our rag while in line at the supermarket. It is not to go prodding thugs and murderers into attacking you."

I rolled my eyes. "I've been asking questions. That's it." And maybe a little B&E. And impersonating an EPA agent. And illegal hacking. But he didn't need to know all that right now.

Felix shook his head. "I want you to drop this story."

"What?!" I sat up straight, ignoring the shooting pain behind my eyes.

"Tina will have something by Friday. We'll print her story, and that's it."

"No way. You cannot do this to me. I've worked too hard on this." I paused. "Besides, I'm almost sure I know the truth about what happened," I added, fibbing just a little.

Felix paused. "You are?"

I mentally crossed my fingers behind my back and nodded.

Felix let out a loud sigh. "And what am I supposed to do, just overlook the fact that you could have been killed tonight if those boys hadn't shown up?"

"I don't know why not. You've been overlooking me all week." I hadn't meant to say it, but the words were out of my mouth before I could stop them.

Felix opened his mouth to retort, but then he must have thought better of it, as he closed it just as quickly, something shifting behind his eyes. Instead, he stood, running a hand through his hair again. "I'm calling Cal," he said. "He'll watch your place tonight."

I rolled my eyes again. "I don't need a bodyguard. I can take care of myself."

"Like you did tonight?" he asked, starting to pace back and forth in my tiny living area. He shook his head. "No, if you're going to be stubborn about this, I'm going to have the peace of mind that Cal is with you 24/7."

I crossed my arms over my chest. "Why is it that a hard-working woman is stubborn and a man is tenacious?"

Felix froze, shooting me another unreadable look. "I'm well aware of your tenacious qualities." His tone was taking on that clipped edge again.

"Then you should know I don't need a babysitter," I shot back.

"Then stop acting like a child," he shouted.

I wasn't sure if it was his tone or the child remark, but the words hit me like a slap in the face. All my fears about Felix not taking me or our relationship seriously—if we currently even had one—came rushing at me with striking confirmation.

"I'm not a child," I said with a calm I didn't know I possessed in that moment. "I'm a reporter. A good one. And bodyguard or no, I'm not dropping this story, and I'm going to write you the best damned article this paper has ever published."

"Allie—" Felix started, his voice softer.

But I waved him off. "If you'll excuse me, *Boss*, I've had a long day, and I've got work to do in the morning."

I quickly turned and went to my bedroom, slamming the door behind me for emphasis.

Angry tears pricked the back of my eyelids as I leaned my back against the door. A few seconds later I heard my front door open and close softly as Felix left.

CHAPTER EIGHTEEN

———

The next morning, I woke with a raging headache and a dry mouth, and every inch of my body ached. My joints were so stiff I was surprised that I didn't creak as I stood up and shuffled to the bathroom.

A steaming hot shower and two ibuprofen later, I was feeling better, but only a little. I decided to leave my hair down in loose waves, since my head felt like someone had taken a baseball bat to it and the knot on the back was still extremely tender to touch.

I wiped the fog from the bathroom mirror and cringed at the reflection staring back at me. My left eye was a gnarly shade of blackish purple, there was a small cut on the side of my bottom lip, and there was a light bruise running along my lower left jawline. It would take an industrial size tube of concealer to cover the mess the attacker had made of my face.

I did my best then applied a little extra mascara and lip gloss to compensate. I tossed on a pair of black capri leggings and a billowy pink spaghetti-strap top and paired the ensemble with matching kitten heels and a hobo bag.

Comfort was the objective of the day where my clothing was concerned.

Cute comfort.

Felix must have had my car driven back to my place sometime during the night, as it was sitting in its designated parking spot for me that morning. I shoved the considerate gesture to the back of my mind, not wanting to read anything into it. At least not before coffee.

I locked my apartment and waved to Cal, in the driver's seat of a black SUV parked at the curb. If he'd been there all night, he didn't look any worse for the wear, raising his hand in a cheerful greeting. I watched him follow me down the street and all the way to the *Informer*.

The last thing I wanted to do this morning was face Felix, but after last night, I was more determined than ever to see this piece through. I parked in the lot and hurried inside. A chill skittered up my spine as the events of the night before flashed in my mind's eye. I shoved those thoughts aside and stepped off the elevator.

I noticed Felix's office was empty and thanked the gods for small favors as I grabbed a cup of coffee and settled in at my desk. I fired up my computer, quickly pulling up my notes.

According to Brodie, Tattoo Guy, who'd attacked me twice now, worked for Sunshine Sanitation. Had someone connected to the company sent him to scare me? Had someone seen me nosing around Sunshine? I hadn't bothered to hide myself when I'd visited under the guise of the EPA. And Shane and I *had* heard someone there the night we'd broken in. It was possible someone thought we knew more than we did about their inner workings.

From everything Shane had dug up, Sal Bukowski seemed like the sort who wouldn't balk at robbery and assault. He also didn't seem the sort to do his dirty work himself—his record was too clean for that. I thought back to the photo I'd seen in the office of Bobby's "fan," Ritchie Mullins. While I knew he wasn't my tattooed friend, the connection to the sanitation company was too much to overlook.

I pulled up Ritchie's social media accounts again, this time paying a little bit closer attention to the details. He didn't mention his sanitation work anywhere, but then again if he was hired muscle for Bukowski's shady dealings, he would hardly advertise it. I idly scrolled through his friends list then checked his friends' friends lists. One name jumped out at me. A Tanya Mullins. She was listed as a friend of several of Ritchie's friends, and after reading a couple of drunken late-night posts from her, I gathered that she was Ritchie's ex-wife and things had not ended well between them.

I raised an eyebrow at my screen. If anyone had dirt on Ritchie—and would be willing to share it—it was an angry ex-wife. According to her profile, she worked for the city of L.A. in an administrative job. I googled the number for the city's main office. Three rings later a gruff voice answered.

"City of L.A. This is Gwendolyn."

"Hi, Gwendolyn," I began. "I'm looking for someone who works in your administrative offices."

"Let me transfer you to personnel," she said in a bored tone.

A sad elevator rendition of an Adele song came on the line while I waited on hold.

"Personnel," came a new voice.

I repeated my inquiry, giving the woman Tanya's name.

"Just a moment," she said, and I heard a computer keyboard clacking. Finally, she told me, "Tanya didn't come in today. Called in sick."

"Do you know where I might find her?"

"I'd assume that she's at home," she answered shortly.

"Thanks for your time." I ended the call and did another quick search online for Tanya Mullins and hoped like crazy that she was listed. A second later her home phone number and address in Echo Park popped up on the screen, and I jotted it down.

I hurried out of the office without a word to anyone and was about to cross the parking lot to my car, when I remembered my shadow. Sure enough, Cal was parked next to my Bug, a cup of coffee in one hand and a newspaper in the other. I paused, ducking back into the building instead. While I didn't altogether hate the safety that Cal provided, I also didn't want him reporting on my every move back to Felix. Or, worse yet, Tina. Plus, it wasn't like I was on a dangerous mission here. I was going to talk to a woman with a cold in the suburbs.

I dialed the number for a cab and doubled back toward the front of the building. Ten minutes later my yellow chariot pulled up to the curb, and I quickly slipped in before anyone on the second floor could chance a glance at me.

* * *

There was a wreck on the 101, so it was almost an hour later that my cab pulled to a stop outside of a modest apartment building in Echo Park. I paid the monster fee, second-guessing my decision to leave my Bug behind, and got out. The building's paint was a pale shade of green and peeling in spots. The window shutters were all a beige color that I'm sure had begun as white but with time and air pollution had turned a long time ago. Overall, the place didn't reek of money, but it was alright. I'd definitely seen worse.

With a quick scan of the area, I spotted apartment 5B on the second level. My low kitten heels made a soft click on the pavement as I walked across the black asphalt parking lot and up the metal stairs to Tanya's apartment.

Tanya's door looked freshly painted but would most likely turn darker, just as the window shutters had. I couldn't help but think that painting was a waste of time. I raised my hand and knocked. The door opened a minute later, and a short brunette woman in an oversized T-shirt and yoga pants with a wad of tissues in her hand peered out at me.

"May I help you?"

"I'm looking for Tanya Mullins," I said.

"I'm Tanya," she answered, her voice nasally, as if her nose was stuffed. "Do I know you?"

"No." I shook my head. "My name is Allie Quick, a reporter for the *L.A. Informer*. I'm wondering if you have a moment to talk to me about a story I'm working on."

"What kind of story?" she asked.

"It's about your ex-husband. Ritchie Mullins."

Her eyes narrowed. "What's he done?"

I was hoping she could tell me. "I'm not sure anything yet," I said honestly. "May I come in?"

She sucked her cheeks in, looking me over for a second. I started to think she was going to tell me no, but then she shrugged and stepped to the side.

"Sure. I have a few minutes. Come on in," she said. Then she sniffled loudly into her tissues.

I followed her inside. The apartment was clean and smelled like coffee. I took a minute to look around. The furniture was deep brown with leather accents and a matching ottoman.

The window treatments were a lighter shade of brown, and the side tables were topped with small clear glass lamps.

"Have a seat." She motioned toward the tall kitchen table. "Would you like a cup of coffee?"

"No, thanks," I said and took a seat in one of the high stools.

Tanya poured herself a cup of coffee, added sugar and creamer, took two aspirin, and then sat down at the table across from me. "Now, what's all this about? You said you have questions about Ritchie?"

"That's right." I nodded. "I'm working on a story, and your ex's name has come up more than once."

"Is he in some kind of trouble?" She looked almost delighted at the prospect.

"I don't know, to be honest with you. Are you close with him still?"

She snorted. "God, no. I haven't seen the lying sack of crap in months."

"I take it you didn't part on the best of terms."

She shrugged. "Do couples ever?"

She had a point. I forced my mind not to flicker to the fight I'd had with Felix.

"What happened?" I asked.

She blew her nose loudly into a tissue. "Let's just say Ritchie's a good-looking guy, and he knows it. Thinks his looks can get him out of anything." She let out a short laugh. "The gag is, they usually do."

I thought back. He hadn't struck me as particularly charming, but then again people didn't usually pour it on for tabloid reporters. "Did Ritchie get in a lot of trouble when you were together?"

"Petty stuff," she said, waving me off with a loud sniffle. "Getting into trouble really wasn't ever a concern of his because he knew someone would always bail him out. I'm not saying he's a bad guy," she explained. "But when it comes to taking responsibility for his own actions, Ritchie falls sickeningly short."

"Humor me," I told her. "What kind of petty stuff?"

"Never anything big, but I had to bail him out for a DUI once. Public disturbances and starting a fight one too many times."

It sounded like Ritchie had a bit of an aggressive streak. "I'm curious…did Ritchie ever work for a place called Sunshine Sanitation?" I asked, taking a stab in the not-so-dark.

Tanya nodded. "Yeah. He was there for a while."

"Why did he leave?" I asked, thinking back to the photo I'd found. Corporate officers usually didn't keep photos of fired employees in their offices.

"I heard from a mutual friend about a month ago that he was on medical leave."

"Medical leave?" I raised an eyebrow her way. Most people didn't take up a part-time job as a personal trainer at a gym if they were sick. The Ritchie I'd seen looked fit, strong, and healthy as a horse. "Was he injured at work?"

Tanya shrugged. "I don't know. But I know better than to believe anything Ritchie says at face value."

That made two of us. I thanked Tanya for her time and handed her my card. She took it with a sniffle, but I had a feeling it was destined for her trash can along with the pile of used tissues.

Traffic had cleared, so the cab ride back to the *Informer* was thankfully cheaper than the one out. While Tanya hadn't exactly given me the proof I needed to hang Bobby's murder on Ritchie, it was looking better and better that the man was involved somehow. I didn't buy the idea of him being on medical leave any more than his ex did. Was medical leave some kind of code for a payoff? It certainly would be an easy way to funnel money to an employee for, say, "taking care of" a guy like Bobby, who threatened to expose them.

After my cab dropped me off, I rode the elevator up, tried to ignore the looks my black eyes elicited from my curious coworkers, and settled back in at my desk.

"Wow. What happened to you?" Tina asked as she rolled her chair over to my desk.

"I had a little run-in with someone who isn't a fan of the story I'm working on," I answered.

"The Baxter story?" she asked. Her eyes narrowed. "You must be getting somewhere."

I took small pleasure in the envy on her voice. "Maybe," I hedged. "How are you getting on?" My mind flickered back to the notes I'd seen the night before on her desk about Henry's big break.

She shrugged and averted her eyes. "Great. Almost ready for print."

I couldn't tell if she was bluffing or if I really was in trouble.

"So what happened?" she asked. "Who hit you?"

I quickly gave her the short version of the run-in I'd had. By the time I was done, something akin to genuine concern shined on her face.

"Wow, that sounds like a really scary ordeal," she said. "Are you okay?"

I nodded. As much as I saw Tina as a rival, the real worry in her voice was heartwarming. "I'll be fine. Just a couple of bruises."

The phone rang on Tina's desk.

"Well, be careful out there," she said before she wheeled her chair around.

"Thanks. I will."

She scooted back over to her desk, picked up the office phone, and started yelling at whoever was on the other end. Her swear pig was going to be full of quarters by the end of that phone call.

My head was killing me, so I popped another ibuprofen and rubbed the back of my neck.

Felix stepped off the elevator, a paper coffee cup in one hand and his phone in the other. He glanced toward my desk and took a step in my direction.

I gave him a look that said I'd slept like crap and was currently wearing a bright shade of *leave me alone*. He immediately changed course and went into his office.

A deep cleansing breath helped clear my head, and the pounding eased a fraction.

The key to Bobby's death was the story he'd been working on about Sunshine. I was sure of it. Maybe it had to do with the dwindling amounts of waste being hauled off the property…or maybe it was something else entirely. Like Sal Bukowski's disappearing trick with the union rep. Of course, with Bobby's laptop and notes gone, I was stuck guessing. On instinct I picked up the phone and dialed Henry's number. While my guesses felt like shots in the dark, Henry had known Bobby a whole lot better than I had. He must have had some inkling of what Bobby was onto, even if it hadn't registered at the time.

Two rings later a perky female voice came over the phone. "This is Tiffany. How can I help you?"

I blinked with confusion, pulled the phone away from my ear for a second, and checked the number.

"Um, Tiffany, hi. This is Allie Quick. I'm looking for Henry Klein?"

"I'm his personal assistant. Can I take a message? Have him call you back?"

Wow. From personal assistant to *having* a personal assistant. Henry was a long way from where he'd been when Bobby was alive days before. Again, I silently wondered if maybe Tina had been on to something about the assistant. I mean, *former* assistant. Maybe all of this Sunshine stuff was just coincidence, and maybe Bobby's death had been much more personal.

"I really need to speak with him. Do you think you can get him to take my call right now please?"

"Okeydokey! Let me see!"

While I normally didn't mind perky, this morning I moved the phone away from my ear just a fraction at her cartoon-range voice.

The phone clicked over to Muzak. I listened to an elevator music rendition of an Aerosmith classic as I waited. Which did nothing to ease my headache.

"Ms. Quick," Tiffany said, coming back on the line. "I'm super sorry, but Mr. Klein is extremely busy."

Of course he was. "Will you have him call me back as soon as possible?"

"Will do! But Mr. Klein asked me to inform you that it may be some time before he gets back in touch with you."

"Thanks," I said and ended the call.

Henry was avoiding me now. Was it that he really was busy with a brand new show…or was he feeling guilty about just how he'd gotten the show and was avoiding the press?

I rubbed my temples as if that might move the swirling thoughts about murder suspects into some semblance of order in my head. When that didn't work, I went to the break room and poured myself a cup of coffee. It wasn't exactly Starbucks, but with enough fake creamer, it worked. I took the cup back to my desk and tapped my pen along the edge of my pink notebook as I sipped.

I mentally laid out what I knew about Bobby's death. The facts remained that Bobby had a story brewing on Sunshine Sanitation. Ritchie, a former employee, had approached Bobby, and Bobby had hit him. A couple of weeks later Bobby met with someone who had the same initials as our shady Sal Bukowski. Then Bobby wound up dead. Throw in the tattooed man, who also worked for Sunshine, stealing Bobby's laptop, and I decided that despite Henry's rise to fame or the wife's big payday, the Sunshine connection was where the smart money was. Sal and Ritchie had to be involved in Bobby's death. What I needed was just one real piece of evidence linking them all together.

If Sal was in fact the SB that Bobby had been meeting for dinner, I supposed that something had gone down at that meal that Sal hadn't liked. Maybe Bobby had refused to keep quiet about whatever he'd dug up on Sunshine. After dinner Sal called his muscle for hire, Ritchie, and Ritchie offed Bobby.

If I could get a look at Ritchie's phone, I could know for certain if Sal had called him the night Bobby had died. I thought about asking Shane to hack into Ritchie's cell records, but after the danger I'd put him in at the recycling plant, I was reluctant to involve him again.

Instead, I drained the last of my coffee, grabbed my purse, and dialed the number for the Oceanside Gym as I walked to the elevator. Three rings in I got a bored sounding woman.

"Oceanside Gym, how may I help you?"

"Is Ritchie Mullins in today?" I asked, hitting the elevator's down button.

"Uh, lemme check," she said then covered the receiver with her hand as she repeated the question to someone else. A few seconds later, she came back on the line. "Yeah, he's scheduled to come in at noon. You want to leave a message for him?"

"No, that's fine. Thanks," I told her, stepping into the elevator as I hung up.

Cal's black SUV was still parked right next to my Bug. He gave me a silent wave, which I returned before stepping into my car. I could have taken another cab, but I was running out of cash. And honestly, I didn't totally hate the idea of having backup to go visit a potential murderer.

By twelve twenty I was parked at the curb across the street from the gym, wondering just how I was going to separate one possibly homicidal personal trainer from his cell phone. If he was like most people, he probably kept it on his person. No way was I stealth enough pick a guy's pocket without him knowing. Amateur lock picking was the extent of my extracurricular abilities.

I stepped into the coffee shop across the street and ordered a vanilla latte, hoping the caffeine would help me come up with a brilliant plan. I was waiting on my order when my phone rang. Shane's number showed up on the readout. I raised an eyebrow at the coincidence, hoping the kid didn't have some sort of psychic abilities. More likely just an unrelenting crush.

"What's up, Shane?" I answered.

"Ohmigod, I'm so glad you're okay!" he practically shouted into the phone.

"Why wouldn't I be?" I asked as I took my latte from the barista.

"Because of your harrowing ordeal last night."

I rolled my eyes. "I'm not sure it was exactly 'harrowing.'"

"Being viciously attacked right in your own parking lot? I'd call that harrowing."

I shrugged even though I knew he couldn't see me. "I guess it wasn't exactly fun." I paused. "Wait—how did you even find out about this?"

"It's breaking news."

I narrowed my eyes at my phone. "Breaking where?" In a city with a crime rate like L.A.'s, I had a hard time believing that a random attack with minor injuries was a leading story on the news.

"Duh. The *L.A. Informer* website."

My mind immediately flashed to that morning and Tina's interest in my "ordeal." I thought a dirty word. Whether her concern had been genuine or not, it seems she couldn't help creating a print-worthy story out of it. While I didn't particularly like being tabloid fodder, I couldn't blame her too much. I'd probably have done the same thing.

"I'm fine," I reassured him. "The tabloids always exaggerate." Especially Tina.

"You sure?" Shane asked. "The article said it was really bad. Harrowing even, babe."

I skimmed over the babe thing, since the kid sounded actually worried. "Totally sure," I reassured him as I left the coffee shop.

"You need someone to watch over you today? I could come, you know, guard your body."

Why did that sound dirty coming from the teenager?

I glanced at the black SUV parked behind my car as I crossed the street. "I'm covered," I told him. "Thanks."

"Well, what are you looking into today? What leads are you chasing down? Any clues to uncover?"

I rolled my eyes at how Scooby-Doo it all sounded coming from his mouth. "Nothing I can't handle. Alone."

"You know, you've got a real independent streak."

"Thank you."

"That wasn't a compliment."

"Don't you have school or something?" I asked as I pushed through the glass front doors of the Oceanside Gym.

"Nope. I had a friend call me in sick when I heard the news about your attack. I figured you needed me more than I needed trig."

Why did I get the feeling Shane took just about any excuse to miss school?

"Well, I'm fine. Thanks."

"Where are you?" he asked. "It sounds noisy."

"A gym," I answered without thinking.

"The one where Ritchie Mullins works?" he asked, his voice perking up.

"Uh…maybe," I mumbled.

"What are you doing there? Are you going to confront him? Interrogate him?"

"I've got to go," I told him, mentally rolling my eyes again. "Bye, Shane." I disconnected before he could protest.

The same brunette was on duty at the front desk as the last time I'd been in the gym. She turned a toothy smile on me as soon as I hung up. "May I help you?"

"Yeah, I'm uh…" I looked past her and spied Ritchie with a client, spotting him on a weight bench. He was wearing the gym's logo shirt, a pair of really tight spandex shorts that made his legs look like tree trunks, and a fanny pack straight out of 1998. "I'm thinking of joining."

"Really? You want to join?" she asked, her eyes going from my heels to the black eye.

I nodded. "I had a little run-in with a bad guy last night." I motioned to my face. "I signed up for a self-defense class this morning, and they suggested I join a gym," I lied. While I still wasn't 100 percent sure how I was going to get a peek at Ritchie's phone, I figured a tour would buy me some time. If I was lucky, Ritchie's phone would be conveniently tucked in the retro fanny pack. How to get it out was still a challenge, but I was up for it.

"Sure," the brunette said. "Let me just see if Justin is available."

"Uh, any chance Ritchie could show me around?" I asked.

She paused. "Ritchie's with a client right now." She spun around, gesturing to the duo at the weight bench.

"No problem. I can wait."

She cocked her head at me.

"My self-defense teacher said Ritchie's the best trainer," I explained.

Brunette shrugged. "Sure. Have a seat." She gestured to the lobby's padded bench. "I'll let him know you're here."

I thanked her then settled in with my latte to wait.

I sipped, tried not to breathe too deeply of the air that was scented with sweat, strong disinfectant, and rubber, and listened to the sounds of weights clanging, ellipticals whooshing, and the occasional grunt from the resistance training machines. I wasn't sure how long I sat, but I was just tossing my empty coffee cup into the trash when the doors opened and a familiar figure stepped in.

I blinked up at the red-haired teenager. "Shane!" I hissed.

His face broke into a wide grin. "Hey, babe."

I narrowed my eyes at him. "What are you doing here?" I glanced guiltily in Ritchie's direction, as if Shane's presence would somehow signal him to a nefarious scheme in the works.

"I'm here to help with the interrogation."

"Shh," I told him, tugging him by the sleeve down onto the bench beside me. I glanced to the brunette, but she'd barely registered Shane's presence. "We are not interrogating anyone," I whispered to Shane.

"Then what are we doing here?" he whispered back.

I sighed. "*I* am hoping to get a look at Ritchie's phone. I don't know what you're doing here," I mumbled.

Shane nodded, ignoring that last comment. "Cool. How are we going to do that?"

I ignored his choice of pronoun. So much for not involving him. In my defense though, he'd totally involved himself. I gave him a palms-up. "Not sure. I'm waiting for him to give me a tour of the gym."

"And what are we looking for on his phone?" he asked.

With a quick glance in Bored Brunette's direction, I filled Shane in on my suspicions about Ritchie being Sal's hired muscle and what I hoped to find on Ritchie's phone.

When I was done, Shane nodded again. "Leave it to me," he said. "You distract the big guy, and I'll sneak a peek at the phone."

"I don't know—" I started.

But I was cut off by a large figure approaching us. "Jill said you wanted a tour?" Ritchie Mullins said, suddenly looking over at us.

I felt my cheeks heat, as if he could somehow know what we'd just been talking about. "Yes!" I said, maybe a bit too enthusiastically.

His eyes narrowed at me in recognition. "Aren't you that reporter?"

I nodded. "I, uh, had a harrowing ordeal last night," I said, borrowing a dramatic phrase from my friend Tina. "I thought maybe I should join a gym. You know, learn a little self-defense? I hear you're the best personal trainer here," I added, hoping to win him over with flattery.

It seemed to work as his eyes softened, and he shrugged. "Sure. I can show you around. Follow me."

I did, quickly scampering after Ritchie as Shane sent me an exaggerated wink.

Ritchie gave me a quick tour of the cardio area, the locker rooms, the pool in the back, and finally the free weights area. Shane wandered along a few paces behind us the entire time. If Ritchie noticed, he didn't let on.

"You say you were attacked last night?" Ritchie asked once we reached the back of the gym, an area full of balance balls, padded mats, and people stretching and doing crunches.

I nodded, watching his reaction. While I knew my attacker hadn't been Ritchie himself, I wondered how much he knew about it. For all I knew, he, Snake Tattoo, and Sal Bukowski were all in it together.

But if he had any intimate knowledge of it, he didn't let on. "There are a couple of moves that we usually show female clients to protect themselves. Just simple things, but they can be effective."

"Could you show me one now?" I asked, seeing an opening.

He shrugged. "Sure, I guess." Then to my delight, he removed his black fanny pack and tossed it in a corner on a spare bench. I followed suit with my purse.

I caught sight of Shane skirting the wall toward the pack. Hopefully, Ritchie's phone was in there, and this wasn't a huge waste of time.

Ritchie's back was to the bench as he stood in front of me with a wide-legged stance. "Okay, imagine I'm an attacker. Where's the most vulnerable part of me?"

My eyes went down to his too-tight pants. "Uh, your…" I trailed off, not really wanting to linger in that area.

Ritchie grinned suggestively. Ick. "Right. Doesn't matter how big the guy is, he's gonna be vulnerable there. So, come at me."

"You want me to, uh, kick you there?" I asked. I was only paying half attention. The other half was on Shane. Out of the corner of my eye, I spied him grab the pack and disappear into the men's room.

"Go for it," Ritchie said, his muscles tense.

Well, if he asked for it…

I moved to kick my right foot up toward his groin. But it only got halfway off the ground before Ritchie caught it in his big, meaty hands, toppling me over onto my butt on the padded floors.

"Lesson one," he said, towering over me, still holding onto my ankle. "Never do what your attacker is expecting." He grinned, clearly pleased with himself.

I mentally rolled my eyes. "Okay. Great. Thanks," I said, trying my best to avoid sarcasm as I took my foot back and slowly stood, thankful I wasn't wearing a skirt.

"Okay, let's try that again," Ritchie said, taking his wide stance in front of me.

"You know, I think I'm good," I told him.

He shook his head. "Lesson's not over. Come on…what was your mistake last time?"

"Doing what you expected?" I guessed.

He nodded. "Also, you left me way too much room to grab you first. I saw your foot coming a mile away. But if you come in closer…" He demonstrated by taking a giant step forward and invading my personal space. "…it's harder for your attacker to grab you."

I swallowed, not comfortable being in such close proximity. "Got it," I mumbled. I looked past him and spotted Shane coming back out of the men's room. "Uh, let me try it," I said.

Ritchie took a step back, taking on his attacker stance again. I watched Shane put the pack back on the bench where Ritchie had left it.

"Okay, ready?" I asked.

Ritchie nodded, his eyes twinkling. If I didn't know better, I'd say he liked playing the attacker.

I took a quick step, coming right up against Ritchie's body. He moved to grab my foot, but I lifted my knee into his groin instead.

I heard a whoosh of air in response. Oops. Looked like someone forgot to wear a cup to work today.

I took a step back, assessing the damage. Ritchie's face looked pinched, but he was still standing.

"Did I get it?" I asked, innocently batting my eyelashes at him.

He nodded slowly. "Yeah. That was it," he grunted out.

Out of the corner of my eye I saw Shane hurry toward the gym's exit.

That was my cue to get the heck out of there.

I grabbed my purse from the bench. "Thanks so much." I gave Ritchie a big smile. "You've convinced me. I'm just going to go sign up now."

Ritchie nodded, still not speaking much. I almost felt bad. That was, if I wasn't 99 percent convinced he was involved in Bobby's murder.

"I'll see you later." I waved and hurried to the front of the gym. I chanced a peek behind me to see if Ritchie was watching me, but he had his back to me, leaning on the bench now in an awkward position. I quickly bypassed the reception desk and hurried outside to my car.

Shane was waiting for me when I reached my Bug and got inside.

"Did you get it?" I asked a bit breathlessly.

Shane nodded. "I was totally stealth, right?"

I couldn't help but grin. "And? Were there any texts or calls from Sal Bukowski?"

Shane shook his head in the negative. "Sorry, babe. If there were, Ritchie deleted them."

I felt my hopes deflate faster than a leaky balloon. Right. Of course he wouldn't keep incriminating information on his phone. Even Ritchie was smarter than that. "Great." I smacked my palm on my steering wheel, feeling like a total doof for thinking this might be my smoking gun. "All that for nothing."

"Well, I wouldn't say *totally* nothing."

I glanced over at Shane. He was doing a Cheshire cat grin.

"What?" I asked. "What did you do?"

"Well...I kinda installed an app on his phone."

"What kind of app?" I asked, allowing that hope to peek its head up just a bit.

"It's like a spyware thing. It tracks all of your calls, texts, any activity on your phone. My parents tried to put it on my phone last year. Thought it might keep me out of trouble." He chuckled at the absurdity of that. I had a moment of sympathy for his parents.

"So, we can track any activity on Ritchie's phone right now?"

Shane nodded. "Pretty much. All we have to do is install the parent app on your phone, and anytime you log in, it should funnel all the data right to us."

"So if Sal tries to contact him again..."

"We'll know about it as soon as Ritchie does."

While it wasn't exactly the sure thing I'd been hoping for, it was better than nothing. I handed my phone over to Shane to install the parent app.

"But won't Ritchie see the app?"

Shane shook his head as his fingers flew over my screen. "Nah. It's designed to be pretty much invisible."

"Then how did you find it when your parents installed it?"

He shot me a *get real* look. "Seriously?"

Right, I was talking to super hacker. Of course he found it. All I could hope was that Ritchie was no tech wizard. And from what I knew of him, that was a fairly safe bet.

* * *

After Shane finished setting up my phone, I sent him home and headed back to the office, with Cal still shadowing me. The first thing I did was pull up the *Informer*'s website and read Tina's article on me. I groaned out loud. It was just as sensational as I'd feared, using lots of ghastly adjectives like "frightening" and "terrorizing." Had she been in her cubicle, I'd have given her about $2.25 worth of swear pig words to let her know just how I felt about her journalism skills. As it was, I decided a kick-butt story on Baxter was the best revenge.

While I was still lacking proof, I started typing up my article on Bobby Baxter's death and Sal Bukowski being the mastermind behind it all. While there were lots of blanks I was hoping to fill in later, Friday was fast approaching, and I all I could do was hope.

My phone dinged with an unusual tone, and I quickly swiped the screen on. Shane's app had registered activity on Ritchie's phone. I opened the app and saw a text had come in for him from a 323 number.

Need to reschedule training session. Sick. Will call on Monday.

I felt my stomach sink. Not a confirmation of dirty deeds. Just a personal training client. I tucked my phone back in my purse and went back to my article.

I grabbed a tuna salad from the deli across the street and ate lunch at my desk. The rest of the afternoon was spent working on the article—adding as much backstory about Ritchie and Sal as I could without incurring the wrath of the legal department. I paused in my furious typing only long enough to check the half-dozen texts Ritchie got throughout the afternoon via my spyware app. A buddy wanting to grab a beer after work. Three more clients scheduling sessions. A girl named Britt who had some suggestive things to say about their "adventure" the night before. Nothing even remotely illegal. At least, I didn't think so. Britt didn't go into "adventure" details.

I was just powering down my computer for the day and about to give up on ever beating Tina to the evidence punch, when my phone dinged once again. I glanced at the app's readout.

And recognized the number immediately. It was a Sunshine Sanitation prefix.

My hands shook as I swiped the screen to read the incoming text.

Port of L.A. Berth 210. 8pm

It had to be from Sal Bukowski! A cryptic message to meet at the docks late at night. This was the stuff of reporter dreams. I almost felt like pinching myself. A payoff for killing Bobby? Maybe an illegal dump site for Sunshine's toxic waste? Or maybe Sal was done using Ritchie and was planning to dump him in the Pacific? Either way, I planned to be there to witness it.

CHAPTER NINETEEN

———

Mr. Fluffykins watched me curiously as I rushed around my bedroom tossing clothing like a madwoman.

Most of my wardrobe consisted of bright, vibrant colors, so finding something that I could wear to conceal myself in the shadows wasn't easy. I stuck with the pair of full-length black leggings I had on, and I rooted around in the closet until I came across a long sleeved black Henley. I managed to find one pair of black boots that didn't have a heel and paired them with a black beanie my cousin from Seattle had left behind when she'd spent the weekend with me last winter.

I pulled my hair up into a loose bun, shoved it under the cap, and looked at my reflection in the mirror. My stealth outfit was actually pretty cute. Cat burglar chic, even.

"What do you think, Fluff?" I turned to model the outfit for him.

My cat tilted his head to the side, meowed, and then turned his back to me and lay down.

"Everyone's a critic," I mumbled.

I checked the clock on the nightstand. It was almost seven, and I had at least a forty-five-minute drive to the docks—and that was only if traffic was thin. I needed to get a move on if I wanted to get into a good position to watch the meeting go down without being seen. I still wasn't 100 percent sure how I was going to ditch Cal, but I grabbed a black cross-body bag from the closet, dumped my purse on the bed, and then stuffed the items into the new bag.

"Hold down the fort while I'm gone, and wish me luck," I called over my shoulder as I hurried out of the bedroom. Mr. Fluffykins meowed a response as I grabbed my car keys and left the apartment. Once outside I locked my door behind me, pressed my back against it, and took a deep breath. My nerves were dancing a samba, and my stomach felt like I'd eaten a bad burrito. I was possibly about to face a murderer and witness a payoff or something else just as nefarious on the L.A. docks after dark...alone. Was this wise?

I closed my eyes, took another deep breath to calm myself down, then opened them and moved forward to the stairs leading down to the parking area. I was fine. I was just going to watch. Maybe snap a picture or two. No one would even see me. I wasn't going to bust anyone. I was just observing. Totally safe.

I'd just stepped off of the last step onto the sidewalk when a gloved hand reached out and grabbed my shoulder.

Adrenaline shot through me, and I let out a scream as I spun around ready to fight whoever was attacking me.

"Whoa! Calm down there, killer."

"Shane?" I squawked and pressed a hand to my chest. "You scared me half to death." I tried to catch my breath as my heart pounded almost painfully against my ribcage. "What in hell are you doing here—" I reached over and whacked his arm for scaring me. "—lurking in the dark?"

"Like I was going to let you go to this meeting alone after what happened to you last night." He shook his head.

"How did you even know—"

Shane rolled his eyes at me, cutting me off. "Dude, I've got the app on my phone too." He held up the device as proof. "Duh."

Duh. Of course he did.

"I can't let you do this. It could be dangerous," I told him.

"Then you shouldn't go alone."

"Shane, you're just a kid."

He frowned, puffing out his chest. "Okay, so how do you plan to protect yourself? You have a gun?"

I scoffed. "No."

"Taser? Pepper spray?"

"No."

"A crossbow?"

"No! Geez, I'm a reporter not a doomsday prepper." I paused, eyeing the backpack he was carrying. "Please tell me *you* don't have one in there?"

He shook his head. "No. But there's safety in numbers, which is why I'm going with you."

I opened my mouth to argue with him again, but he ran right over me.

"Look, you can argue all you want, but the fact remains I'm going to be at berth 210 at 8 p.m." He looked down at his phone again. "Which is coming right up, so we better get a move on."

I shut my mouth with a click. As much as I didn't like this arrangement, he was right. If we didn't get on the road, we were liable to miss whatever Sal and Ritchie were meeting for.

"Fine," I said. I looked up at Cal's SUV parked across the street. He was reading a paperback in the driver's seat, strategically parked to keep a close eye on my Bug. "But we're taking your car," I told Shane. "Where are you parked?"

Shane grinned at me as he led the way around the back of the building. "Whatever you say, babe."

While I'd put the Port of L.A. into the GPS in Shane's Mom's minivan and had a vague idea where it was, I'd never actually been there myself before. As we pulled up almost an hour later, I realized the place was huge. It looked like a virtual city filled with jutting docks and waterways, dotted with cruise ships, cargo ships, and large shipping crates. I squinted in the dark, pointing out the signs and looking for berth 210. After winding through the maze of small roads connecting the inlets of slips, we finally found the right one. Even if I hadn't read the number of the berth, the huge containers, stacked near the water, bearing Sunshine Sanitation's cheery logo would have clued me in that we were in the right place. Shane parked as close as we could get, about a block away beneath a burned-out streetlight.

We walked down the street in silence until we reached the berth. Three large ships and a barge were docked along the low cement walls. We turned left and walked along the shadows in the opposite direction from the ships. Large containers were lined along each side of us. Forklifts and other machines were dispersed among the containers. Pale light shined down on the cement beneath our feet from dim lights lining the walk.

"This place is creepy," Shane admitted.

"Agreed." I nodded my head. Not even the sound of the calm water lapping against the docks or the smell of salty sea air soothed me. Despite the humidity and the long-sleeved shirt I wore, goose bumps dotted my skin.

We reached a smaller rust red shipping container situated just past the empty barge. I wasn't sure exactly where to expect the meet-up, but this looked like as good a place as any to keep an eye on the walkway in.

"Back here," I said, leading the way behind the container. Shane followed and knelt down beside me. We had a perfect view of the ships as well as anyone coming or going from the berth.

"What time is it?" I asked.

Shane pulled out this phone, the pale light feeling way too bright in the darkness. "Ten past eight."

"Looks like they're running late."

"Or we've missed them," he added.

I frowned, hoping he was wrong.

We settled in with our backs against the shipping container and waited.

Half an hour later we'd seen nothing but a few gulls land on the water. I looked over at Shane and shook my head. "I can't believe they're a no-show," I said. "Let's get out of here."

The night was a total bust, and I was so frustrated my head was pounding with every beat of my heart. I stood to brush the dust off my legs, when I heard the sound of a big truck pulling up.

"Is that them?" Shane whispered.

I squatted back down quickly and peeked around the container. Two big trucks were backing up toward the barge. Once they were a few feet away from the edge, they stopped, and a large machine pulled up beside them.

Shane leaned against my back and looked over my head to get a better view. A few minutes later Ritchie hurried down the dock toward the trucks.

Bingo! "There's Ritchie," I whispered.

"What are they doing?" Shane asked.

"I'm not sure." I pulled the camera app up on my phone and zoomed in, watching as the back of the truck opened up. "Wait—is that trash?"

Shane was still leaning against my back, so I felt his nod rather than saw it. "Yeah. Looks like it," he answered.

Compact squares of multi colors sat neatly stacked in the back of the large semitruck. "What are they doing with it?" I asked.

"Beats me."

A forklift pulled up beside the truck started moving the compressed squares of garbage onto the barge.

"I don't get it," I said and started snapping pictures, careful to make sure I got clear pictures of Ritchie, the trucks, and especially the trash squares. "Sunshine Sanitation is a recycling facility. All the garbage should be at the plant, being processed into new stuff like egg cartons and crappy brown paper, right?"

"So why are they putting it on a ship?"

That was a great question. And why was Ritchie—who was supposed to be on medical leave—apparently supervising the whole thing? I wiggled farther around the corner of the container, trying to get a better angle to get Ritchie in frame. I zoomed in on him, snapping photos of his face under the dim lights as he directed the guy on the forklift.

Then, almost as if he could feel me, he spun around, his eyes meeting mine through the lens.

I immediately dropped the phone from my eyes, finding myself staring across the expanse of docks at Ritchie.

"Uh-oh."

Ritchie yelled to someone, pointing toward our hiding spot.

"Oh crap. We've been spotted," I said, shoving my phone into my boot. "Run!"

I grabbed Shane's arm and tugged him along. We sprinted the other direction from the men, through a maze of shipping containers. I heard a loud pinging noise hit the metal as we ran past.

"They're shooting at us!" Shane shouted as he ran beside me. He stumbled, and I grabbed his hand, practically dragging him along with me.

My lungs were bursting with the exertion, and my heart threatened to beat right out of my chest. I heard footsteps behind us, several pairs, pounding the pavement.

We sprinted to the car. Shane fumbled to hit the key fob but ended up dropping it on the ground. I picked it up, my fingers feeling like they were made of jelly as I unlocked the minivan and shoved Shane into the passenger seat. I quickly turned the ignition and put the car in gear. Shane buckled up while I peeled away from the curb. Tires screeched as I whipped onto a side street, heading across the Cerritos Channel back toward the 110.

I was officially freaking out. We'd been shot at! Whatever we'd seen, Ritchie had been willing to kill us to keep it quiet. My palms were sweaty, and my grip slipped on the steering wheel. Shane's complexion looked positively ghostly beside me, his breath coming hard and fast.

We'd just crossed the East Basin when a car sped up behind us so close that the headlights illuminated the interior of the minivan like daylight.

Shane spun in his seat. "They're after us," he yelled, his voice cracking on the last word.

He steadied himself with a hand on the dashboard as I made a sharp right turn. I looked in the rearview mirror. Thanks to their close proximity and brightness of the lights, I couldn't see a thing.

"Is it Ritchie?" I asked.

"I dunno," Shane responded. His voice was high and sounded as panicked as I felt. "But whoever it is is gaining on us."

My thoughts whirled as I struggled to come up with a plan that wouldn't result in getting us killed. The car behind us floored it. I heard the rev of his engine as he kissed our bumper. We skidded sideways. I held the steering wheel in a white-knuckled grip and struggled to keep the car on the road. Our attacker eased back but kept his headlights close enough to have me squinting at the road ahead.

I pushed the accelerator, taking the next turn so fast I feared we'd be on two wheels, and hit the freeway. I quickly merged on, losing the car behind us in traffic for a moment. I kept one eye on the rearview mirror and the other on the road ahead. For a minute, I thought we were safe.

Then I saw Ritchie's mustang cruising along in traffic two cars behind us on the right.

Shane must have seen it too. "He's following us," he croaked out.

I nodded. "I'll see if I can lose him," I said, pulling to the left, into the Fast Track lane. I figured the ticket was worth it. I zoomed ahead a few cars then abruptly pulled back into the right, hoping to hide between two SUVs.

Neither of us spoke as we drove north, exceeding the speed limit by as much as traffic would allow, holding our collective breath. Shane sat sideways, still watching the back window, his eyes looking big, scared, and distinctively childlike. Five minutes later he let out a sharp breath. "He's back."

I bit my lip, trying desperately not to let out the panicked sob I could feel in my throat. He was stalking us, biding his time in traffic until he could get close enough to get off a shot. I had a bad feeling that the second we veered off the freeway—and onto a street with fewer witnesses—we were toast. We had to get off sometime. And apparently Ritchie knew it.

My mind reeled a mile a minute as we merged onto the 101, still heading toward Hollywood. Though, I didn't really know where our destination was. I couldn't drive home. I couldn't take Shane home. I could drive to a police station, but even if I knew where one was, I had a bad feeling we'd never get there in one piece unless it was directly at the off-ramp.

I leaned harder on the accelerator, whipping in and out of traffic, probably incurring lots of middle fingers from my fellow drivers as I tried to think of something—anything!—to keep us from ending up as another L.A. drive-by statistic.

"Where the heck are the CHP when you need them?" Shane said, his eyes glued to the headlights behind us.

I froze. CHP. That was it. I knew exactly where they were.

I yanked the steering wheel to the right and skidded across two lanes of traffic. Shane slid in his seat, knocking into the door.

"Whoa, watch it!"

"Sorry," I mumbled, looking up at the freeway signs. The overpass with the speed trap was just three exits away. I said a silent prayer to the gods of speeding tickets that the CHP was in his usual spot and not napping on the job. Then I gunned the engine and watched the speedometer climb. 70, 75, 80, 85. I felt the car start to rattle as I pushed it to its limit.

I glanced in the rearview. Ritchie's mustang accelerated easily, coming up behind me hot and fast.

"Here we go..." I whispered, flying past the overpass, Ritchie quickly gaining on me.

I was going too fast to see if the CHP was on duty, but a second after we passed the speed trap, Ritchie right behind us, I heard the sweet sound of sirens filling the air.

Flashing lights shined behind us, but I didn't dare slow down. Neither did Ritchie, pulling almost close enough to touch my bumper again.

Up ahead, I spotted the exit for the *Informer*.

"He's gaining on us." Shane turned around in his seat again to get a better look.

"Hang on," I said and made a sharp right off the freeway, slamming the brakes as I slowed for the turn. My tires squealed, Ritchie swerved, banking off the guardrail as he adjusted to follow us, and the sirens behind us intensified as the CHP officer tried to catch up.

I swerved left at the cross street, pulling away from the heavier traffic. While it was late, the roads were never empty in L.A. And the last thing I wanted was to injure an innocent bystander in our high-speed chase.

Ritchie swerved behind us, the CHP hot on his tail.

I gunned the engine then made a hard left at the next intersection, barely missing a pickup truck in the next lane. Ritchie clipped it but kept coming.

"This guy is relentless," Shane said. "What's he gonna do, shoot us right in front of the cop?"

I wasn't sure, and I didn't want to find out.

I turned right again and saw flashing lights up ahead of us. The CHP had called for backup. I said a silent thank-you and slowed as I approached the lights and two black-and-white police cars parked in our path.

Ritchie skidded to a stop behind me, and the CHP's car skidded to a halt sideways in the road behind him, effectively blocking us both in.

Shane and I jumped out of the car with our hands in the air at the same time as the officers did, their guns drawn.

What ensued was nothing short of chaos. Ritchie got out of his car and tried to run, but he was tackled by two police officers. It took another three to wrestle handcuffs onto the bodybuilder and shove him into the back of a squad car. Shane and I were a little more cooperative, compliantly letting the officers cuff us as we tried to explain just why we'd led them on a high-speed chase through L.A. traffic. Someone finally decided they'd sort it all out at the station, and we were driven in separate cars the few blocks to a nearby precinct.

I spent the next few hours giving statements, showing the officers the photos I'd taken, and trying to explain just what we'd been doing at the docks without giving up anything too incriminating—like hacking into databases or minor B&E.

Being that he was a minor, the police called Shane's parents, and I felt a pang of sympathy for the harried looking older couple who arrived and immediately wrapped the kid in a big bear hug. Guilt rushed through me at the danger I'd inadvertently put him in. I vowed never, ever to let him ride shotgun with me again. My days of having a teenaged sidekick were definitely over. And from the way Shane started tearing up as he hugged his mom, I had a feeling he'd had his fill of thrill seeking as well.

A plainclothes officer took me into a small room with a wooden table, a couple of folding chairs, and a huge video camera mounted in the corner to sign my official statements. I did, unable to keep from glancing at the camera, feeling self-conscious that my every move was being recorded as some sort of evidence. After I went over everything for the tenth time that evening, the officer left me alone. I'm not sure how long I waited in the unnerving interrogation room, but by the time the door finally opened again, I was starting to nod off from total exhaustion.

"Allie." I looked up to find Felix's frame in the doorway.

My first thought was humiliation that this was the equivalent of the police calling *my* parents. My second was that he looked amazing. Someone had obviously gotten him out of bed with the unfortunate call that his employee-slash-maybe-girlfriend had been taken in for questioning, as his hair was mussed, his chin covered in a healthy dose of sexy stubble, and his uncharacteristic T-shirt and jeans rumpled and looking like they'd been hastily picked out of a hamper and thrown on as he'd rushed out the door.

I jumped up from the table and threw myself into his arms, just barely able to hold back the sob of relief at seeing a familiar face.

His arms went around me and held me tightly—the first thing that had felt like safety to me since Shane and I had pulled up to berth 210.

"You okay?" he finally asked, pulling back and letting his eyes scan my face. Though how he thought he could tell any new bruises from the old ones, I didn't know.

I nodded, feeling my hair bob up and down.

"What happened?" he asked, easing me back down into one of the folding chairs. "We got people calling in to our tip line that you were involved in some sort of car chase?"

I let out a shaky breath and relayed to him the events of the evening, starting with Shane installing the app and ending with the handcuffs all around as we rode to the station. Felix sat quietly, only nodding here and there where appropriate. When I finished, he rubbed a hand across his face, as if I'd aged him a couple of years since he'd arrived.

"And where was Cal during all of this?"

I shook my head. "Not his fault. I snuck away in Shane's car."

"Shane." He paused, the name sinking in. "The guy who keeps sending you flowers?"

"*Kid*, not guy."

Felix nodded, letting that detail go for now. "You turned all the photos over to the police?"

"Yeah," I said reluctantly. "I told them everything."

Felix raised an eyebrow my way.

"Well, almost everything," I mumbled, knowing when to invoke my right to remain silent.

"It should be enough to put Ritchie Mullins away."

I perked up. "Did they charge him?" The police hadn't filled me in much and had kept the three of us separated since we'd arrived. Which was fine by me—I'd be happy if I never had to set eyes on Ritchie Mullins again.

Felix nodded. "I called a contact of mine in the DA's office on my way here. He said they've charged him with attempted assault with a deadly weapon for now. But more charges are likely to follow, depending on which parts of his story check out."

"His story?" I said, jumping on the words. "So he's talking?"

"Not much at first, but when the DA started mentioning murder, conspiracy, and fraud charges, Ritchie decided he wasn't getting paid enough to take the fall for everyone."

"Everyone being Sal Bukowski and Sunshine Sanitation?"

Felix grinned. "You seem to already know what Ritchie was up to."

I couldn't help smiling back. "What can I say? I'm a good reporter."

Felix let out a chuckle. "No argument from me on that point."

"But I'll admit I don't know everything he was up to— what was with the trash cubes at the port?"

"Well, according to Ritchie's confession, Sunshine Sanitation began cutting some corners shortly after receiving their new contracts from the city."

I nodded. "They started disposing of less waste instead of more."

Felix raised a questioning eyebrow at me. "And you know this…?"

"You don't want to know," I told him honestly. "But I thought they were dumping the extra chemicals."

Felix shook his head. "Actually, it turns out they were never processing the recyclables to create the waste in the first place. Instead of running it through the plant, they were simply compacting the trash into those cubes you saw, loading it onto a cargo ship, then dumping the recyclables in the middle of the ocean."

"Seriously?"

"Seriously," he answered. "Turns out dumping trash illegally is cheaper for the company than actually recycling it."

"So Ritchie and those guys we saw were loading the ship after dark, presumably to keep it on the down-low."

Felix nodded. "That's what he says."

"Bobby must have uncovered their scheme while working on the recycling story," I said, pieces falling into place. "And threatened to expose them on his show."

"According to Ritchie, he did. That's when Sunshine turned the problem over to Bukowski. Apparently, Ritchie describes Bukowski as something of a 'fixer' at the company, taking care of unpleasant problems."

I thought of the missing union rep and shuddered, wondering if Bukowski'd had me on his radar as a "problem."

"So Bukowski sent Ritchie to confront Bobby?" I asked, remembering the very public altercation at Beverley's.

"Correct. Bukowski offered Bobby money for his silence, but Bobby wasn't having it. I guess he felt he'd make more in the rating boost than Sal was offering. So the altercation with Bobby at the restaurant was a warning for Bobby not to do the show. When Bobby hit Ritchie, Ritchie was instructed to press charges in hopes that the bad press might put a damper on any future airings of his show, especially the exposé on Sunshine Sanitation."

"Only it had the opposite effect," I pointed out. "Bobby got more press, not less."

Felix shrugged. "I guess Bukowski didn't know much about how Hollywood worked."

"So then Bukowski met Bobby for dinner at DeVitto's to try to convince him one last time...and when that didn't work, he killed him."

Felix shrugged, running a hand through his hair. "That's where your guess is as good as anyone's. The police picked Bukowski up a couple hours ago, but he's lawyered up and isn't confessing to anything. Ritchie says he has no idea who actually killed Bobby, but he didn't do it. He's pointing a finger at a guy named David Parks, one of Bukowski's hired muscle at Sunshine, as the person who stole Bobby's laptop from the studio in an effort to cover up the recycling story."

"And who attacked me in the *Informer* parking lot to shut me up," I added. "Tattoo Guy."

Felix nodded. "He's being brought in now, but so far it sounds like he's denying pulling the trigger on Bobby as well."

I shook my head. "Well, I'm sure the police will sort out which one." I stifled a yawn, realizing I'd been up all night.

Felix must have noticed. "Let me take you home," he offered.

"I'm free to go?" I glanced up at the camera.

He nodded. "Unless there's anything illegal you'd like to confess to?" I was pretty sure he was at least half kidding.

I gratefully grabbed my purse and stood, feeling the evening's toll in my sore muscles. Shane and his parents were nowhere to be seen as we made our way out of the precinct, which I hoped meant he'd been let go already and was at home in his bed like a good kid should be. I let Felix lead me out to his junker in the parking lot, and we spent the short ride back to my apartment in silence. For once, I didn't mind when he left me at the door with a chaste peck on the cheek and a promise to check in with me the next day. I stumbled inside and fell asleep on top of my bed, fully clothed, just as the sun was starting to peek through my blinds.

CHAPTER TWENTY

It was after noon before I awoke the next day, groggy and disoriented by the late hour. I took a quick shower, pulled my hair back into a simple, high ponytail, and went with an extra short skirt and extra low-cut, flowy pale violet top to make up for the fact that I'd slept most of the day.

I pulled up my article on Sunshine on my laptop as I sipped coffee at my kitchen counter, filling in all the gaps with the juicy details from the night before. Then I quickly sent it off to Felix. No matter what Tina might have had up her sleeve, this time I knew I had her beat. I almost felt bad for her.

Almost. She *had* scooped me the last two times, so I figured we were even.

I finished my coffee, grabbed my purse, and headed out to my Bug. Noticeably absent was Cal's SUV. I guessed with the not-so-sunny contingents from Sunshine Sanitation all in police custody, it was a lot safer out there today.

I pulled out onto the street and headed toward the freeway. While I was dying to see the look on Felix's face as he read my killer story, there was one stop I wanted to make first.

As I'd drifted through dreamland the night before, Marilyn Baxter's tear-stained face had haunted me. I felt bad for suspecting that she'd been involved in her husband's death—all but accusing the grieving widow. I mean, who was I to judge how someone grieved? If pedicures and sunbathing helped her through it, so be it. Granted the number of zeros on her husband's estate would help her remember him fondly, but it wasn't going to bring him back. So while I was pretty sure the police had already filled her in on Bukowski's involvement in his death, I felt I needed to personally share any details I could with her. If only to give her some sort of closure. I felt like I owed her that at least.

As soon as I hit Marilyn's street, I spotted Shane skateboarding on the sidewalk outside his house. I waved as I pulled up to the curb outside the Baxter residence.

Shane skated over and kicked his board up as he rolled to a stop in front of me.

"'Sup," he greeted me. In true teen fashion, he looked like he'd bounced back from the night's ordeal a lot quicker than I expected to. He didn't even look tired.

"You okay?" I asked.

He nodded. "Sure. Mom said I could take the day off school for a mental health day. Though, if you ask me, I think she's the one who needs it more."

I bit my lip, feeling that guilt wash over me again. I really owed his mom an apology muffin basket. Or big pink teddy bear. "I bet she was worried sick about you."

His jovial expression darkened a bit. "Yeah. I feel bad. But I'm fine, so, you know, she'll be okay. Though…" He trailed off, looking down at his board.

"Yes?" I prompted.

"Look, it's been cool hanging out with you and all, but I probably shouldn't help you out anymore. I mean, it's not that I don't want to help, but I kinda promised my mom I'd stick close to home for a while."

I tried not to smile at his earnest tone. "I understand," I told him.

His grin returned. "Thanks. Besides, I've only got, like, three more months left to enjoy being a kid. Might as well live it up before I have all that responsibility and stuff, right?"

This time I couldn't help the laugh that escaped me. "Totally," I agreed, nodding. "But thanks for everything," I added.

"No prob. See you around, Allie," he called before skating away.

I watched him go then pulled my car up to the gates of the Baxter estate. I hit the intercom and waited as a female voice came on the other end.

"May I help you?" it asked with a heavy Spanish accent.

"Allie Quick from the *L.A. Informer*," I said into the speaker. "I have some information for Mrs. Baxter about her husband's death."

There was a pause, then a beep, and the gates slowly opened. "Please come in," the voice told me.

I made my way through the open gates and up the cobblestone driveway and parked behind the same pool service SUV I'd seen the last time I'd been by. I rang the front doorbell once and waited. A moment later the door opened, and Marta, the housekeeper I'd met before, smiled out at me.

"Ms. Quick. Please come in," she said, standing aside. If she noticed I was the same "neighbor" she'd talked to before, she didn't mention it.

"Thank you. I was hoping that I could have a word with Mrs. Baxter."

"Of course. Come in. Come in. She's in the yard." She waved me inside and closed the heavy wooden door behind her. "If you'll just wait here, I'll get Mrs. Baxter for you," Marta said as she led me down a hallway and opened another thick door. She motioned me into the study I'd seen from the street.

"Thank you," I said as she turned and closed the door behind her.

The smell of old books and papers permeated the air. I turned in a complete circle and took in my surroundings. The room was quite beautiful. Very masculine with thick, dark wood accents, a heavy desk, leather desk chair, and floor-to-ceiling bookshelves lining the walls. The side wall was all glass and looked out over an immaculate side garden that put my one tiny Bonsai tree to shame. Out the front windows, I had a clear view of Shane's house. He was still skateboarding on the street.

I could spend hours in that garden if given the chance. The roses looked divine.

I shook myself away from the view and back to the real world. I heard who I assumed were the housekeeper and Marilyn talking in the hallway and turned toward the door.

But as I did, something caught my eye.

On the desk there was something partially shoved under the keyboard, almost as if hidden in a hurry. My curious nature got the best of me. The women were still talking in the hallway, so I tiptoed the three steps to the desk and slid the paper out from its hiding place.

A pair of plane tickets. One way to New Zealand. The top one held the name Marilyn Smedfield. With a quick glance toward the door, I shifted the bottom one. The name on the second ticket was listed as Chad Davies. I froze, my mind going to the SUV in the driveway. Would this be Chad Davies of Davies Pool Maintenance?

The room suddenly felt eerily still, my vision narrowed to the two plane tickets, and my head swirling. Why would Marilyn be taking the pool boy to New Zealand?

The housekeeper's remark about infidelity in the Baxter household came rushing back to me. At the time I'd assumed she'd been talking about *Bobby* being unfaithful. But what if it hadn't been the husband stepping out, but the wife…

"Ms. Quick?"

I heard Marilyn's voice behind me and instinctively shoved the plane tickets back under the keyboard and whirled around, adrenaline shooting through me.

"Mrs. Baxter, it's so nice to see you again." I gave her my best attempt at a friendly smile.

She returned it with one that wasn't nearly as sincere. "Marta said you wanted to see me?" Her eyes flickered to the desk behind me. "That you had some information for me?"

"Yes. Right. Of course. I do." I cleared my throat, my brain still whirling with images of Bobby's dead body, Marilyn's crocodile tears, and the plane tickets. "I, uh, assume the police have been in touch with you."

She nodded, her perfectly sculpted updo, not moving. "They called me this morning." She was dressed in a pair of white linen shorts, a thin halter top, and gold sandals—the perfect outfit for lounging by the pool and admiring your pool-boy-slash-lover.

I shoved that thought away, trying to focus on the conversation at hand.

"Then you know they have employees of Sunshine Sanitation in custody in connection to your husband's murder?" I asked, suddenly doubting if they were the guilty parties.

She leveled me with a pointed look. "Yes. You have no idea how relieved I am to hear my husband's killer is behind bars."

Now that statement I believed—at least the relief part. The killer part...

I cleared my throat again. "Yes, well, I just wanted to make sure you had heard and to, uh, personally tell you again how sorry I am for your loss." I made a move toward the door.

Marilyn stepped in front of me. "Really?"

"Um, what?" I asked.

"Are you *really* so sorry for my loss?" she asked, her eyes again flicking to the not-so-hidden plane tickets. "You know, everyone says that, but I think it's mostly a hollow sentiment to get them out of an awkward situation."

I laughed. Awkwardly. "Oh, well, yeah, I guess sometimes..." I trailed off as she took another step toward me, so close I could smell her lunch mimosa on her breath.

"Why did you really come here, Ms. Quick?" she asked, narrowing her eyes at me.

I tried to take a step backward and came up against the desk. "Look, I'm just a tabloid reporter—"

"Yes. A nosey little reporter." She scoffed. "You people used to be Bobby's lifeblood, you know? Keeping his name front and center in the public's mind."

"Happy to help?" I said, though it squeaked out more as a question.

"Who knew you'd be so much trouble in the end?"

"End?" I asked, not at all liking the sound of that word.

Then Marilyn surprised me by throwing her head back and laughing. It was loud and shrill with a slightly maniacal edge to it. Instead of breaking the tension, it caused a chill to run up my spine. Then she quickly skirted around me and pulled something from a desk drawer.

"Don't move." Before I could even take a step toward the closed door, she had a gun leveled at me.

I froze, my heart suddenly pounding so hard I feared we'd both soon be able to hear it. "Is that Bobby's gun? The missing one?" I asked, my voice surprisingly calm for how panicked I felt.

She nodded. "Not so much missing as being kept safe."

My eyes darted around the room that I knew must have been searched by the police after Bobby's death. "Someone else was keeping it for you," I guessed. "Your boyfriend? Chad?"

Her red lips curled into a wicked smile. "So you did see the plane tickets. I suppose I should have kept them hidden a bit better, but I didn't expect a surprise visit from the press."

That was me. Full of surprises. I glanced behind Marilyn toward the window, hoping to catch the attention of Shane skating by. Not that I wanted to put him in any more danger, but if I could somehow get him to call for help…

As if she could read my mind, she reached behind her and pulled the blinds shut with her free hand.

"Look, it's none of my business if you have a hottie on the side," I told her. "Your prerogative, right?"

Her eyes narrowed again.

"So, you know, enjoy your trip, and I'll just be on my way…"

"Don't play dumb with me," she sneered. "I know you know."

After how stupid I'd been to dismiss the obvious suspect in all of this, I didn't feel like I was playing much at all. In fact, I was mentally kicking myself on so many levels. Tina had been on the right track all along by suspecting the wife, while I'd been on a wild, recycling goose chase. Granted, several bad geese were now behind bars thanks to me. But one homicidal housewife was still on the loose.

And pointing a gun at me.

"Tell me why you did it," I said, stalling for time. "Why did you kill Bobby?"

She did a nonchalant shrug. "He left me no choice."

The calm, clear admission sent another chill up my spine. And told me that Marilyn had no intention of letting me leave this room alive. I felt my breath come fast as my eyes scanned the room for anything I could use as a weapon. Stapler. Paperback books. Pen holder. Nothing that could compete with a gun.

"What do you mean you had no choice?" I asked, trying to keep her talking. And not shooting.

"I didn't lie to you when I said Bobby stopped paying attention to me. All he cared about was that stupid show. So left to my own devices, I found my own hobbies."

"Like Chad."

She grinned. "Have you seen him? That body of his is quite the fun playground."

I swallowed down a shiver of disgust, wondering if Chad knew he was sleeping with a murderer. "I'm guessing Bobby found out?"

She nodded, an almost sad look on her face. "I guess he wasn't paying as little attention as I thought."

"And he asked for a divorce?"

"At first I thought I could put him off. Maybe change his mind. My powers of persuasion aren't totally lacking," she told me. "I used to be an actress, you know."

"But Bobby wasn't biting."

She shook her head, that sad look crossing her face again. "I really did love him. It was all his fault. If he'd just spent more time at home, maybe fewer nights at the studio. If he'd just looked at me the way he did when we first married…" She trailed off, lost in her own thoughts for a moment.

I took the opportunity to take a step closer to the door. And another. I was where I could almost reach the handle, when she seemed to focus back on me, leveling the gun again.

"But it had to be done," she said, the finality in her voice scary. "Thanks to that stupid prenup, if Bobby went through with the divorce, I'd get nothing. Nothing! Five years of being his arm candy. Do you know how hard it is to look like this?!" She gestured to her perfectly sculpted body. "Hours of Pilates, giving up carbs, laser treatments, Botox, Restylane, hair extensions, gel nails, facials, waxing, seaweed wraps. It's endless! I've worked *hard* for this money, and there was no way I was going to let some sleazy lawyer take it all away from me."

I bit my lip, wondering how long it would be before the housekeeper walked by. Would she hear us? Would she realize her employer had gone loco?

"So you followed Bobby the night he had his meeting with Sal Bukowski, and you killed him," I surmised.

She shrugged. "Honestly, I had no idea who he was meeting. I just figured it was less messy to kill him while he was out than in the house." She wrinkled up her nose, like killing her husband was no problem, but getting blood stains out of her rug—now that would be icky. "Unfortunately, now I don't have much of a choice with you."

Uh-oh. I eyed the door again. It was almost within reach, but there was no way I could get it open and get out before she could pop off a single shot.

"What about your housekeeper?" I asked, hearing desperation in my own voice. "She'll hear the gunshot."

Marilyn gave me wan smile. "No, dear, she won't. I sent her off to pick up groceries for dinner."

Well, that was inconvenient. "Chad?" I asked, thinking of the SUV in the driveway.

Marilyn shook her head. "You know what I love most about Chad? He doesn't ask questions." Her smile dropped, and she took a step forward. "And he knows when to keep his beautiful mouth shut."

"Sounds like a keeper," I said with levity I certainly didn't feel. I glanced again at the door. If I dove, she'd catch me. I had to distract her somehow.

"If only I could trust you to do the same," Marilyn said, clearly not meaning it at all. In fact, if I had to guess, there was something akin to excitement in her eyes. She was enjoying this. The woman really had lost it.

It was obvious there was no reasoning with her. She took a step toward me. I felt my heart leap into my throat. It was now or never.

I made my eyes go big and round, feigning a look of horror (which wasn't too hard, considering the circumstances) and pointed behind her. "Ohmigod, look out!"

On pure instinct, Marilyn turned.

I quickly took a big step toward her, invading her personal space like Ritchie had shown me at the Oceanside Gym. She realized she'd been duped just as my knee came upward, slamming into her groin.

She made a grunting sound, but considering she had far less "vulnerable" stuff in that area than Ritchie had, it was only a momentary stun. She twisted her hand around, pointing the gun toward me. I grabbed her wrist, trying to point it away. We locked in a tug of war, the gun direction the prize.

Unfortunately, Marilyn did a lot more Pilates than I did. She was gaining, the gun barrel slowly moving in my direction. I acted quickly, letting go of her arm at the same time I shifted behind her, jumping on her back.

"What the—?" she said, whipping around.

I wrapped my legs around her stomach and held on for dear life. She spun around in circles, screaming.

"Get off of me!"

Fat chance of that. There was no way I was letting her go. I had a tiger by the tail. I dug my fingernails into her face, hoping the pain and her vanity would convince her to drop her weapon, but she didn't. Instead, she brought the gun up over her head, toward me. I reached out and grabbed her wrist in one hand and struggled to hold myself on her back.

"I'm going to kill you!" she screeched and with her free hand clawed at my fingers in an attempt to stop my assault on her face.

Marilyn stood up straight then rammed herself backward toward one of the bookshelves. My body slammed painfully into the shelves, volumes of books toppling down around us. The air left my lungs, and I gasped for breath, but I didn't loosen my grip.

She stumbled under my added weight but took several steps forward before taking another ram at the bookcase. My head slammed into the shelf, and my vision started to swim.

Stunned, my arms went weak, and I slid off of her back, falling to the floor on my butt.

Marilyn spun around and aimed the gun at me. Scratches ran across her face from one side to the other, and blood trickled down her chin. "Time's up, blondie," she growled through clenched teeth. She took a step toward me.

I felt around on the floor beside me for a weapon, for anything to fight her off with, but all I felt were books.

Marilyn took a single step toward me. Then another.

I took a deep breath…and kicked out with one leg, catching her ankles.

Marilyn's feet flew out from underneath her. She fell onto her back, her head hit the hardwood floor with a sickening thud, and the gun went off. Plaster fell from the ceiling into my face. I jumped up and pounced on her, going for the gun.

But even stunned, Marilyn was way stronger than I was. She easily rolled me over, straddling me. She wrapped her slender hands around my neck and squeezed slowly. Firmly.

I couldn't breathe. My lungs felt like they would explode at any minute. I tried to pry her hands from around my neck, but she held firm. Her face snarling down at me started to waver and then blur.

"You should've left me alone. You should've stayed out of my business. You should've dropped the story when you had the chance," she said through clenched teeth as she squeezed tighter.

I stopped trying to pry her fingers from around my throat and felt around on the floor beside me. My vision was going dark, and my lungs burned. My fingers flailed, reaching for anything. Finally they brushed something hard and curved. I didn't know what it was that I'd found, but it was better than nothing, so grasped it and swung with all of my might.

Potting soil and green leaves exploded all around us. I'd hit her with a potted plant. As cheesy action flick-esque as it was, it actually worked. Marilyn's expression morphed from full of hatred to suddenly slack. Then she fell to the side and hit the floor. She was out cold.

I got to my hands and knees, scooted the gun across the floor far away from Marilyn's body, and took in huge gulps of air until my vision cleared.

Then I called 9-1-1.

CHAPTER TWENTY-ONE

———

Marta, the housekeeper, came home to find that paramedics and half a dozen police officers had converged on the Baxter residence. After having a mild freak out, followed by a string of Spanish curses, she'd cooperated fully, saying she'd always thought there was something a little off about her employer. Poor Chad had been clueless the entire time, waiting by the pool for Marilyn to reappear, with a pair of earbuds in his ears blasting death metal. He'd only realized it wasn't a typical lounge day when an officer had burst through the patio door with gun drawn. As it turned out, Marilyn really had kept her boy toy in the dark, and Chad had no knowledge of her murderous tendencies. She'd simply told him that they were taking a long vacation to New Zealand, and he'd been happy to tag along with the free ticket.

After coming to, Marilyn was cuffed and hauled out to a waiting police car, all the while screaming and shouting for her lawyer. Though, after the police took my statement, it was clear even the best lawyer wasn't going to get her off. The officer assured me that her confession coupled with the missing gun was more than enough evidence to get an indictment.

The paramedics looked me over on site and determined that I was going to have some (more) bruises and be sore for a few days, but other than that I was okay and cleared to go home. Which, with a promise to the officer in charge to come into the station to give a more formal statement the next day, I did.

The first thing I did was take a long, hot shower that eased some of the soreness from my muscles. Everything hurt from the tips of my hair to the ends of my pedicured toes. But I couldn't deal with pain right now—I had a story to turn in. I dressed in a pair of comfy purple sweats and pulled out my phone. Next, I sent a batch of pictures that I'd taken of Marilyn unconscious next to the missing gun to Cam. Hey, I'd had to do something while I'd waited for the police to arrive. It might as well be to the *Informer*'s benefit. Then I quickly pulled out my laptop and typed out the *real* story of Bobby Baxter's death. I'd just put the finishing touches on it and emailed it off to Felix, when a knock sounded at my door.

I got up from my sofa with a groan, feeling those bruises set in already. I was *so* taking a sick day tomorrow. I peeked through the peephole and saw Felix standing on my front step, running a hand through his permanently disheveled hair.

I frowned and opened the door. "What are you doing here? I just sent you my story," I told him.

"I know. I just got it." He held up his phone as evidence the email had gone through. He paused, eyes assessing my face and neck. "Why is it every time I see you, you have new bruises?" While the words were an attempt at light and conversational, his tone was thick with something that in any other man I might have said was emotion. But I knew stoic, British Felix didn't do emotion.

I shrugged, going for light and breezy right back at him. "What can I say? I guess I'm just a tough chick."

He cocked his head at me, more emotion in his eyes. "Are you?"

The concern had tears I'd yet to shed at being almost killed backing up in my throat. I shook them off, clearing it loudly. "Did you want to come in?" I asked, pulling the door wider and stepping back to allow him entry.

He did, closing the door behind him as his eyes swept my apartment and immediately settled on the giant pink teddy bear sitting in the corner. In his defense, it was hard to miss. "Your, uh, sidekick isn't here?" he asked.

I shook my head. "Shane's retired. He's just gonna be a kid for a while."

Felix nodded. "Smart move."

"So why are you here?" I asked. I know, I was being cool. But I was tired of playing the guessing game about where I stood with Felix.

He ran a hand through his hair again and paced to the other side of the room, like the direct question made him uncomfortable. "I heard about what happened at Marilyn Baxter's place." He paused. "I had to hear about it through the tip line. Why didn't you call me?"

That was a loaded question. "I…" I decided to go with the truth. "I thought you'd care more about me getting my story in quickly than a personal call."

His sandy eyebrows drew together. "Allie, there's nothing in this world I care about more than you. Don't you know that?"

The air whooshed out of me in a rush, my heart beating fast. "No," I said honestly.

His frown deepened, and he took a step toward me.

But I took one back, not quite ready to accept his statement yet. "Then how come you've been so standoffish lately?"

"Standoffish? I don't understand."

I rolled my eyes. "Canceling on me for drinks, hardly speaking two words to me all day at work, assigning me a bodyguard instead of staying over yourself," I said, ticking off my list of evidence.

Felix let out a loud sigh, still looking confused. "If I recall, it was *you* who turned me down for drinks the last two times. You haven't spoken two words to me at work either. Not to mention the flowers and gifts you've been getting from your…friend."

I opened my mouth to respond, but quickly shut it with a click. I hadn't thought of it like that. "I told you they were from Shane. He's just a kid."

Felix nodded. "I know. I get it. It still doesn't feel nice, but I get it."

I let out a big sigh. "Okay, so all of this is great, but let's be honest. There have been problems between us for a while."

Felix frowned again. "Problems?"

Did I really have to spell it out for him? I felt myself blush. "You…never want to stay over. With me. You know, like to sleep. But not sleep. "

The corner of his mouth hitched up momentarily at my obvious discomfort, but it quickly settled back into the frown. "You're right," he admitted on an exhale.

There it was. The admission I'd been dreading. He just wasn't that into me.

"Look," he continued, "things between us started…fast."

I felt myself blush harder, knowing he was referring to the one-night stand that had started our relationship.

"I just wanted to slow them down a bit. Especially considering our circumstances."

"You mean that we work together?"

"I mean that you're a full decade younger than I am, Allie."

I bit my lip. So he *had* been thinking that. I was a kid to him. Usually I loved being right, but this conversation was making me rethink my stance on that. All I felt at the moment was hollow, knowing my worst fears were being confirmed.

"I know I'm young. And inexperienced. And I'll admit there might be one or two times where I have acted childishly—" I started, angry at how desperately I was trying to make my case for us to stay together.

But Felix cut me off, holding up a hand. "Let's face it, Allie. I'm old."

I froze midsentence. "What?"

"I'm old!" He threw his hands up. "How ridiculous am I going after a beautiful, smart, young girl like you? What men my age do that?"

"You're not that old. What are you, forty?"

He shot me a pained look. "Thirty-eight."

Oops. "I don't understand—" I started, still trying to play catch-up.

But he didn't let me finish. "I'm old enough that people notice. *I* notice. Don't you think I see people's reactions when we go out? They're laughing at me, Allie. They're laughing at the poor old guy with the hot girl who's probably going to lose interest in him any second now and move on."

For some reason I was having a hard time processing what he was saying. "You're worried what people think about you dating a younger woman?"

He shook his head. "No. I'm worried about what *you* think." He took a step closer to me. "I'm worried you'll see me as...old. That...that you'll move on and leave me heartbroken."

I couldn't help it. I burst out laughing. I'm pretty sure it wasn't the reaction he'd been expecting, but the absurdity of the situation was too much. All this time I'd been worried that Felix thought I was too young, when he'd been worried that he was too old.

"Allie?" he asked, that frown reappearing.

"Oh, kiss me, you old fool!" I told him, not waiting for him to make the move. I wrapped my arms around his neck, pulling him close.

He didn't resist, pressing himself against my chest as he kissed me long and hard. His lips were soft yet firm, and I melted against him as he threaded his fingers into my hair. When we finally came up for air, Felix traced his thumb over my eyebrow, down over my cheekbone to my jawline then cupped my face in the palm of his large hand. It might have been the single most tender gesture I'd ever experienced.

"I must look a mess," I whispered, feeling his eyes intent on my face.

He slowly shook his head. "You look amazing."

If he hadn't been holding me up, I might have melted into a puddle of purple goo right there on my brown renter's carpet.

"So any chance you'd like to go out with me tonight?" I asked. "Maybe make up for those drinks we've been missing?"

He slowly shook his head, his eyes not leaving mine. "No, I think we should stay right here."

"I have an extra toothbrush. In case you want to stay over?" I asked, hoping I was catching his meaning right.

A soft grin spread across his lips. "Where else would I go?"

A shiver went down my spine. Mr. Fluffykins was definitely sleeping in the living room tonight.

ABOUT THE AUTHORS

Gemma Halliday is the *New York Times, USA Today* & #1 Kindle bestselling author of the High Heels Mysteries, the Hollywood Headlines Mysteries, the Jamie Bond Mysteries, the Tahoe Tessie Mysteries, the Marty Hudson Mysteries, and several other works. Gemma's books have received numerous awards, including a Golden Heart, two National Reader's Choice awards, and three RITA nominations. She currently lives in the San Francisco Bay Area with her boyfriend, Jackson Stein, who writes vampire thrillers, and their four children, who are adorably distracting on a daily basis.

To learn more about Gemma, visit her online at
www.GemmaHalliday.com

Not only is Anna Snow a wife, mom, and lipstick junkie, but she's also a multi-published *USA Today* bestselling author of several romance, mystery, erotica, fan-fiction, paranormal, chick-lit, and thriller works. Anna began writing as soon as she could hold a pen and hasn't stopped since. She loves life and can think of nothing she enjoys more than spending time with her family and friends. She loves archery, reading, writing, kitties, spending time outdoors, and did I mention kitties? *Big grin* Anna also loves to hear from her fans and answers all correspondence she receives.

To learn more about Anna Snow, visit her online at:
http://www.annasnow.info

Other series in print now from Gemma Halliday...

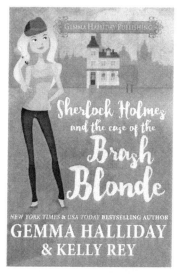

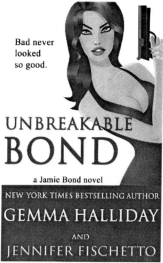

www.GemmaHalliday.com